Dear Gerry & Elaine,

I hope you enjoy Mis[sing]

Let's also hope it brings out ......

both of you!

MISSING GRETYL

A Comedy Novel

With the best of wishes,

love

Si Page

x

Si Page   Eph 3:16-21

Grosvenor House
Publishing Limited

This book is published by
Grosvenor House Publishing Ltd
28-30 High Street, Guildford, Surrey, GU1 3EL.
www.grosvenorhousepublishing.co.uk

A CIP record for this book
is available from the British Library

ISBN 978-1-78148-814-0

Simon would like to thank

Family

To my dear wife, Solana. I'm sorry if for the last eighteen months it has felt that you have indeed been married to a twin of Gretyl Trollop. For my mood changes, I would also like to blame the characters in this book: Dave Sodall, 'Sharkie' Lovitt and Arti Chokes. Let's hope the hard times were all about developing character (and paying the mortgage). Thank you for your love, friendship, endless patience and belief in me. I love you.

My dear children, Ruben and Freddie. You are a source of inspiration for me and a key reason why I worked so hard on this novel. I love you, my special boys. Now, please go tidy your toys and stop picking your nose.

My supportive parents. For bearing with me and supporting my family during a huge career change and an unknown future. My dear sister, uncle, aunt, cousins and even a lovely mother-in-law (yes, that bit is absolutely true). In fact, to everyone else in our family, thank you for being there, wherever you are, all over the world!

Friends

There are so many to mention and I will try to thank you all personally in time. However, I would like to note my special thanks to the following people:

Tony & Sam, you have inspired Soli and I with practical help, fantastic artwork and last but not least, prayer for the success of this book. You are the real deal.

To my editor and published author, Dr. Mark Stibbe, your feedback, corrections, mentoring and encouragement have been invaluable to the success of this book. To the talented proofreader and scriptwriter, Dee Williamson, thank you for the final eyeball! To Kate Astley, for your almost bonkers enthusiasm and advice. Norman Marshall, a funny, kind friend who introduced me to Arti

Chokes. Thank you. I've learnt that teamwork has great value, but a good working friendship is priceless. For everything else, I use MasterCard.

To my friends, your input and support for this book has been important to me. My thanks to Lee-Lye M, Claire T-H & Andrew H, Mark & Louise L, Kevin & Lesley W, Judith S, Gerry T, GP T, Nicola H, John M, Nina F, Karl W, Ranjitha G P, Janine D, Simon D, Barney W, Glenn & Nadette I, Mark and Abbie B, Kirstie B-L, Ruth & John F, Ken B and the many other friends, businesses and professionals who have kindly helped with accurate information for this novel.

Thanks to the excellent stand-up comedian (and sit down author) Andy Kind and the fabulous funny man and actor, Bobby Ball. I love the fact that both of you are not ashamed of being men of faith who are also very funny.

Finally, last but not least, to my Maker, JC. You gave us the gift of humour (well, some of us?) Thank you. You inspire love and laughter. Without you, I wouldn't like to think ...

To you, my dear reader and my last 'finally' (honest). Thank you for purchasing this book. I sincerely hope you enjoy reading it. After all, time is a precious commodity and I hope I have used both of ours well. Missing Gretyl was written for your pleasure as well as mine.

Contents

CHAPTER 1

Silence of the Frogs

Albert Trollop adjusted the crotch of his blue striped pyjamas and staggered into the kitchen, yawning loudly. He leaned over the work surface to flick the switch of the kettle and scratched his bottom within inches of his wife's nose.

'Usual date with death this morning is it, dear?' Albert asked.

'Why, are you taking me out then?' Gretyl hissed.

'I would dear, but in your present state, it would be cruel to the neighbours.'

Gretyl leapt to her feet and reached towards Albert's neck. Using a deft side step that any drill instructor would be proud of, Albert deflected the blow and watched his wife fall with a thud to the floor.

'I'll only take you out if I can find a bag large enough for your head,' he growled.

Flat on her back, Gretyl kicked out with a sweep of her left leg, but Albert was ready for it. He caught her by the ankle and dragged her toward the bathroom, her head bouncing on the carpet.

Gretyl spat with rage but her saliva reached no farther than her own stubbly chin.

'Get your filthy hands off me!' she hollered.

In defiance, Albert held onto both legs and dragged Gretyl through the door into the bathroom. Hoisting her up by her ankles, he dropped his wife head-first into the toilet bowl and pulled the chain.

Gretyl tried to scream, but her cries turned into splutters as the flushing water flooded her gawping mouth.

Albert chuckled as he left the bathroom, turning for a moment to look at his wife's ungainly handstand, her florid dress now draped around the toilet bowl like a tacky lampshade.

A broad smile lit up Albert's face as he strutted back into the kitchen.

'Ribbit, ribbit, ribbit, ribbit!' The sound of Gretyl's ornamental frogs only served to remind Albert in the most sinister fashion that his work was not yet finished.

Covering his ears, Albert muted the sound of the awful chorus and stomped off to the closet to retrieve an old cricket bat nestling behind some Wellington boots.

Seizing the ageing willow with both hands, Albert lurched wildly at the gloating collectibles.

'You'll go the same way as her!' he declared, as he swung the old bat ferociously at the mocking frogs and watched with delight as their shattered limbs flew apart in every direction.

Albert took a deep breath and sat down on the sofa, surveying the landscape of broken pottery and china.

'Is this what deep contentment feels like?' he sighed, closing his eyes.

Albert heard the whistle of the kettle and sat up, rubbing his eyelids. With a crushing sense of disappointment, he suddenly realised that he'd only dozed off at the kitchen table and Gretyl had not drowned in the toilet after all.

'Just a dream,' he muttered.

'Just a bloody dream.'

The air was filled with the smell of sizzling bacon and spitting sausages. 'I won't be getting any of that,' Albert thought. The meat was always carefully marked in the fridge with a black felt tip pen, 'GRETYL'S'.

Albert was agitated by the unholy sound of Gretyl's chomping, not to mention the ghastly sight of her swollen cheeks and the food trapped in her dentures. In protest, he lifted his daily broadsheet in front of his face to obscure the view of the mutilation before him.

Whistling the melody of an old wartime song, Albert tried in vain to drown out the offensive racket coming from his wife's mouth.

'Oh, I can't wait for Shop Galore. I wonder what I'll spend your money on today, Albert Trollop? There is a car boot this Saturday as well.'

Albert groaned in protest and struck up an angry drum beat on the table with his knife and fork.

Gretyl bellowed, 'Why don't you get off your backside and clean the kitchen, get the hoover out, wash the windows and finish with the toilet. The cleaner will be here in ten minutes.'

'Clean this, clean that, mop this and wipe that. What's the point of home help? All she does is sit on her bum and drink my tea.' Albert whined.

'It's about time you got off your boney arse,' snapped Gretyl.

'Oh look, my horse is running at the three thirty at Newmarket – it's called Wedded Misery,' Albert interjected.

'Well, you're the one responsible for the misery.'

Albert lashed back, 'Love, you'd think misery was an Olympic sport, the way you practise it.'

Albert was saved by the doorbell. It was Sally, the twenty year old home help, deluded daydreamer and wannabe footballer's WAG.

Gretyl greeted Sally at the door with a fresh cuppa. 'How are you, luv? Got any gossip for me?'

'Nah, not really ... erm, actually, yeh. I was having a cappuccino with one of the Spice Girls this week. She's with a footballer, y'know. Anyway, she's been with her new fella for a few weeks now and she told me she fancies having a baby with him. Apparently, he's got really nice blue eyes. She wants to name it Blue Bear if it's a boy or Damson Berry if it's a girl.'

Wide eyed, Gretyl bit into her crispy bacon and considered the repercussions. 'Well it's fashionable nowadays to have kids with different dads. In my day, those women were called slappers.'

Albert lowered his newspaper and raised his eyes to the ceiling, muttering under his breath, 'I'd rather pass kidney stones than listen to this.'

'Are you still here? Go bugger off to that allotment of yours.'

Albert ignored Gretyl and stood up from the table, walking over to the fridge. He opened the door and apart from the meat products, he was greeted by a lonely china frog sitting smugly on top of a lurid green butter dish.

'Y'know what, love. I think I would have a better chance of being fed if I moved in to my allotment shed.'

Gretyl laughed. 'Why bother coming back, then?'

Albert ignored his wife and grabbed his trouser clips, making his way to the front door with his folding bike.

'You know what they say,' Albert said. 'Be careful what you wish for ... be careful what you wish for.'

CHAPTER 2

Memory Lane

Albert took the few steps out of his modest, 12th floor high rise flat into the decaying elevator, holding his breath to mask the acrid stench of urine. His bicycle and saddlebag barely squeezed in.

'Booyaka, Booyaka, y'know it's right, innit,' blasted from the headphones of the young hoodie standing in the corner of the cramped lift.

'Stone the crows son, you'll ruin those eardrums,' Albert thought to himself.

The old people on the estate didn't mix well with the younger generation. Often referred to as 'the wrinklies', they may as well have been invisible – especially after the recent news of poor ol' Rupert on the third floor who was found rotting in his flat after being dead three months. Nobody seemed to notice or even care.

As the dim light flickered in the lift shaft, Albert began to reminisce – as if the cinematic roll of a projector was playing back scenes of his life - the loud scrapes and creaks of the lift only reminding Albert of his own frailty.

'We both need a service,' Albert murmured, as the lift descended.

Albert bent down and pulled up his trouser legs, applying his bicycle clips before his daily pilgrimage to the Potter Vale Allotment. Such was his devotion that he had never missed a day at his vegetable patch since his retirement. No weather forecast could quell his enthusiasm for peaceful solitude.

The short ride to his daily appointment was one of the highlights of Albert's day.

'Morning guv'nor,' Albert shouted.

'Alright Albert – see ya just after one!' Stan yelled back.

Albert continued on his bike, past Stan's Grocery Store, the oldest local business in the area.

Stan Jones would always leave the shop for an hour and join Albert at the local bookmakers for a rendezvous they had kept faithfully for over a decade.

Albert smiled as he relished the cherished daily meeting with his oldest friend.

Whether it was the smell of the local pie and mash shop, the sight of the Dick Turpin Pub or the familiar sounds of the outdoor street market, Albert was deeply proud of his own Cockney roots and always looked forward to his meander down memory lane.

At the same time he knew that London had drastically changed and was still changing at a pace. The few remaining shops that had survived the years of modernisation and new owners had a special place in Albert's heart and often brought a smile to his wrinkled face.

This didn't mean Albert was completely set in his ways. For one thing he welcomed the influx of the mostly Asian and Eastern European folk on his estate. From the little he understood, he respected their sense of community and family values and they, in turn, seemed respectful of his age. He was touched that some of them even managed a 'good morning', which was more than could be said for most of his white neighbours.

Albert lived by his original digital Casio watch that had survived eleven battery replacements and a few decades of hard graft. It was programmed each day for the early morning trip to his vegetable patch, midday lunch and 1pm at the local bookmakers with Stan.

His wife Gretyl, on the other hand, lived by the chime of her mantelpiece clock and kept to her routines with a metronomic predictability.

Sporting a different wig for every day of the week (bought from the local charity shops and car boot sales) the fake mink coat with golden handbag was Gretyl's 'going posh', trademark appearance. In the summer months she would sweat rather than dress down, with an ice cream in one hand and a mascara smudged handkerchief in the other for wiping her dripping mush.

Gretyl was always trying to roll back the years, but in an attempt to keep a modicum of peace, Albert had given up making any comments about her appearance. A few of the neighbours had taken fate into their own hands after calling her, 'Mrs Mutton dressed up as Mutton.' Much to Gretyl's amusement, they hadn't endured the test of time and had either died or moved out.

Albert arrived at the allotment and unlocked the door to his shed, the storehouse of his fondest memories. His large, heavily padlocked chest kept photos (amongst other things) of his early childhood, young sweethearts and his time serving with the Middlesex Regiment in Korea in the fifties.

Though the conflict was to be later known as The Forgotten War, Albert's harsh experiences as a POW ensured that he would never forget those who died.

'Miss you buggers.'

Albert raised a small glass of whisky every morning to his departed friends. Over forty soldiers had died from his regiment but sixty years later their faces were still honoured within the sanctuary of Albert's memory. Their photographs were lovingly placed upon the wooden shelf every morning, then taken down and padlocked away safely at the end of each visit.

Despite the pain of war, Albert believed they were the best years of his life.

In his shed he honoured the dead.

'We will remember you,' he sighed every day.

CHAPTER 3

Toenails & Handbags

'Beep! Beep! Beep!' It was midday and Albert's Casio watch alerted him to the lunch (consisting of buttered cream crackers) awaiting back at the flat.

Routine was something Albert had learned to love as a young soldier but the monotony of his marriage was slowly suffocating him. Most days he feigned deafness to nullify any conversation with his wife.

Gretyl was eating at the table, with sandwich in one hand and a pair of scissors in the other.

'Snip, snip.'

In one fell swoop a crusted toenail flew towards Albert, landing in his milky tea.

'Flaming Nora, woman! Do me a favour. Next time, make my tea in a bowl so I can drown myself in it.'

Incredibly, this wasn't the first time the flying toenail had made an appearance at lunch and after five decades of marriage, Albert expected nothing to change.

Now on his last cracker, he was desperate for the one o'clock beep which signalled his reprieve.

Albert turned his face away and looked at a small portable television standing on the kitchen work surface. It was connected to a free digibox that Gretyl had picked up for £1 at her local car boot sale. This purchase had given Gretyl access to a world of TV soaps and supposedly 'free' shopping channels - which were in fact anything but free to Albert.

Agitating Albert as usual, Gretyl's mantelpiece clock had chimed for a whole minute, the cuckoo hooting to remind her there were at least six shopping channels transmitting imminently. She rushed toward the TV, grabbed the remote control and beamed its signal onto the screen.

'This Golden, Paris/New York Handbag, especially designed for you, the modern 'independent' woman, will catch men in its glare. Studded with over 100 diamond-like stones, the faux crocodile skin bag gives you the animal magnetism you desire. You will think you are dreaming when we tell you its knockdown, bargain price, just after the break ... Stay tuned and get on the phone ... wait ... I hear the buzzer, folks. Callers, this is incredible ... place your order during the adverts and we will send you an exclusive, free mystery gift with a recommended retail price of £19.95.'

Albert took a deep sigh as he observed the determined look on her face.

'Ooh, a free mystery gift!' yelped Gretyl.

Before the price had even appeared, she was dialing the memorised premium rate number.

Albert watched as his wife withdrew a credit card.

'I wouldn't mind, but you've got at least a dozen of those handbags.'

'If you weren't so tight, you'd have got me satellite TV; that's got over 40 shopping channels. Then I wouldn't have to buy the same thing every week, would I?'

Albert considered the flawed logic of her argument but knew it was pointless fighting with her.

'Hello, Gretyl', answered her usual telesales operator. 'So which bag is it this week?' he asked.

His sarcastic tone eluded Gretyl.

'Oh, erm, the one on the TV?' she replied.

The young, cocksure agent was bored with mocking her so he hurried her along.

'We have your credit card details on file. We'll send you the gold-studded crocodile skin clutch bag, complete with our free gift of the week - erm, the stunning silver Parker Pen.'

Gretyl's tone was one of disappointment. 'Oh, I thought it was a mystery gift.'

'Er, right,' the operator replied. 'Well, we'll send you a mystery gift instead. Forget what I said before. Speak to you soon. Bye.'

Over the years and on numerous occasions, Albert had seen Gretyl use the free gifts as his Christmas presents. He had already received several Parker pens, a digital clock and a small garden shovel from the previous year's collection of mystery gifts. Gretyl, however, had saved her biggest insult for the recent birthday card she had made for him. It read:

'I saw a turd the other day and remembered your stinkin' birthday!'

The front of the card was poorly illustrated with Gretyl's attempt at crayoning a pile of brown faeces. The inside of the card read:

'Hoping this Birthday is as crap as all the others! Love, the Mrs.'

Albert's eyes gazed up toward the artex ceiling.

'Beep! Beep! Beep!'

His deliverance had come. It was time to meet Stan at the bookies.

CHAPTER 4

Soddall in Canvey Island

After his vending machine business went belly up, Dave Soddall was looking, in his own words, for 'a new scam to put them on the map'. Living on the dole and housing benefits was proving hard enough and he knew the long term prospects were in his own words, 'crap' and 'not good enough for his family'.

Over the years, Dave had always found it difficult making a living and never seemed to profit from his scams. It wasn't that he minded overcharging or even telling a few porkies to make money, but he hadn't shown the same stomach for the big scams like his brother Tony, who lived in the Costa Del Sol, off the loot of a bank heist.

Although the Soddalls also lived by the seaside, the weather in their home county of Essex was not exactly Mediterranean and Canvey Island was certainly no tourist's paradise.

Sharon had been married to Dave for nearly twenty years, first meeting her husband at Totties nightclub where she worked behind the bar for his brother Tony. He had obtained the club through somewhat criminal means and gave Dave a job working on the doors. It had been a job of convenience for Dave before Totties was sold on and he was soon left out of work and on the dole. Tony also refused to share any of his good fortune with his brother, resulting in some ill feeling and bad blood between them for a number of years after.

Back then, he had a very muscular, if short, stocky frame, but it had wilted somewhat over the years and he could only be described now as short and portly.

Dave's once taut biceps now hung low like a bloodhound's jaw, while his green, red and blue tattoos had faded and stretched on his flabby arms. Sharon often joked that Dave's rippled, lean chest, once boosted by body building pills, had found a new master - the

KFC family bucket. The family complained that they rarely got a taste of it, especially when Dave held it firmly in his grip on the couch while watching the football on the TV.

'Ere Kev!' Dave hollered as he lay sprawled out on the worn couch, staring at the TV. 'Fancy buying your ol' man one a' these posh 'ouses?'

Kev with one finger up his nose looked vacant and glanced at his Dad with the usual look of, 'What's he on about? Whatever?'

Dave was enjoying a few beers and watching 'Posh Tarts, Rich Farts' on terrestrial TV. It was normally Sharon who watched this show, daydreaming about coming into money and escaping the two bed council house that hadn't seen any home improvements since their wedding day.

Sharon often moaned that Del and Rodney Trotter's flat on the TV series 'Only Fools and Horses' had a more modern décor. Dave always replied with the same mantra:

'Babe, our financial breakthrough is just around the corner. I can feel it.'

'You're right about it just being around the corner,' replied Sharon. 'The only chance of us coming into money is if you go to the corner shop and buy a lottery ticket.'

Dave motioned to Kev. 'Son, do me a favour and throw me that cushion so I can bury my face in it.'

Sharon turned to Kev.

'Don't you dare. I haven't finished with your father yet.'

Dave used his wobbly bottom lip trick to gain some sympathy, at which point Sharon grinned before letting out a loud cackle.

Dave sprawled out as usual on the couch and began to daydream again. He liked the idea of playing Al Pacino in the lead role in 'Scarface', or Robert De Niro in 'Heat' and 'Raging Bull', but he knew deep down he wasn't rotten enough to be a gangster. He didn't mind a scam, but he wouldn't want to physically hurt anyone. A good doorman, yes, but they'd have to be asking for it before he would use his fists to teach them a lesson.

Dave looked over at Sharon's outstretched, shiny legs on the sofa.

'Waxing again Love? I can't see a single hair on those lovely pegs.'

Sharon laughed. 'Y'know me, babe. I love my mani, pedi and all my other cures. Will you let me do your hairy back?'

Dave grimaced as the noise of the wax strip ripped through the air.

'Na. It'll ruin my caveman image. I'll pass on the offer, thanks love.'

Kev was 16 years old and was the brains of the family - which was not saying much. Fed up with his parents' prospects, he knew that he had to make something of himself or risk getting stuck on the dole and living in the same dump-like council accommodation. He wanted to get his hands on some serious cash like his Uncle Tony, without getting caught.

Penny up the wall, selling knocked off DVDs in school, fake designer T-Shirts - that's how Kev made extra cash, but he knew he needed an angle, a scam, a lucky break like Uncle Tony who owned five luxury villas in the Costa del Sol.

Removing his finger from his nose, Kev stood up from the chair, walked to the end of the lounge and then slowly back towards his Father.

'Dad, you know you said there are plenty of ol' folk with money who don't know what to do with it?'

Before Dave could answer, Kev continued. 'Well, it's not like they need it at their age is it? I mean, the really old ones don't stay around for long.'

'This ain't the flamin' Krypton Factor. What are you gettin' at?'

'That posh village you mentioned ... y'know, the one where you told me it's full of senile ol' folk and money. Where is it Dad?'

'Somewhere outside London, I think, with loads of trees and grass. Why do you want to know?'

Kev smiled. 'Old people - they like holidays, don't they? Y'know, coach trips to the seaside 'n' stuff.'

'Listen son, if you want to work at a holiday camp, be my guest. Maybe you could be a rep for the over 60's.'

Dave let out a real belly laugh.

'Dad, I'm serious. Why don't we take a load of rich ol' senile people to Uncle Tony's in Spain and sell 'em his posh villas - y'know, like time share stuff.'

Dave replied, 'Nice idea, son, but how would we get the pensioners to buy it?'

'That's the beauty Dad. They don't pay for it, they win it. We phone them up, tell them they've won a holiday, get a deposit off them for say, er, travel insurance and stuff, and use that money to hire a coach. We then take them to Uncle Tony - he uses his charm to sell the villas he's built in Marbella and we all split the profit.'

Dave began to sober up as he thought of his son's idea, the neurons in his brain firing in unusually rapid fashion.

'Flipping heck, son!'

The room fell silent as Dave hit the mute button on the remote control, looked at his wife and said, 'I think he's got something, luv.'

Sharon knew that Dave was serious now and couldn't remember the last time he'd turned the TV down in order to say something.

For Dave, this moment was an epiphany, as if destiny had knocked on the door. Furthermore, the idea passed his own ethical test. After all, they would be loaded and no one would get hurt.

'Son, darlin',' Dave replied. 'I've got it!'

Before they could reply, Dave said at the top of his voice, 'This will be our first family business together, so let's give it the family name, "Costa Soddall Travel".'

Sharon laughed out loud at the suggestion.

'It's great eh. What ya' think? The business will have our surname on it.'

Kev thought about it for a moment.

'Dad, we need a motto or some-fin' underneath it like, "Where holidays in the sun Costa nothing".'

Kev's laughter was infectious. The Soddall family was now bonded like a pack of wolves as they imagined just how much money they might make with Tony's villas.

'Costa Soddall Travel' had been officially launched - though its name would never appear in the registers at Companies House.

CHAPTER 5

Bet Paddy

Albert entered the 'Bet Paddy' betting shop and spotted Stan sitting at the counter with his small blue pen behind his ear, coffee in one hand and the Racing Telegraph in front of him.

'Who do you fancy for the two o'clock at Newmarket, Stan?'

Albert loved the lingo and the sporting patter, although he wasn't anywhere near as knowledgeable as Stan with the runners.

'My Fair Lady, joint second favourite, with decent odds of three to one. She won last time out and the going was good, so she should do well today.'

Albert folded his betting slip, tucked a liquorice sweet inside it and along with two pound coins, handed it to Sonja at the counter.

'Here you are, my darling.'

'Aw, thanks love. How are you today, Albert?'

'Can't complain. Well, I could but I won't. I got my allotment and second home here with you, so what more could an old man ask for?'

Sonya smiled warmly at Albert and the small, tight community that existed amongst the local punters.

Though Albert had met Stan at the bookies every day for over ten years now, he wasn't one for choosing the horses based on their form, preferring to choose them by name. Stan, however, would always try to convince Albert of the folly of this kind of bet.

'Albert, you have to make a calculated gamble. Get to know the form.'

Albert smiled.

'Stan, how long have we been doing the accumulator bet? Has either of us hit the jackpot yet, mate? I like my system and you stick with yours. Anyway, every time I choose the name of an old hag, I feel like I am getting one over the missus.'

Stan and Albert had often discussed the dream of winning the accumulator. They heard of one lucky punter who placed a small bet on Frankie Dettori to win all of his seven rides at Ascot Race Course. As he won each race the bet accumulated, delivering him a win of over half a million pounds. If the jockey had lost just one of his races, the customer would have walked away with nothing.

'You know me Albert, always living the dream that one day before I croak, I might be sipping champagne on a yacht in the French Riviera.'

Albert replied, 'Yeh, but you said your missus would drive you nuts. Being nagged is just the same wherever you are, whether you are on a boat or in your council flat.'

'Who said anything about taking the missus? I fancy one of those beach bunnies.'

Albert grinned.

'I used to think Gretyl might benefit from a bit of sun, but I soon came to the conclusion only a taxidermist could help.'

Albert and Stan laughed out loud like two naughty schoolboys.

Billy, a friendly local who also spent his lunch breaks in the betting office, interrupted the laughter with his own news and sat down beside Albert.

'Albert, have you seen this photo?' asked Billy, pointing to the front page headlines of the newspaper.

'What, the black silhouette of a person?' replied Albert, a little confused.

'Yeh, it looks like him, doesn't it?' said Billy.

Stan interrupted. 'Looks like who? What are you on about?'

'Y'know, the footballer who's been having it away with that supermodel,' he replied.

Albert chuckled. 'That's just a black shape of a person. It could be anyone - the Prince of Wales, even Humpty Dumpty!'

Billy looked embarrassed. 'Yeh, but everyone knows the Prince of Wales doesn't play in the Premier League and Humpty Dumpty is just a nursery rhyme.'

Stan sighed. 'Billy, you've got the brains of a rocking horse.'

'Well, while we're talking about football, did I tell you that I'm gonna write to the FA?' Billy asked defensively.

Albert chuckled again. 'Well if you're applying for the manager's job, you couldn't do any worse than the bloke we've got now.'

'No, it's about bald heads,' replied Billy. 'I've been thinking about it. How can they control the ball properly with a shiny head? Surely, the more hair they've got, they can cushion the ball better, don't you think?'

Stan looked up from his newspaper. 'Are you serious, Billy? I'm worried about you mate!'

'Maybe the players who don't have much hair could borrow one of my wife's wigs for the match?' teased Albert.

But Billy was not to be put off.

'Remember when Kevin Keegan, Glenn Hoddle and Chris Waddle played for England?' he asked excitedly. 'They scored some lovely goals with their full perms. I bet if you asked them, they'd put the headed goals down to their hair.'

Stan and Albert burst out laughing together.

'Billy, you crack us up mate,' replied Stan. 'Maybe you should write to the Football Association, but you know what reply you'll get from them? FA mate, I tell you!'

The tune from Mission Impossible blasted out of Billy's phone.

'Er, yes love.' answered Billy. 'I'm not in the pub, honest. I just popped out for a pint of milk. I'll be back in five minutes.'

Billy said goodbye as he ran out of Bet Paddy.

Albert turned to Stan. 'You know what. Win or lose today, we do have a right good laugh in here.'

CHAPTER 6

Small Minded

Gretyl grinned as she checked the calendar for the third time that evening. Battersea Car Boot Sale was on Saturday as usual from 7am to 6pm. Her excitement charged the air like pheromones and Albert could only dread what newly acquired rubbish would clutter the house by tomorrow evening.

From left to right, wall plates and shelving covered every conceivable inch of the tiny front room. The Royal Family took pride of place above the small portable TV set, whilst Walt Disney figurines, porcelain frogs, miniature cottages and a whole array of farmyard animals filled every flat surface. Now a weekly ritual, Gretyl would attempt to find some space to fix a new shelf to the wall, rearranging ornaments to suit her mood. Whatever the changes, her much loved frogs would end up dominating the room.

Albert frowned as he watched the glee on Gretyl's face.

'Don't bring back any more frogs, love. There's absolutely no room left on the shelves and I'm forever tripping over the stupid things.'

Gretyl snapped, 'Well, you never turned into a handsome prince when I kissed you, so I'm still looking. Anyway, you should look where you're going. Last time, you broke my Freddie the Frog door stop with your size tens.'

Albert bellowed, 'That Freddie the Frog you called a door stop was a china ornament.'

'Well it became a door stop after you couldn't find me any more wall space for Freddie. It's your fault he's dead.'

Before Albert could stop himself, he added, 'I wish they were all door stops so I could tread on the flamin' lot of them.'

Albert knew that the apocalypse would be preferable to Gretyl's wrath, so he grabbed the newspaper, locked himself in the toilet and sat with his elbows and knees together, wedged between the small radiator on one side and the toilet roll holder on the other.

He knew it wasn't safe to come out until Gretyl had calmed down. The building would have to catch fire before he'd come out and he would need to see the smoke before he believed it was a genuine fire. Gretyl was in the habit of setting off the fire alarm in the kitchen in an attempt to scare him out of the bathroom.

Albert could hear Gretyl pacing outside the small 4x3ft toilet. She had recently blocked it off from the main bathroom after complaining that the sight of it spoiled the ambience of her bath time. Albert knew better though. Gretyl must have thought that if she made the toilet area ridiculously small, Albert wouldn't want to read his paper in there for long periods of time. She was wrong.

The small toilet door folded inwards, proving near fatal for anyone whose body mass index was anything above perfect. Albert could only surmise that Gretyl's large, double jointed frame had learned to squat and wipe. She was stubborn enough to choose this inconvenience rather than admit she was wrong for partitioning the toilet from the rest of the bathroom.

Bang! Bang! Bang! Bang!

Gretyl peeped out of the curtain window. It was Mrs Cooke, her heavy drinking and obese neighbour standing at the door.

'Albert, can you get that.' shouted Gretyl. 'I'm in my nightie.'

Albert immediately recognised the familiar thud on the door as Mrs Cooke's particular and irritating signature. He opened the bathroom door and walked into the hall to let her in.

'Good evening, Mrs Cooke. Is everything okay?' enquired Albert.

'Couldn't be better ... well, apart from one thing,' she replied, barging past him into the kitchen. 'It's my plumbing! I can't flush the damn thing. My toilet has been blocked since this morning and it's full now.'

Albert tried hard to prevent himself from picturing Mrs Cooke's stuffed toilet bowl.

'I'm desperate to use the loo. Can I borrow yours?'

At this point Gretyl walked in, unable to conceal the amused look on her face.

'Of course you can, love. Off you go,' said Gretyl, pointing her towards the toilet.

Mrs Cooke opened the door and panicked, unsure how she would fit on the seat. She had no choice but to try and enter. The alternative was to have an accident right where she stood.

Albert scratched his head. He could barely fit in the toilet himself, let alone the prodigious Mrs Cooke. She had a voracious appetite that would threaten the reserves of any 'eat all you can' buffet restaurant.

Having managed to enter the toilet by standing on it first, she closed the door. After several loud knocks and clunks, Mrs Cooke began to cry out.

'Someone, help me!'

Albert ran to her aid.

'Mrs Cooke, I'm trying to open the door but you seem to be wedged behind it.'

Gretyl listened in. 'Albert, is she hyperventilating?'

Albert shrugged his shoulders. 'Mrs Cooke, please try to relax and breathe slowly. We'll have the door open for you in a minute.'

Albert heard a loud thud against the door. Worried that Mrs Cooke had fainted, Albert tried to get her attention, but she offered no reply.

Albert looked at Gretyl. 'What if her body is wedged between the toilet bowl and the door? You should have had the door fitted so it opens out.'

Gretyl ignored Albert's rant and made an emergency telephone call.

The Fire Brigade and Ambulance service arrived within minutes and after removing the door, found Mrs Cooke unconscious, her tights wrapped around her ankles, a sight that Albert Trollop would not forget easily.

CHAPTER 7

Cacamamie

Young Kevin Soddall was now surfing the internet, looking for photos of large, 'fifty persons plus' seater coaches. He had come up with the idea of using his computer to sign write a picture of a coach with the name of their new business, 'Costa Soddall Travel'.

Meanwhile, Dave Soddall was looking into the various means of raising some serious cash from the old folks they would soon be calling on in the retirement village of Poncey Bridge.

Pad and pen at the ready and formidably armed with two coffees, three Kit-Kats and an XL bag of McCoy's crisps, Dave's attempt at an hour's work only produced one word: 'Savings'.

Dave was well aware that he needed a better angle than asking flat out for people's savings. The problem was that he knew more about knitting than he did about financial services.

Slumping despairingly amongst the settee cushions next to Sharon, he looked to the television for some inspiration. With perfect timing, a smooth voice began to tickle Dave's ears:

'What are houses? More than bricks or mortar, they become the homes which provide some of our very best memories. Our children move on, we watch the family blossom, but the best memories are far from over. Some say life begins at 40, but with Banking Direct, it starts when YOU say so! If you are over 55, there is a simple way of unlocking the equity in your property without leaving your home. Yes, incredibly, you can release anything from ten thousand pounds up to 45% of your property value. Whether it's for that dream holiday, new conservatory, comfy retirement or nest egg, why not use the equity in your property to serve you? After all, you deserve it and it is of course, yours to spend. Remember: you're sitting pretty with Banking Direct.'

Dave gulped, staring at the screen in astonishment. 'Flippin' 'eck!'

Dave wanted to find a golden nugget for his plan before he discussed it with his brother Tony and this was it. Surely the old folks would think nothing of releasing some of the cash from their own properties? After all, they could sell the idea that they would be buying a future holiday home for themselves and their grandchildren as well.

Dave smiled as he suddenly realised that this was probably the best idea he'd ever come up with in his life and that its ambitious scope stood a good chance of attracting his brother Tony's involvement.

The memory of Tony laughing at his plan to sell soiled nappies as fertilizer, had earned him the nickname, 'Cacamamie' (caca meaning poop in Spanish). Dave's inspiration for this failed scheme had come after watching a documentary about the South American Cultures. It showed how some tribes used their own excrement as manure and mixed it with other organic material on their gardens. Dave had figured that baby poo could offer a pure and environmentally friendly way of supplying the large yuppie community.

Tony's response to this madcap venture had been to tell Dave that the idea was 'crap' and had been 'dung' before. Humiliated, Dave had just hung up the phone and didn't speak to his brother for the next two years.

This time, Dave now felt armed with the perfect tool to remove some serious cash from wealthy pensioners, so he plucked up the courage to dial the international number and speak to Tony.

'Holà, buenas tardes. Cómo puedo ayudarte?'

Dave took the opportunity to use his full repertoire of Spanish. 'Erm, Hola, Tony por favor.'

Dave looked over at Sharon and winked at her.

'Un momento por favor, señor. Cómo se llama?'

'Erm, ce, yes love ... whatever, er, can I speak to Tony please?'

Sharon laughed as Dave stuttered. A few minutes passed until Tony answered the phone.

'Hello, who is it?'

'Tony, it's your brother Dave. How are you, mate?'

'Doing good mate, doing good,' Tony replied. 'All the better for hearing your voice ... Carmen, Maria, get your hands off. I'm on the phone. Hold on ... give me a minute, Dave. These women can't keep their hands off me.'

Tony had always fancied himself as a bit of a playboy and loved to brag about his endeavours in the sun, but this time, Dave was having none of it, preferring to use the mute button on the telephone while he went over his sales pitch again with Sharon.

The plan was about to unfold and Tony's payday would now depend for once on Dave's involvement.

CHAPTER 8

Ain't No Pleasin' You

Gretyl sat up in bed and, inspired by her recent bowl of Brussels sprouts, released a windy blast of gas in Albert's direction. Throwing the quilt over his head, she grabbed hold of the items of her outfit which had been prepared the night before and which had earned her the nickname 'The Bag Lady'.

Her musty, faded clothing was torn, overstretched and stained with grease patches, while the baggy cardigan with missing buttons barely covered her money belt. The small change jingled with every step.

Albert woke up distressed. Not only was the smell under the covers unbearable, but last night's dream was proving a bigger challenge. In his latest dream quest to poison his wife, the wrong dosage had been administered and Gretyl just ended up having a good time.

Albert raised his head above the covers and prayed loudly for Gretyl's benefit. 'Lord, look upon my wife today, as only thee can. As she travels out today, may an asteroid come her way, with liquid fire, to torment her, I pray. Thy will be done. Amen.'

Gretyl gave Albert a two fingered salute and walked over to the record player, reaching down for her favourite Chas & Dave LP. Another of her favourite rituals before the car boot sale was to play 'London Girl'.

'Give me a London girl every time

I've gotta find one I've made up my mind

Give me a London girl every time

I want a London girl

Marry a girl from London town, and you know you can trust 'em

They'll darn your socks and wash and mend, your trousers if you bust 'em

There all good cooks and they got good looks and they won't lead you a dance

I'm gonna find a London girl, if I get half a chance.'

Albert had his own, childish rebuttal and loved to play it when Gretyl left for the car boot. The song, *'There Ain't No Pleasing You'* would always bring a smile to his face.

Both Albert and Gretyl shared the same love of Chas & Dave. The cockney rhyming slang band hit the music charts in the early 80's and were famous for their pub sing-along, humorous, boogie-woogie piano style.

Back in the 1950s, Albert had enjoyed listening to a young Gretyl belt out some of the Vera Lynn and Gracie Fields favourites. Try as he might to remember better days, this was no comfort to him today.

Albert picked up Chas & Dave's *'Mustn't Grumble'* LP, lifted the needle on the record player and moved it to his favourite track:

'Well, I built my life around you

Did what I thought was right

But you never cared about me

Now I've seen the light

Oh darlin', there ain't no pleasing you

You seem to think that everything I ever did was wrong

I should have known it, all along

Oh darlin', there ain't no pleasing you.'

The kettle finished boiling and Albert reached for his West Ham United FA Cup Winners 1980 embellished mug. Not only proud of his London roots, Albert was a fanatical supporter of the West Ham United football team.

Albert loved to recollect the 1966 world cup, relishing the fact that England's goals in the final were scored by West Ham Players. He was a regular season ticket holder from the 1960s through to the late 80s and still loved listening to the game on his radio at the allotment.

Albert enjoyed living in the past. The sadness he felt at home was kept at bay by his hobbies and memories.

This morning, the words *'Ain't No Pleasing You'* echoed in his head:

"Cause I ain't gonna be made to look a fool no more

You done it once too often, what do you take me for

Oh darlin', there ain't no pleasing you

Yeah, if you think I don't mean what I say

And I'm only bluffin'

You got another thing comin'

I'm tellin' you that for nothin'

Oh darlin' I'm leavin'

That's what I'm gonna do-oo...'

'The Bag Lady' was the name given to Gretyl by those Battersea car boot faithfuls that traded on the stalls. Gretyl loved using her disguise to deceive the naive, one-time-only sellers to part with their items far more cheaply than they may have intended.

Traders arrived from 6.30am, with the general public following at 8am, but this time Gretyl had a plan to sneak in with the early traders. Ready to feign injury, she limped agonisingly at a snail's pace, wheezing past the queue of vehicles as they waited at the gate entrance.

Gretyl looked at the vehicles to see if she could spot any new faces. Stopping alongside a small van, she spotted an empty passenger seat.

The young driver looked toward Gretyl, who was bent over, appearing to be in some distress.

The lad wound his window down.

'Are you alright?'

Gretyl replied, 'Oooh no. What's your name?'

'Pete.'

Gretyl's web had caught its young prey.

'Pete, I really need to sit down and catch my breath. Do you mind if I just rest myself in your passenger seat?'

Pete took a hard look at Gretyl's appearance, desperately trying to think up some excuse but couldn't find one. He hoped she didn't smell as bad as she looked.

'Sure.'

As Gretyl sat down, she dropped the facade and relaxed.

'Oh, thank you, young man. This was just what I needed before walking around the car boot.'

'No problem. I thought you were having a heart attack.'

'A bit of the ol' angina, that's all. You don't mind if I just have a little rest here, do you dear? Is this your first car boot?'

'Yeh, my Gran died recently and I'm doing her house clearance. Got rid of the furniture, but this is just the small stuff – ornaments, pictures, plates and the like.'

'How lovely, Peter. You are a good boy.'

Pete looked embarrassed at Gretyl's flattery.

'To be honest, I didn't have the heart to throw it all. I phoned the local charity shop and they told me they were chockablock and didn't have any space until next week.'

Gretyl replied, 'Aw, how sweet. You just wanted the stuff to go to a good home, eh? It's not even about the money darling, is it?'

Pete blushed at the question.

'Erm. No, not really. To be honest, I should be at the footy today, but I promised my family I'd sort it.'

Gretyl smiled as the window of opportunity opened right in front of her eyes.

'Do you mind if I take a wee peep back there and look at your dear grandma's stuff?'

'No, by all means.'

Gretyl climbed into the back of the van, rummaging through the boxes. To her delight she noticed that the plates, figurines and cutlery were very much to her taste.

Gretyl moved a large cardboard box and found the pictures that Pete had mentioned.

Her face lit up.

One large painting depicted a quaint cottage set amongst green hills and a bright blue sky. This was Gretyl's dream, that one day, somehow, whether through the lottery or the discovery of some ancient artifact at a car boot, she could enjoy the comforts of a luxury residence or a posh holiday somewhere over the rainbow.

Over the years Gretyl had become bitter, resenting the fact that Albert had no desire to take a holiday with her. She had become bored with life and despised his lack of ambition to travel outside London.

Gretyl returned to the front passenger seat of the van.

'Pete, did you say you wanted to be at the football today? How much would you want from me to take this stuff off your hands? I have a small garage that isn't far from here. These things would make it so much more like a home for me. You could drop it off later.'

'I was hoping to take about fifty quid,' Pete said sheepishly.

Gretyl opened her moneybag and looking intently inside, rummaging through her coins.

'On a good day, you might make that at a car boot, but not with this stuff. If the weather's bad, you'd be lucky to cover the fifteen quid stall hire.'

Gretyl glanced out of the window before adding nonchalantly, 'You might sell the stuff over two or three weekends though.'

'I couldn't do that,' Pete replied. 'I play for a local club on Saturdays.'

'Well, how about I try and help you out. If you just want to get off, I can offer you twenty quid and all you have to do is drop the stuff off later.'

Pete paused, rubbed his chin, and stared out of the window for a moment, before turning to Gretyl.

'That sounds okay. Write your address here and I'll drop it off after my football match. How does six o'clock sound?'

'That's fine. Enjoy the game, dear.'

Gretyl stepped out of the van, delighted that she had captured such a great haul before the car boot had even started.

CHAPTER 9

Green Fingers

Albert enjoyed an early start at the allotment and was surprised to hear several knocks on the door of his shed. It was Sajan, complete with a mug of tea and a Rich Tea biscuit.

Sajan was a young Asian lad who worked his own allotment next to Albert's. Barely 18 years old, he had just left school and achieved six 'A' level passes.

The Panesar family had great hopes for their son's future and would sit up most evenings to discuss whether he should pursue a career in law or medicine. Salary, working hours and career prospects were all weighed up, including further opportunities for a PhD or equivalent. They were immensely proud of their son and Sajan knew it, but no academic success could remove the fear that plagued him.

Sajan's parents rented the allotment for him for his 16th birthday after a terrifying spell of bullying at school. Sajan had lost a lot of confidence as a result and was now becoming a recluse, with no friends his own age.

Over the few years, Sajan had enjoyed the safety and solitude of his vegetable patch and a friendship had slowly developed with Albert.

Feeling unable to talk to his parents about the bullying, Albert had become a source of wisdom and encouragement for him.

For his part, Albert didn't socialise a great deal with the other gardeners. For him, the allotment was a private place where he could cherish his memories and keep fit in his old age. It had also helped him earn some extra cash; he sold the fruits of his labours to his best friend Stan who owned the greengrocers.

Albert welcomed Sajan into his small allotment shed. He grabbed the wooden stool, wiped the seat with his hand and invited him to sit down.

'Thanks for the tea, son. I noticed your vegetables are doing well.'

Sajan smiled bashfully. 'Thank you. Block planting the cabbages has worked well with the mint and garlic chives. My parents love to use the herbs with their curries.'

'Can't say I ever tried a curry myself ... more of a fish and chips man, me.'

Albert smiled and dipped his Rich Tea biscuit in his mug.

'Well Albert, I'll bring you a sample of our vegetable curry. I think you will like it.'

'Thanks son. I'll let you know what I think. Maybe I'll give it a try.'

'Can you tell me about this picture on the shelf?'

Sajan pointed to a wrinkled black and white photo of a group of soldiers who were seated, cleaning their weapons behind a Navy ship.

Albert took a deep breath, reached for the small bottle of whisky and poured a strong measure into his mug of tea.

'I'm sorry, I shouldn't ask,' said Sajan, concerned that he'd hit a raw nerve. He hadn't asked about Albert's photos before, though he had wanted to.

'It's okay, son. These photos are very precious to me. That's why I keep them under lock and key in this wooden chest.'

'Why do you keep these photos here in your shed?'

'I like to have a drink with the boys down here. It's my own space and it's away from the wife. Best days of my life they were ... and the saddest as well.'

Albert paused, lifting his mug in the air to salute his friends seated on the shelf.

Sajan noticed Albert's eyes were sparkling and teary. He smiled respectfully.

'What's it like to fire a rifle like the one in this picture?'

As Albert began to reply, Sajan was all ears.

'Well, the boys and I were issued with the Lee Enfield Mark 4 as our main rifle. It was the fastest bolt action rifle in the world. She was a reliable and rugged weapon and could fire thirty aimed rounds a minute at someone over 200 metres away.'

d you ever kill anyone?'

bert sighed and looked down at the photo he was holding.

on, when there are men who are trying to take your life and the lives of your friends, you don't think twice. If you think, you're dead. I lost a number of good friends, but you know what? The people we shot had families as well. Everybody lost somebody back in those days.'

Sajan sat pensively, staring down at the floor.

Albert detected some deep and emotional pain in Sajan, unaware of the vengeful plans that had been running through the young lad's mind.

'Remember this, Sajan. Whatever pain we inflict upon others, good and innocent people get hurt in the process.'

Sajan seemed disturbed by Albert's words.

'So who teaches them a lesson?'

Albert sipped from his mug.

'What goes around, comes around, I say. Nobody appointed us judge, jury and executioner.'

Albert paused.

'Believe me son ... vengeance is a bittersweet pill, best avoided at all costs.'

CHAPTER 10

Knock Down Price

Tony returned to the phone. 'So, how's life going in Canvey, Dave? What you been up to? Making any money?'

'Er, to be honest bro, still in the same council house. Same wife, kid and debts.'

'Nice one, nice one. How are the Mrs and the little fella?'

Tony, disinterested, continued to pick his nose and flick the contents out of the large double doors, toward the swimming pool.

'That little fella is now a six footer with pimples and hairy armpits. Sharon is, well, still Sharon, moaning about the house and lack of money as usual.'

Tony rolled a bogey on his finger and flicked it at his large Alsatian dog.

'Nice, nice. Anyway, what makes you call after such a long time mate? The last time we spoke you told me about selling a load of baby crap to some yuppies on allotments.'

Tony let out a large laugh but Dave refused to be put off by it for once.

'Got a far better idea this time for you, bro. This is one that could make you some serious money.'

Dave knew that Tony would be surprised by his directness and confidence.

'Go on. I'm listening.'

It was now or never.

'Tony, how would you like it if I brought a group of wealthy ol' folk to Marbella to spend their large sums of cash on your holiday villas?'

Tony blew up on the phone. 'Who's told you? Are you taking the Mick?'

Flummoxed at his brother's response, Dave replied, 'What are you talking about? I thought you had built them to sell on?'

'So you haven't heard anything?' replied Tony.

'No. What's up?'

'Well, after bunging the local town planner a wad of cash (he's supposed to run things here), it turns out that the planning license he gave me isn't worth the paper it was written on.'

Dave listened intently. He knew Tony had invested his 'bent' money in the popular and 'authentically Spanish' old town area of Marbella. As far as he knew, Tony was made for life.

Tony continued, 'Well, this muppet called Carlos got his fingers caught in a load of other scams. The government investigated my planning permission and next thing I know, the police turn up at my door with a demolition order, telling me my villas were built without a permit and they're gonna knock 'em down. I have ninety days notice!'

Dave paused and then began to make his pitch to his brother.

'Tony, all the more reason then to get these ol' folk to stay in your villas before they become rubble. You can offer them a knock down price when they stay.'

Now it was Dave's turn to have a laugh at Tony's expense.

Tony was listening ... thinking.

'And how do you suppose to bring them over here? What's your angle?'

'Don't you worry about that one, Tony. I've got it sorted. I've been planning it with Kev. He's doing a website, letterhead and brochure design. You'll love the business name - Costa Soddall Travel.'

Tony cackled over the phone at his brother's childish attempt at humour. That was until he realised that Dave wasn't joking.

'Are you serious?'

'As serious as the Pope. I know where the money is and I know how to get them over to you. All you need to do is wine them, dine them, spoil and gut them at the end of it all.'

Tony paused before replying with an unusual urgency and gravity.

'Dave, if you can bring them over and we can sell these villas, I will seriously make it worth your while. The rooms are ready. Fit for the Queen, mate. I tell you, I spent everything I had on them, before I got this letter. We've got stunning views, complete with Jacuzzis and swimming pools here. I'll even have one of the girls cook up some fresh bread in kitchens, to give a new and welcome atmosphere for the ol' croaks.'

Dave could hardly contain his excitement.

'I know we can do this Tony. You could sell sand to the Arabs. These ol' folk would be a walk over for you.'

'Dave, if you bring any men on the trip, I'll make sure that their young housekeepers are so fit, they'll fake illness just to stay indoors with them. Give me spinsters or widows and I'll make sure I hire some local escorts to do the gardening in nothing but tight shorts, popping in regularly for cold drinks.'

CHAPTER 11

Ernie's Nest

Gretyl scanned the traffic as it moved towards the entrance of the car boot sale. Not content with one van load of mixed items for the day, she spotted a girl who had packed her Ford Fiesta so full that the rear windows were completely obscured. Gretyl figured that she was either a new face to the world of car boots, or a first year student lost on her way to university.

Walking slightly ahead of the car, Gretyl was ready for her next dramatic contrivance. As the car moved forward she fell to the ground in pain, feigning a collision with the vehicle.

'Oh my God!' shrieked the blonde in the car.

'Are you okay? I didn't see you. I mean, er didn't think I ... are you alright?'

Gretyl hobbled over to the driver's door, wincing.

'It's not your fault dear. I think I was about to cross the road when you drove over my foot. Do you mind if I sit down in your passenger seat?'

The slim young woman reached over to open the door and Gretyl gently manoevered herself into the passenger seat, ready to be chauffeured to the field where the stalls were being set up.

It was now 7.30am.

'Let me offer you a helping hand with your stall, dear,' Gretyl said.

'If you're feeling up to it, I could do with some help,' the young woman replied.

A few moments later Gretyl was rummaging through the boxes in the back of the car. Within seconds she had located a large china mug with a frog embellished on it.

'Oh how wonderful. You didn't know that I collected frogs, did you? Let me just count out my change for the morning and see what I can offer you for it. I'll just check if I have enough. That is if you don't mind, sweetheart?'

The girl called out, her head buried in the boot of the car.

'You can have it. Call it quits for running over your foot. Actually, I'm glad that I haven't done you any damage. You must have been lucky.'

'Life, my dear, has nothing to do with luck and everything to do with opportunity. You have to make the most of every moment. If you hadn't driven over my foot, this lovely frog may never have jumped into my arms.'

'Well, I can't argue with that.'

'No. You mustn't. If this little frog hadn't found a home today, that would have been bad luck.'

Gretyl added, 'I'll be on my way, now dear. Don't forget my advice now, will you? Bye.'

It was approaching 8am and the field was set up with over one hundred stalls, laid out in six long rows. For Gretyl, the first priority of the day would be the ice cream van, with the burger stall coming a close second.

Gretyl spent so long scouring the mix of cheap antiques, clothing and other household toot, that she demolished her ice cream long before reaching the third stall.

To appease her gargantuan appetite, Gretyl silenced any dissenting stomach gurgles with her customary hot dog with extra onions, drowned in dollops of ketchup and mustard sauce.

Gretyl then ordered her usual double Flake 99 with extra raspberry and chocolate sauce, along with her childhood favourite - sugar coated hundreds and thousands.

Bill, who had served as an ice cream vendor on the site for nearly eight years, was accustomed to Gretyl paying for her ice cream with mostly copper coins. But this morning even he was losing his patience with Gretyl.

'Please love, you aren't going to stand there and count one hundred and forty pennies are you? My customers will die of heatstroke before you're finished.'

Bill snatched the large handful of change, refusing to count it and threw it in his cash tin.

The crowd broke into applause, while Gretyl stormed off, adorned with a moustache made of ice cream.

'Take a look at that boat race.' 'The bag lady is back.' 'State of that and the price of fish.' The bystanders barked comments which stuck to Gretyl like chewing gum on the bottom of a shoe.

A new stall in the distance caught Gretyl's eye. Her face lit up as she saw what looked like a collection of head wigs.

Gretyl's heart skipped a beat as she read the sign:
'PRELOVED WIGS FROM THE RICH AND FAMOUS!'

Gretyl's fascination with wigs had begun back in her pub singing days. She had quickly discovered that not only her image but her whole personality was transformed every time she wore a different wig.

Each hairpiece had its own name and personality and with a collection of over twenty hair styles, Gretyl had narrowed it down to wearing her favourite seven from Monday to Sunday.

Monday – Marilyn Munroe Classic Blonde Bombshell wig.

Tuesday – Gracie Allen, the famous Hollywood comedienne of the 1950s with her finger curls and wavy hair.

Wednesday – Ginger Rogers, the soft, gentile, red-head.

Thursday – Raquel Welch, the bouffant brunette.

Friday – Cher's long curly locks.

The weekend brought out Saturday's special – Tina Turner's straw-like and frizzy nest.

Sunday – Pat Butcher from the BBC TV soap series, Eastenders. Bleach blonde and scraggy hair (also used on car boot days).

As Gretyl strode eagerly towards the stall, the trader's voice grew louder and louder.

'Come and look at these lovely syrup of figs, ladies and gentleman. Expect the best at Ernie's Nest.'

Gretyl accelerated to the table where she was greeted by a burly and hairy tattooed man.

Ernie's shirt was violently displaced from his trousers by his enormous belly. Even Gretyl couldn't help feeling a little intimidated by his unkempt appearance and manner.

'Alwight luv. I can see that you're a wig lover. That's a lovely bit of rug on your head.'

'I beg your pardon,' replied Gretyl. 'What you just called a rug is my Millano dusty blonde, pixie cut. You've probably seen it on TV.'

At six feet three inches, Ernie loomed over Gretyl as he looked down at her greedy face.

'Ah, course I have! Sorry me luv. I meant rug in the best possible taste. It was me ol' man who used it when he said how lovely me mother looked. You, my dear, look lovely, like you were born for the best wigs.'

'Oh, really?'

Gretyl noticed a laminated booklet on the table with photographs of famous people, all of them apparently wearing Ernie's wigs. Even the least discerning eye could see that he had superimposed his wigs onto the faces of celebrities, but Gretyl wanted to believe she was about to buy quality, even at a car boot sale.

This morning, Gretyl was allured by the scent of celebrity.

'And may I say what a lovely boat race you have for it. Two secs, luv; I have somethin' very special to show you.'

Ernie bent down and retrieved a wig from a sodden cardboard box at the rear of his stall.

Gretyl grimaced at the sight of Ernie's blotchy, spotty bottom that popped out from the top of his jeans with unnerving ease.

'I'd refuse to sell this lovely little blonde nest to anyone who didn't look like Marilyn Munroe, God rest 'er soul.'

Gretyl reached for a hanky and wiped the sweat from her brow. Keen to look in every direction but Ernie's, she spotted a black bob cut style wig, unlike anything else in her collection.

'I like this wig, but it feels a bit different. I only buy real hair and not synthetic. Is this synthetic?'

Ernie turned around and pulled his trousers up.

'No dear. That's real hair from Japan. Feels different eh? My sources told me it was owned by a wealthy geezer's wife. Multi-millionaire I understand.'

Gretyl seemed impressed by the provenance of the wig.

'Well, I like it, but I have plenty of wigs and don't really need any more. It doesn't feel like real hair.'

'Have you ever owned a Japanese wig?'

Gretyl had no idea of the origins of any of her wigs.

'No,' replied Gretyl.

Adopting a softer tone, Ernie pressed in for the sale.

'They're different to us, y'know; different eyes, skin colour, hair. It's real quality, human hair. I should know. I've been in this game for years.'

Gretyl ran her fingers through the strands of the wig, considering for a moment whether she'd be comfortable wearing a wig previously owned by a foreigner.

'I tell you what luv, if you want it, it's yours for twenty quid. I shouldn't let it go this cheap. The celebrity who owned it would have paid hundreds for it. Posh people don't wear cheap, do they luv? I can tell you don't wear cheap.'

Ernie quickly smothered the beginnings of a sardonic grin as he scrutinized Gretyl's decrepit Sunday outfit.

'Celebrity, you say. I'll give you a tenner for it.' replied Gretyl.

The trader smiled.

'Done!'

Gretyl rummaged through her bum bag, feeling for her stash of coins.

'I've done some good business today,' she thought. 'Especially, as it's barely eight in the morning.'

Striding proudly to the burger van, Gretyl celebrated her morning success like a champion athlete, an odorous wave of burgers washing over her like a champagne baptism.

CHAPTER 12

Forgotten War

Albert took a stroll out from his wooden shed and looked with great pride at his row of cabbages.

'I see you're keeping your patch intact?' said Mr Singh, the Allotment Inspector.

Albert was never quite sure with Mr Singh if this customary statement was an observation or a command.

'Mr Singh, you always have the best interests of the Greater London Council and its neighbours at heart,' Albert replied sarcastically.

The Inspector pulled on the lapels of his black trench coat.

'You know me, Mr Trollop. Just doing my job, keeping the riff-raff out.'

Albert sighed as Mr Singh opened his satchel bag to reveal a large A3 size poster with a picture of his huge black boot stepping on a cornucopia of slugs, snails and caterpillars with the words:

'YOU WILL BE HELD RESPONSIBLE.'

'There will be plenty of these notices up around the site. You can tell the others, I expect my instructions to be obeyed,' snarled the Inspector.

Mr Singh loved to issue citations for the slightest appearance of caterpillar or weed.

Albert retaliated.

'Don't worry. If I spot any offenders, I'll march them over to the tardis and lock them in there, ready for your interrogation!'

The tardis was an evaporating and dehydrating toilet which converted ninety five percent of its human waste into a safe, pathogen free material without the need for water, chemicals or electricity.

As the Inspector walked off, Sajan had just arrived at the allotment.

Keen to continue his conversation with Albert, Sajan knocked on Albert's shed and entered, finding him with a large photo album open upon his knee. Amongst what appeared to be hundreds of photographs, Albert was looking at one particular photo of an old sweetheart.

'I'm sorry Albert, I didn't mean to interrupt again.'

Albert didn't reply immediately, as if caught in time, his eyes fixed intensely on the album. It looked to Sajan like he'd been crying.

Sajan shuffled uncomfortably.

'It's alright son. Take a seat. I was just, y'know, thinking about the past. You do a lot of thinking when you get as old as me, though I don't expect someone as young as you would understand that.'

Albert smiled before continuing.

'It's important that you make the right choices early on in life. You tend to see everything through rose-tinted glasses when you're young.'

Albert looked down at the photograph and sighed.

'Her name was Betty,' he said.

Albert paused for a moment and handed over the album to Sajan.

The photo had worn around the edges and the bottom half of the photo was barely recognisable.

'She was my childhood sweetheart from school. I found out when I got back from being a POW that Betty had married two years after I had been captured. I don't blame her though. Everyone thought I was dead. She was married several weeks before I returned to London.'

Sajan often wondered why he'd never seen any pictures of Albert's wife in the shed so he asked, 'Did you meet your wife soon after you returned?'

'Yes. Gretyl sang three nights a week at the Ship and Shovel. I buried my head in the bottle when I came back from Korea. I began to take note of her a few weeks after that and ended up getting her pregnant. Back in those days, it was the done thing to marry the girl, so I did.'

Sajan blushed.

'Gretyl was barely eighteen years old when we were married, and was a looker, of sorts, back then. She had curly blonde hair, eyelashes as big as a paint brush, bright red lipstick and legs up to her neck.'

Sajan laughed nervously.

'Let me give you a word of advice, son. Not all that glitters is gold. When life rubs off that golden paint, you won't always like what's underneath.'

Sajan opened his mouth slowly, took a deep breath and looked down.

'Albert, I have never really um, had a girlfriend. My parents never approved of me talking with girls. They said that it would get in the way of my education and career prospects. To be honest, I find it so hard to talk to anyone these days. In fact, you're the only person that I chat to.'

Albert smiled.

'Son, I understand. I don't want to intrude or anything, but if you ever want to talk about stuff, you know where I am.'

Sajan looked pensively at the floor for a moment.

'What's it like being a prisoner of war?' he asked.

Albert took his time to reply. Apart from Stan, he hadn't spoken to anyone else about his time as a POW.

'We lived in appalling conditions. Some of the men died of malnutrition, some dysentery, others from torture.'

Sajan couldn't disguise his mixture of shock and curiosity.

'At times, death seemed like a close companion, but a few of us dared to believe that one day we would be back home. Nearly two years of hunger and cold, sickness and disease was enough to finish off the best of the men. Korea has some of the most precious and painful memories for me.'

Sajan was now captivated.

'Albert, the people that ill-treated you ... did you want to kill them? Do you still hate them?'

'What do you think, son?' replied Albert.

'I think you wanted them dead. You wanted them to feel your pain.'

Albert paused before he added, 'The bitterness and pain fed some of us with the constant desire for revenge, but it didn't do us any good. It seemed to eat at our souls.'

Sajan's eyes welled up.

'The only one who kept us sane was a soldier we called Gunner. A super bloke, he was an honest, funny and religious lad. He coped better than all of us and often read Bible verses about hope and salvation. Converted a few of us, I can tell you. So in answer to your question, no, deep down in my heart, I know that I don't hate them.'

'But how can you really forgive those who hurt you?'

Albert's eyes began to fill with tears.

Sajan shifted uneasily in his seat and made as if to leave the shed.

Albert poured himself another shot of brandy.

'Son, when you know the pain of taking another man's life, it's not easy to live with. I used to justify it, but nowadays, I think not only of the friends who died by my side, but all of those who lose their life in war. I think about the lives of the families that are forever changed, because of the horror of war.'

Sajan wiped his eyes.

Albert continued. 'I've learned over the years that when I hold any bitterness or resentment, it only makes me feel worse. Hurting people end up hurting people.'

Albert smiled at Sajan. 'Let me share some words with you that my friend Gunner said to me in camp: 'We need to forgive our enemies. For if we truly forgive, we not only free ourselves, but we show our enemies how to be free as well. The most powerful weapon in the world is forgiveness, and only the truly strong can use it.'

CHAPTER 13

Plan for a Scam

After Dave Soddall had spent an hour in the loo weighing up his call with Tony, he called a family meeting together. To his surprise, rather than the usual groans, his request was met with an air of interest and expectation by Kevin and Sharon.

Dave revealed a set of hand written motivational notes that he'd scribbled while sitting on his preferred seat of inspiration ... the toilet.

Sharon began to laugh.

'Aw, honey. I didn't know you could read and write.'

Dave ignored the wind-up and pressed on with his speech.

'We will remember this day. Just like when Churchill gave that speech about beating the Germans (and yes, the ball did cross the line), this day marks our finest hour. No more will we bow down to those who have more than us, for we will have more than them! From now on, it'll be takeaways every night for the Soddall family.'

Sharon giggled.

'I love your ambition, honey. A lifetime of takeaways ... wow baby!'

Dave ignored Sharon's mockery, while Kevin remained typically unimpressed.

'Dad, what are those brown smudges on the paper?'

Before he could answer, Sharon let off a foul mouthed burst.

'You dirty git. You wrote that while sitting on the throne, didn't you? Have we run out of toilet paper, or what?'

'What are you on about love? I needed some inspiration, so I took a bag of chocolate Maltesers with me.'

Kevin expressed his repulsion (he wanted those Maltesers), while Sharon breathed a sigh of relief. Dave, oblivious to their reaction, continued reading:

'There is still a way to go yet. We've an ocean to swim, a hill to climb and a road to walk. We must work hard to make this work, rise to the challenge, row to the finish line and get a medal for a bloody change.'

Unable to control his laughter, Kevin spat his Cola on the floor, earning him a clip round the ear from Sharon.

'Dave, what you on about? You know I can't swim, and I don't wanna go mountain climbing.'

Kevin fell to the floor, holding his stomach in spasms of laughter.

'You muppet, he's speaking metaphorically, mother, not literally.'

Sharon looked embarrassed and pretended that she hadn't heard.

Dave continued.

'Ok, that's it. You don't deserve my wisdom, any of you. Kev, you'd rather wear the same ol' hand-me-down clothes from last year? Tottie, don't you want that lucky break we've always dreamed of? I'm telling you, we pull this off, and darling, we can redecorate. Kev, you can go buy yourself a little car. We'll never need to collect newspaper vouchers for cheap and tacky caravan holidays.'

Dave handed Sharon and Kevin their basic job descriptions with a list of things to do. Sharon would be the sales agent on the phone, chatting up the ol' folk. Kevin's role involved creating the marketing and any print they would send out. This included the website, sales letters, fake photos and anything that Dave found more intellectually challenging.

Kevin immediately began to tap away on his laptop and made a start on the web domain, costasoddalltravel. co.uk with a banner declaring, 'Where Great Holidays in the Sun Costa Nothing'.

He also designed a logo, which consisted of a large bosomed woman sitting under a palm tree.

This received a hearty 'thumbs up' from Dave.

Dave, who now dubbed himself the mastermind of the project, made a phone call from his bathroom HQ to an old friend.

Peter Lovitt, known as Sharkie, was a successful but dodgy mortgage broker. Most of his wealth came from a bygone era when there was little legislation in place to stop his outrageous commissions and crooked financial deals.

Dave invited his old friend to come round and take part in his scheme.

Sharkie was now on his way.

Kevin busied himself by gathering information from the Internet about the retired members of the village they were about to target. Dave knew this would impress Sharkie and was quite sure he'd never turn down the opportunity to make money.

Dave rummaged through his wardrobe and hurriedly dressed in his Sunday best for the business meeting, only to be cruelly reminded by a broken trouser zip that it was more than several sizes too small. All he had to wear now was his wrinkled, once white, short-sleeved shirt covered in Brut aftershave and KFC-stains, a yellow and brown Simpsons tie and grey tracksuit bottoms.

'I'll just have to invent some story about me trousers being ruined', Dave thought to himself.

The doorbell rang and Sharon rushed to firm up her cleavage in the mirror before answering.

Peeling back the curtains to take a look, she saw Sharkie, standing six feet two in a pin-striped blue suit, open neck white shirt and shiny leather shoes. His face was handsome, clean shaven, with blue eyes and short black spiky hair. Sharon stood there, spellbound by such a fresh offering of eye candy on her doorstep.

The front door swung open and Sharkie looked at her eyes and then moved slowly down from her chest to her legs.

Sharon's cheeks flushed, charmed by his drop dead gorgeous looks and suave, confident demeanour.

Her temperature rose faster than the needle on a formula one racing car.

Sharkie stood ogling for what seemed an eternity.

'Hi. You must be Sharon. You're flipping gorgeous.'

Sharkie landed a huge kiss on her lips that lasted moments longer than was decent but moments shorter than was desired, by both of them.

Sharon broke away and stuttered in a nervous school girl voice:

'Please, come in.'

Sharon led him into the lounge. Feeling a bit light on her feet, she sat down in the three-seater settee and tapped the cushion next to her, encouraging Sharkie to take a seat.

Meanwhile, Dave anxiously checked himself in the bathroom mirror and cleared his nose of a few unsightly crustaceans.

Dave stomped down the brown carpeted stairs and greeted Sharkie.

'Hey, Sharkie. You haven't changed in years. Still looking good I see.'

'Wish I could say the same for you Dave. What happened to those muscles, mate? That tattoo on your arm looks like the woman's jugs are tickling her feet.'

Sharkie let out a loud, confident laugh, while Sharon cackled giddily.

Ten years ago, Dave would have gladly chinned the cocky git for such a comment, but he needed Sharkie to work the old folk with the equity release idea, so he kept silent.

Sharkie's face squirmed, as a waft of Dave's breakfast after-burn escaped from his jogging bottoms and caught his nostrils.

Dave stretched his shirt over his sagging belly and gazed at the ceiling in a forlorn attempt to draw attention away from the smell.

Sharon was sat next to Sharkie in red high heels, black see-through tights, a white short skirt, and a red low cut blouse that left little to the imagination.

Averting his eyes from Sharon's dangling earrings and cleavage, Sharkie looked at Dave, wondering what had turned this once pumped-up man into a couch potato.

Dave noticed Sharkie looking at his dirty jogging bottoms.

'Sharon darling, are my trousers dry yet? I feel a bit of a dick sitting here in me bottoms.'

'You haven't worn any trousers, love, for the past six years. You've lived in those filthy things ever since.'

Dave looked indignant.

Sharon continued with her jibe.

'I'd put them out for the bin man, if it weren't for the fact that you'd probably just sit in your dirty underpants the whole day.'

Dave had expected Sharon to go along with his excuse for his bottoms, to impress Sharkie.

Dave snapped defensively, 'That's nice. I'm talking about me black suit, aren't I?'

Sharon winked at Sharkie, suggesting she wasn't quite finished teasing just yet.

'Ah, yes love, do you mean the one you got married in? I thought you were saving it for your funeral? Won't matter what it looks like then dear, when I cremate you in it.'

Sharkie, not one for small talk, cut to the chase.

'Okay, so let me get this right. You told me on the phone that you want to sell your brother Tony's holiday properties to some rich ol' folk from Poncey Bridge and you want me to get the money out of 'em. Correct?'

'Right so far, mate,' Dave replied.

'Apart from targeting their savings, you also want me to offer them an easy way to release money from their own properties, like a lifetime mortgage through an equity release scheme. Correct?'

Sharkie fiddled with his Hugo Boss cufflinks.

'Yeh, I saw on TV that with a lifetime mortgage, they can release money from the value of their houses. Apparently, the loan doesn't get paid back until they are dead or in nursing homes when their property is sold, so they've got nothing to lose.'

Sharkie interjected.

'Well, the good news mate is that a few years ago, I became a specialist lifetime mortgage advisor for several companies that offer the equity release scheme. I used to earn good money just referring them, but I found out there were big bucks to be made setting them up. How many old croaks are you planning to take to Marbella?'

Sharkie's attention shifted again to Sharon, who was staring into his blue eyes. She could almost taste the champagne on her wet lips, wrapped up in his soft white dressing gown, the warm Mediterranean breeze caressing her face as she gazed into the beautiful, deep blue sea from her balcony.

'Tony has five villas, so enough to fill them. He's gonna work his magic selling them to the ol' folk. You can follow them up and show them just how easy and painless it is for them to own them. Obviously, you'd have to come to Marbella with us. All expenses paid, of course.'

Dave hoped he had impressed Sharkie and paused for his reply.

'Yep, sounds fine by me. Plenty of top totty in the Costa, I tell you mate. There's a few birds I could knock up while I'm there.'

Dave put on a sober voice.

'Sharkie, there's something I need to tell you about the properties. They're gonna be knocked down. The Spanish authorities said my brother's building construction was illegal and they've given him ninety days' notice before they bulldoze it all. Tony stands to lose the lot. That's why we need to get these ol' folk out there on their free holiday and flog 'em the posh villas while they're still standing.'

Sharkie put his hand into the top pocket of his pin-striped suit, pulled out a cigar and what looked like a solid gold lighter. He lit the stump, sucked several times on its shaft and puffed the sumptuous aroma into the room.

Rather than be deterred, Sharkie seemed enticed both by Tony's predicament and the eye contact from Sharon.

Dave noticed in the corner of his eye that his wife was ogling Sharkie. 'Na,' he thought to himself. 'She's probably thinking, like me, that pretty boy here is our meal ticket if he can help make this happen.'

The smell of the Cuban cigar was making Dave think of a holiday somewhere warm.

'As long as she's not sitting on pretty boy's lap throwing her lucky dice in some flashy casino,' Dave thought.

Dave wondered if the aroma of Sharkie's Cuban cigar was taking his wife somewhere that he couldn't. He imagined a casino, Sharon sitting on Sharkie's lap and throwing a few lucky dice on the table. Whatever she was thinking about made her blush as she darted from the lounge to the upstairs bathroom.

Running the cold tap, Sharon threw handfuls of cold spray over her face, as she tried to cool down from the Adonis sitting on her sofa.

After Sharon dried her face with the towel, she came back down the stairs and into the front room again, choosing this time to sit on the single chair and out of Sharkie's direct gaze.

'Love, what's wrong with you? You look like Chuckie's bride,' said Dave.

Sharon suddenly realised that her mascara and make-up must have run all over her face. Having been in such a daze, she'd forgotten to check the mirror.

'I'll go get the kettle on,' Sharon said, squirming with embarrassment.

The two men looked at each other and burst out laughing.

'Anyway, back to business,' replied Sharkie. 'As long as Tony's got the paperwork in place to show them when they arrive, we can sell them. As far as the equity release is concerned, the whole thing's a walk in the park. There are no surveys needed. Just a simple signature on the application forms and when the offer is made from the lender, it normally gets signed off by a solicitor. Then the cash lump sum is released.

Sharkie paused and took a puff of his cigar before leaning back in the couch with a smug grin.

'I love it,' he concluded. 'It's bent and yet I'm clean selling it.'

'Will a solicitor have to get involved?' Dave asked nervously.

'Na, it's normally recommended that they do, but we can work that to our own advantage. You see, solicitors don't make any checks on the properties themselves. They just bring the two parties together to make the deal happen. Not only that, but I know a few solicitors who would gladly turn a blind eye and sign it off, if the price was right for them, of course.'

Sharkie looked intently at his friend before asking, 'What you earning out of this, Dave?'

Dave stood up and flexed his dirty waist band.

'Hmmn. Apart from a wad of cash, let's just say a move out of these trackie bottoms for a start.'

CHAPTER 14

Silver Spoons

Gretyl smiled as she mulled over her first triumph at the car boot. She'd already gained another frog for her collection, along with a van-full of goods that Pete agreed to sell for £20 so he could get off to football.

Gretyl couldn't wait to sort through the paintings, plates, figurines and cutlery, but it was only 1pm and she had five hours to wait before they would be delivered to her lock up.

In an attempt to kill time, Gretyl made a visit to 'Gary's Top Nosh Caf' (famous for its spelling mistake) and stood at the counter, eager to gorge herself on another meal.

'I'd like three sausages, 2 bacon, 2 eggs, mushrooms, black pudding, chips, beans, two slices of bread, a pot of tea and lemon meringue pie. Oh and please hurry if you don't mind. I've had a busy morning and need to put some coal in this fire.'

Saturday afternoons were Gretyl's favourite time of the week. After her lunch, she would scour the field, looking for folk who were packing away and might sell their remaining wares for next to nothing.

Having dispatched her lunch, Gretyl returned to the field where one stall had particularly caught her eye. Clearly a wealthy woman's 'brick-a-brack', the goods had been carefully unpacked from a Range Rover and laid upon a trestle table, dressed with a Burberry patterned tablecloth.

The stall holder saw Gretyl approaching and in disdain flung her scarf around her neck.

Gretyl scanned the table and saw that most, if not all, of the delicate and expensive items had not been sold and were definitely overpriced for a boot sale.

'Blimey,' Gretyl muttered.

The Wedgewood plate stood out with a £105 price tag and a collection of silver spoons had £195 on the ticket.

Gretyl raised her eyebrows.

Celia Thorpe-Khan, the chairlady of the Muswell Hill Ward Cancer Research, thrust her chest out so that Gretyl could see her badge.

Her contempt was evident. Gretyl had seen that look many times before, so she picked up the charity sign on the table and scoffed, 'It's such a lovely charity and so worthwhile. Raised much money today, have we dear?'

Gretyl had a good idea of the number of items the lady started with. She surmised that the same number was still on the table.

Celia sensed her cynicism and replied, 'One does what one can. I'm sure you understand.'

'You look like a lady who's frequented many charity venues,' she added.

'I've given thousands to charity,' Gretyl retorted, as she remembered the thousands of items in her garage lock up.

'I've helped the spastics, deaf as a post and blind as a bat. I love giving to third world charities, me. Charity begins at home, but you can't ignore those little pot bellies on TV, can you?'

Gretyl wiped her nose and gave it a long and hard pick before she fingered the Wedgewood China plate.

Celia took one look at Gretyl's grime encrusted hands and snatched the plate back.

'That plate cost me one hundred and twenty five pounds,' she sneered.

Taking an antibacterial wipe from her top pocket, she frantically polished away the smudged fingerprints until she could see the reflection of her own face.

Gretyl felt the insult immediately.

'Love, let's be honest. You should be glad I'm even interested in this load of shite. It's no wonder you've sold bugger all.'

'Our charity ward has raised over forty six thousand pounds so far this year,' Celia replied defensively. 'I couldn't possibly expect someone like you to appreciate what I have so generously donated.

Raised much money yourself? I think not. You look like someone who just takes from charity.'

Gretyl continued her attack.

'Put it this way, love. I've spent more money in charity shops than you have on that tight face of yours, and I know Botox ain't cheap!'

Celia snorted like an indignant mare.

'You have some nerve. It's my taxes that pay for your type.'

'Taxes? You can barely raise a few quid at a car boot! I can see you now, sitting on your fanny at the top table of your little group saying, "I raised £2.70 at the car boot sale, sold a box of Earl Grey tea to Mrs Botox-wreck, another loyal supporter of ours."'

Celia pulled out her Chanel handbag, withdrew her cheque book and taking her diamond crust studded pen, wrote out a cheque in front of Gretyl.

'Cancer Research Foundation ... two hundred pounds... now that ought to do it. You see my dear, rich 'birds' like me can always 'buy' themselves out of trouble.'

She raised her cheekbones, pouted her lips and flaunted the cheque in Gretyl's face.

Gretyl laughed. 'Come on, luv. We both know that it's all show. When I go, you'll tear the cheque up. Probably bounce if they tried to cash it anyway.'

Fuming with rage, Celia grabbed her designer handbag and with one mighty swing, struck Gretyl around the head, a few of the shiny studs scratching her face.

Gretyl did not need to retaliate.

The assault was witnessed by an off-duty police officer, who approached the stall and offered his hand to Gretyl as she lay on the wet ground. He took out his warrant card and showed his ID.

'Excuse me madam. My name is PC Lineker. I witnessed the incident. What's going on here?'

Gretyl sat up on the grass, took a tissue out of her pocket and wiped her cheek.

'Brilliant', she thought to herself as she wiped red marks from her lips. 'Some of the ol' claret on my tissue. Blood money's worth more than her silver spoons. I'll milk the ol' cow now.'

'Can you stand up?' the police officer asked.

'Oh dear, erm, where am I?'

Taking his hand she stood, shaken, unstable and on the edge of tears.

'Oh officer, at my age. I've never been so humiliated.'

'I find that very hard to believe,' Celia interrupted. 'I would have thought you were quite used to it.'

The police officer turned towards Celia.

'Madam I witnessed you assault this lady with your handbag. You have caused a minor injury, for which I could take you to the police station. What do you have to say for yourself?'

Gretyl now saw the opportunity to play her trump card. The trap was laid and Celia was caught smack bang in the middle of it.

Gretyl placed her hand gently on the officer's arm.

'I'm sure that we could settle this amicably and out of court. I wouldn't want the name of the Chairlady of the Muswell Hill Ward Cancer Research to fall into disrepute. You know the local newspapers, always naming and shaming local lawbreakers. It might even cost her prestigious role as Chairlady of such a wonderful charity. I wouldn't wish that on her.'

Celia's face drained before she regained her composure and addressed the officer.

'I'm sure there's a simple solution. This lady was enquiring about the silver spoons and I would be more than happy to recompense her with them.'

Gretyl placed her blood stained tissue on the table and held the cutlery to her ample bosom.

'Why that's very gracious of you, my dear. I want you to know this ... these spoons are finally going to a good home!'

CHAPTER 15

Polish a Turd

It was now 4.30pm and Albert took down the photographs from the shelves of his allotment shed, placing them carefully into his heavily padlocked wooden chest. He threw an old tablecloth over the chest and put his mug, kettle and newspaper over it, using it as a small table.

Albert filled his carrier bag with some of his latest produce from the allotment. Eager to reach Stan's shop before closing time, he closed the shed door, locked the heavy padlock and set off on his bicycle.

Albert entered the store to the ring of bells. Stan greeted him with a heavy cough and a tired smile.

Albert was startled by how frail his friend looked.

'Stan, you gotta cut down on the cigarettes,' he said. 'You look terrible.'

Stan's furrowed brow and wrinkled face oozed beads of sweat.

'I'm ok Albert. Just have a bit of a cold on my chest.'

But Stan now began to cough violently. Grabbing a wooden stool, he collapsed onto it.

Albert rushed over and steadied Stan, helping him to sit upright.

'You don't look good mate. Have you got any chest pains? Do you want me to call for an ambulance?'

'Na, don't be silly. Like I told you mate, it's just a chest cough.'

Stan took a tissue to his mouth and coughed inside it, making sure that Albert did not see the bloody phlegm within its folds.

'You stay there, Stan. I'll put the kettle on. How's that sound?'

Stan lifted his head and smiled.

'That would be lovely, mate. Just need a good cuppa down me and an early night. Think I might have to cut down on my sex life, though.'

'Stan, mine went off the boil years ago!'

Albert laughed amid the noisy rattle of the kettle.

As the steam rose from the kettle spout, Albert remembered an image from over sixty years ago.

The ship, HMS Ceylon was docked in the quayside in Pujan, South Korea. Her tubular horn blasted while Albert sat listening to the Bagpipers of the Argyll and Sutherland Highlanders.

'Taking a trip down memory lane?' Stan asked.

'I've been thinking a lot lately about my time in Korea. The 29th of August, 1950 to be exact. That's when we joined forces with the Scottish battalion. We were amongst the first allied ground forces to join the Americans and South Koreans.'

'What's brought that up?'

Albert smiled at his friend.

'There's a lad at the allotment who often pops in for a cuppa. He's been asking a lot of questions lately. Got me thinking about stuff.'

Stan looked concerned. 'Well if it's too painful to talk about, just tell him.'

'Actually, Stan, it's strange, but I'm happy to talk about it with him. I think in some way, it's helping both of us. He even got me talking about Gunner Jones. Did I ever tell you about him?'

'Remind me.'

Albert passed Stan his mug of tea.

'Gunner was an army regular who, by the time he arrived in Korea, had already fought in different campaigns during world war two. He was as fit as a horse and strong as a mule and here I was, a scrawny bloke swamped with my seven pound rifle and tropical kit, while he made light work of carrying his 23 pound Bren machine gun with ammo.'

Stan sipped his hot tea and nodded knowingly.

'Y'know what really impressed me? How he cared for the lads. He was a right good laugh as well.'

'Funnier than you, Albert?'

'Way funnier. Those days were so hard, that if we hadn't have laughed, we would have definitely lost our marbles.'

'I thought you had already lost yours, mate!'

'That's down to spending too much time with you!'

Albert continued. 'I remember Gunner doing some of our sentry duty in temperatures as low as minus 25. Just so a few of us could curl up in our holes in the ground and get a couple of extra hours' sleep.'

'When you get to our age Albert, you realise how special your mates and your memories are,' Stan commented.

'That's true. Our food rations were a joke at the best of times, so what did Gunner do? He'd often be seen bartering or gambling for luxuries like coffee and chocolate with the Americans. Fed us all, best he could.'

Albert grabbed a few chocolate digestives from the biscuit tin while Stan got up gingerly from his stool to cash up for the day.

'He sounds an amazing bloke,' said Stan, handing his friend three £1 coins in return for some of his prized tomatoes, radishes and lettuce.

'One of the best,' replied Albert. 'You're a good mate, Stan. We've shared some right laughs over the years, haven't we, mate.'

Stan dipped his biscuit into his hot tea.

'We've kept each other sane, Albert.'

Albert smiled as he watched Stan devour his biscuit. Smeared around the mouth, crumbs in the corner and remnants on the chin, Stan didn't come up for breath whenever he ate.

'You're too right there, Stan. If it weren't for you, I'm sure I would have throttled Gretyl by now.'

Albert's conversation was temporarily and rudely interrupted by an image of Gretyl's prodigious mouth, gobbling all in its path.

It was Stan who brought a welcome end to the picture.

'Your trouble and strife has done wonders for my marriage,' he said. 'Made me grateful for Janice. It's cost me a fair few quid in flowers though!'

'Your Mrs is an angel. Mine? Well ... you can polish a turd, but it's still a turd.'

Stan looked puzzled.

'What's that about a turd, Albert? You got a problem with the water works, mate?'

'Nope, me bowels are fine, mate. One look at the wife and my digestive transit never breaks down!'

CHAPTER 16

The Lock Up

It was now 6pm and Pete pulled up outside Gretyl's garage with a van full of items from his gran's flat.

Feeling a bit mugged for accepting just twenty quid for the lot, he consoled himself with the thought that he did get to play football and that the old woman was taking the stuff off his hands.

Gretyl stood outside the garage, puffing a long cigarette. Her lips were smudged with a shade of red gloss and no longer sporting the bag lady look, she proudly stood waiting in high heels. Her tight, long beige Mackintosh coat was bulging at the seams, barely covering what was concealed underneath and leaving little to the imagination.

Pete took another look at Gretyl's face and was brought back to reality.

'Blimey. Is that the same woman I saw earlier?' he thought to himself. 'I'd hate to think what lurks underneath that.'

Pete caught a smile from Gretyl as she squeezed her hand inside her coat pocket and withdrew a remote control. He couldn't believe his eyes. The woman he earlier took for a tramp was now unlocking her garage remotely.

The metal slatted door rolled up to reveal what Pete could only describe as a TV set from one of the soaps. The garage appeared more like a front lounge, complete with shelving, furniture and a huge number of wall plates, ornaments and pictures.

'No wonder she was so keen to buy my stuff?' he thought.

Pete opened the back door of the van and lifted the large cardboard box, complete with picture frames and all manner of household fare. He proceeded to the garage and looking toward the back of the lock-up, spotted a double glazed window and door.

'This must be how she ventilates this place? Maybe she does live here?' he wondered.

Gretyl now spoke with an air of authority.

'Young man, please be careful when you unpack everything. I'll show you exactly where I want it to go.'

Pete was now feeling a little intimidated.

'Erm, sorry, but I haven't got time to unpack it all for you. Where do you want me to put the box down?' he asked nervously.

Gretyl walked slowly toward the young man, staring in a menacing way into his timid eyes.

'Surely you don't expect a woman of my age to unpack all this? Anyway, I'm hardly dressed for it. I need you to put some shelving up for me before you go. You want to earn your fifteen quid, don't you?'

'Fifteen quid! I thought we said twenty? I tell you what. You can keep the stuff. Forget the money. I'm sorry, I have to go.'

Pete clocked Gretyl's grin. 'That's one crazy old cow,' he thought as he dashed past her to his van and left the scene.

Gretyl was now alone in the garage and like a treasure hunter jealously guarding a secret she turned to the box and took hold of the one thing that especially caught her eye. It was a painting of a beautiful thatched cottage set in the most picturesque of surroundings. Gretyl sat on her leather stool and stared into its dream depiction of her perfect world, her glamorous, perfect world. Gretyl dreamed of a place where the green hills glistened with morning dew and the sun broke through the sky with the promise of perfect happiness. As usual, the daydream would soon end with a reality check. It was just a picture in a frame.

Gretyl resented the fact that all she possessed in this world was a London lock up and a rented flat full of ornaments. Having no savings to speak of, Gretyl knew she had no real prospect of climbing the social ladder.

'Oh well. Better get back in time for me soaps,' she conceded.

CHAPTER 17

Trackie Bottoms

The meeting between Dave Soddall and Sharkie had been a success. Plans had already been made to meet up again to iron out times, dates and strategies for their excursion to Marbella. Dave had also asked Sharkie to speak to his brother Tony, figuring that Sharkie would get more money out of Tony than family would.

'See you later Sharon,' Sharkie said.

Sharkie left the house while Sharon sat in the kitchen, drinking hot chocolate and sulking after her mascara disaster.

Dave clapped his hands together in excitement.

'Tottie, we've done good business today my love, good business I tell ya'. Got a good feeling about this, a good feeling - something I haven't felt before.'

Sharon looked up at Dave from the kitchen table, her cheeks stained with black mascara.

'Maybe you should stop scratching your crotch, or should I say ... your brain,' she mocked.

'Aw, come on love. We were just havin' some fun when I said earlier that you looked like Chuckie's bride.'

Sharon sobbed. 'Y'know what Dave? Every day, every week since we've been married, I've made an effort with how I look, but you never pay any notice. And look at you. Your trackie bottoms look like they're about to run off to the tip.'

Dave smiled and put his arms around his wife.

'Don't you like my trackie bottoms?'

'Get off! There you are again, trying to make a joke about everything. For the record, your minging bottoms are a disgrace. Tell you what - you can have my Primark vouchers if you'll go out and buy yourself a pair of jeans and a decent shirt. At least it'll get you off that rotten couch.'

'Love, if my trackie bottoms offend you that much, I'll change them, but I do notice you.'

'Yeh, right,' sulked Sharon.

Dave tried to put his arms around Sharon again.

'I love the new blonde stuff you've put in your hair. Your legs are so smooth, they look like polished table legs. Your white teeth are in better condition than me mum's bone china tea set.'

Sharon began to let out a hint of a smile.

'Dave, you're beginning to sound like your father. Anyway, your mum's bone china tea set is chipped. Do you really love my teeth?'

'Hun, I could nibble those lovely gnashers. Come 'ere.'

Dave picked Sharon up and perched her on his knee, trying to kiss her neck for a second time.

Sharon let her dumpy, badly dressed and forgetful husband kiss her.

At that moment Kevin walked in and couldn't hide his disgust.

'Ew. Spare me the details.'

Dave looked like the cat that got the cream.

'If it weren't for your mother's hot passion, you wouldn't be here.'

Sharon cringed as she looked at Kevin, embarrassed by the mental image her son was now desperately trying to erase.

'That's way too much info, Dad. Anyway, I've been working on the website and it's looking good.'

Kevin placed the laptop on the table.

Dave looked surprised. 'Crikey, son. It looks like Thomas Cook made it.'

Kevin gave a cocky look.

'I told you dad, ain't much I can't turn my hand to. I copied the look of another travel website that sells holidays in Spain.'

In large, bold print, the words 'Costa Soddall Travel' sat at the top of the web page with the slogan in italics, underneath: 'Where holidays in the Sun, Costa nothing.'

The website was adorned with impressive photos of the beach, luxury property and shopping markets, but what took centre stage was a dominating photo of a coach, signwritten with the Soddalls' business name and slogan.

'Son, how on earth did ya' get that coach sign-written with our name and logo?'

'That was easy, dad. I copied the photo of the coach from the Internet, opened a photo editing program on my laptop and added the name and logo to the picture.'

Dave took one long and proud look at his son.

'I've added a few things up in my head and I reckon we could make hundreds of thousands out of this.'

Sharon's jaw dropped, while Kevin's eyes, like saucers, stared in amazement at Dave's projection.

'How do you work that out Dad? Are you serious?'

Dave flashed a confident, cheesy grin and extracted a half torn envelope from his joggers. It had some numbers and columns scribbled on it.

'Okay. Tony has five villas that he reckons are worth over £2 million each. I figured if we only sold them for half of their value, that works out as, erm ... hang on.' Dave squinted at his notes and tried to make sense of the sums.

Kevin looked up at the ceiling in disgust and let out an exaggerated sigh. 'If the five villas are sold at half their value, it's five million quid.'

Dave gave up trying to work out the math with his fingers and thumbs and scratched his crotch in excitement.

'Son, I can't wait to show Tony this web thing you've done. He'll be blown away. Then he'll really know we mean business.'

Dave picked up the phone, blew a loud kiss at Sharon and dialled Tony.

Tony answered the phone, recognising the Canvey Island area code.

'Hello.'

'Tony, it's your brother, Dave. How are you, mate?'

Before Tony had time to respond, Dave blurted out the entire details of his meeting with Sharkie, even down to the mascara accident with Sharon. Dave felt that he finally had the respect of his brother.

This respect was intensified further when Dave told Tony to look at the website for Costa Soddall Travel.

'Blimey Dave. You really are pulling this out of the bag mate. It looks amazing. I'll send over all the images and info I have for the villas. Do you have an email address?'

Dave passed the phone to Kev.

'Hi Uncle Tony. Send the email to sales at costasoddalltravel. co.uk and I'll get the photos up online straight away. Were gonna get rich together, eh uncle.'

Tony replied, 'We have to move fast and get them old folk over here asap. Where are we up to?'

Kev passed the phone to his dad.

'Tony, we just have to iron out times and dates and we'll start on the phones straight away. My broker, Sharkie, is on board and he'll get the ol' croaks to sign on the dotted line. One thing though. You're gonna have to fund their travel to Marbella and I need you to speak to Sharkie about our deal.'

'Okay, get back to me with the numbers you want to bring over and give my number to your mate. Let's speak soon. Cya.'

Dave yelled out to Sharon, 'Did you hear all that, love? Soon you'll see me as head of the family and call me Don Corleone. This Papa's gonna make his family proud and rich!'

'That's great, Don,' replied Sharon. 'First things first though. No more crappy caravan vouchers, or you'll find a horse's head on your pillow!'

CHAPTER 18

Reading Material

It was Monday and time for the Marilyn Monroe Classic Platinum Blonde Bombshell to make its appearance. Gretyl's husky voice was now accompanied by such a swagger that it looked like her hip joint would soon pop out of place.

Albert couldn't wait to pop out to the allotment himself. Of all the characters that Gretyl acted throughout the week, Marilyn Monroe was by far the most annoying.

Not content with the Marilyn hairpiece, a flick of the hand accompanied every exaggerated word, while her plastic cigarette looked quite ridiculous, drawing attention to the black mole above the left corner of her mouth, crudely drawn with eyeliner.

Gretyl started her Monday morning drama with the compulsory viewing of old video cassettes like, 'Some Like It Hot' and 'Gentleman Prefer Blondes'. Albert had loved these old films until Gretyl had decided to impersonate them so appallingly.

'Curling Me Softly' was the only hair salon within a thirty minute walk that would accommodate Gretyl's needs and exacting requirements.

Gretyl picked up the phone and dialled the salon.

'Good day. It's Mrs Gretyl Trollop.'

'Morning Mrs Trollop,' replied the salon assistant.

Gretyl snorted. 'Young lady, I can assure you that my name is pronounced 'Trollope' without an 'e' on the end.'

The salon assistant held the palm of her hand over the telephone mouth piece and whispered to the senior stylist and owner, 'Cathy, it's that trollop of a woman on the phone. Can you speak with her?'

Gretyl had earned herself a reputation with the salons in the town and only Cathy could tolerate her.

'Good morning, Mrs Trollop. How can we help you this morning?'

'I've purchased a designer black bob style wig and it's really quite exquisite. I'm told it's all the rage with Japanese millionaires and you know I don't do cheap. Well, my Mondays belong to Marilyn, but today, it must be today, I need you to dye and curl this wig for me.'

Cathy replied, 'The only time I have available is our first appointment at 9.00 this morning. That's in half an hour? Is that ok?'

'Absolutely dear, can you send a car over for a quarter to nine?'

Cathy looked to the ceiling. 'Erm, Mrs Trollop, it's not possible for us to pick you up. I suggest you call a taxi? Would you like the number of a firm we use?'

Gretyl looked disgusted. 'A mini-cab? A mini-cab. I only do Hackney Carriage my dear.'

'I understand, Mrs Trollop. Then we will see you in half an hour. Bye bye.'

Gretyl loved the special attention she received at Curling Me Softly and had placed one of her own royal family china cups in the salon for the sole use of her appointments. She had also left a small wooden box with a coat of arms on the lid, complete with a range of herbal teas to suit her mood. Gretyl always expected her hot beverage on arrival and would loudly compliment the staff for their attention to detail.

Monday appointments would also include 'The Very Best of Marilyn Monroe' CD playing in the background for her arrival.

Several minutes later Gretyl was waiting outside the flats when she was greeted by the honk of a car horn, signalling to her that it was time to leave.

'Where am I taking you this morning, luv?' asked the driver.

Gretyl let out a deep sigh.

'Young man, I am not your 'luv' as much as you may wish me to be ... and what's the point of your office asking me the destination, when I have to repeat myself to you?'

The taxi driver replied, 'Well, I like to check that the girl in the office took down the details correctly.'

Gretyl applied the Red Taboo lipstick to her thick pouted lips and paused for a moment.

'Does your office have a problem ignoring clients?'

'Look, do you want me to take you to the hairdressers in South Street or not?'

'No young man, I do not. I would like you to drop me outside Home Bargains, which I am sure you know, is a few shops before the Curling Me Softly salon. I would normally ask to be chauffeured outside, but I noticed your car lacked the appropriate waxed finish, so you will drop me a few yards away.'

Already irritated by a non-paying customer and another passenger who had vomited only an hour previously in the rear seat, the driver hit the CD button on his stereo and turned the volume dial up to maximum, selecting 'Drum and Bass'.

The noise was deafening. Gretyl's repeated requests for him to turn the music down were ignored and met with derision from the cabbie.

The taxi now had its front and rear electric windows completely wound down and locked from the driver's controls.

Not wishing to be associated with an unwashed Vauxhall Astra and its riotous lyrics, Gretyl grabbed the nearest magazine from the seat pocket and held it up over her face as the car moved at a snail's pace along the High Street. To her horror, however, Gretyl quickly realised that she was holding up a Playthings Uncovered magazine.

'Flamin' Nora!' Gretyl yelped in disgust as she threw the magazine out of the window.

As his pornographic magazine struck the head of a passerby, a look of shock replaced the driver's cocksure grin.

The vehicle was now stationary at the traffic lights. The assaulted victim approached Gretyl's window, dour faced and wearing a clerical collar.

'I do believe this is your magazine. Maybe you'd like to tell me why you decided to throw this filth at me?'

Before Gretyl could even mouth a response, the priest - a Father O'Driscoll - recognised his assailant and raised his bushy eyebrows.

'I do believe it's Mrs Trollop, isn't it? I haven't seen you at confession for some time now.'

Gretyl was flushed with embarrassment.

'Father, I can assure you that I do not own this magazine. It's his,' she said, pointing to the driver.

'Mrs Trollop, I saw you reading it in the taxi before you threw it in my face. Maybe you should think twice before buying such disgusting material.'

The shame of the accusation reduced Gretyl to a momentary, stunned and unaccustomed silence.

'I'll be expecting you at confession next week, Mrs Trollop. May God have mercy on your soul. Good day to you.'

Gretyl exited the back door with a mighty slam.

'That will be three pound sixty if you're getting out here,' said the driver.

'I tell you what. How about I phone your boss and tell him about the magazines you provide for your passengers, eh?'

The taxi driver shoved his hand out of the window and extended a single fingered gesture towards Gretyl.

'Luv, you don't need a salon for that rug on your head. You need a vet to put that pup out of its misery!'

Gretyl took off her red stiletto and threw it at the taxi. With little time to spare, she retrieved her shoe from the pavement and hurried to the salon, her heels pounding like hooves on the pavement slabs.

CHAPTER 19

Salon Surprise

Cathy answered the phone in the salon and discovered that Frankie hadn't checked in for the school breakfast club.

'But I dropped him off at eight this morning. Don't tell me he's playing truant again?'

This wasn't the first time Cathy had been called out to collect her son.

Cathy called the girls together in the salon.

'Ladies, I've got to leave you with the salon for the next hour or so. I'll be as quick as I can. Gretyl is due any minute now. Kirsty, you're the only stylist available, so you will have to take care of her. It's simple. Just do what she asks you to do. Don't question her. It's not worth the hassle. She's more than eccentric, so it's best just to get your head down and get the job finished. Okay?'

Kirsty was an 18 year old junior stylist who lacked confidence at the best of times. Leaving her with Gretyl would be the biggest test yet of her apprenticeship.

Gretyl arrived late at the salon and pushed the door open to the sound of electronic wind chimes.

'Good morning Mrs Trovoke.'

Gretyl turned around and looked towards the door.

'I'm sorry, what did you call me?'

Kirsty's lip began to tremble. Before she could reply, Nancy brought over Gretyl's very own china cup with her variety box of tea bags.

'Mrs Trollop. How are you?'

Encouraged by the correct pronunciation, Gretyl replied:

'Why, I am very well young lady. Thank you for having my tea ready. It's good to see that you value clients such as myself.'

Gretyl was seated towards the rear of the shop. Unable to control her gassy bowels, her cooked breakfast infused the salon air while the young stylist looked startled and held her breath.

Flatulence was a common problem for Gretyl at the best of times, but now fuelled with the customary eggs, bacon, beans and black pudding it had clearly taken on a potency that would make an aspiring dictator proud.

Gretyl took the wig out of her bag and handed it to the young stylist.

'My dear, as you can see, I am wearing a very expensive designer bob hairstyle and I would like it coloured strawberry blonde. Then I would like you to blow dry it, style it and add some curls to it with those heated tongs. Meanwhile, here is the CD I would like you to play, thank you.'

Kirsty looked disgusted as she ran her fingers through what seemed to be a synthetic wig.

'Erm, Mrs Troll, Mrs Trollop, are you sure you would you like me to dye this, erm wig?'

'Those are the instructions I gave you my dear. Now be careful with it. As you can see, it's very fine hair that was previously owned by a Japanese millionaire. Now pass me the chart so I can choose the right colour match please.'

Kirsty passed the colour chart and awaited Gretyl's instructions.

'There it is dear, this one. I'll call her Goldie Hawn.'

Kirsty took the chart and box, complete with wig from Gretyl. Setting it upon the wig stand, she now began the transformation of Gretyl into a new, Asian wonder.

CHAPTER 20

Mourning Storm

Albert sat in his shed with his feet up on the wooden chest, enjoying his third cup of tea for the morning.

Normally the allotment would be teeming with individuals by 10am, but heavy showers were now flooding the site as the sky thundered and cracked overhead.

When the heavens collapsed, Albert often thought back to his time in Korea. As an old soldier, he had to cope with radical changes in temperature, such extreme cold where a frozen egg proved almost impossible to crack with a rifle butt and bearded men were known to remove inch long icicles from their face before they ate. The blistering heat of the Korean summer proved no better, bringing with it an invasion of mosquitoes and other insects.

In comparison, Albert's shed housed the luxury of a small fan, a heater, bench, wooden chest (which doubled as a table) and a large cupboard full of teabags, long life milk and sugar. This little retreat was more than a comfort to Albert.

Amid the sound of heavy rain pellets pounding the shed roof, Albert rose from his chair, startled. This was the third time he thought he'd heard someone calling his name, albeit, faintly.

'Who'd be outside in this downpour?' he asked himself.

Albert pulled back the curtains covering the small window and looked toward the gate of the allotment. To his surprise, he could see in the distance a lady with an umbrella. It looked like Stan's wife, Janice.

Albert moved fast, grabbing his flap cap and zipping up his parker anorak, walking briskly toward her. What on earth was she doing here? To the best of Albert's knowledge, she'd never visited the allotment before.

As he drew closer, Albert could see that Janice looked as white as a sheet and clearly had no makeup on. Stan liked to joke that she never went out without spending an hour in the bathroom first and wouldn't be seen dead without mascara.

Janice fell to her knees in the rain, her loud, eerie wail rising from the sodden ground.

'He's gone ... Stan, he ... he's, he died in his sleep. He's gone, Albert.'

Albert now ran the final few metres toward her and removed his coat, placing it over her shoulders. His voice began to shake.

'Janice ...'

Albert stood frozen, as if paralysed. It wasn't like he was unfamiliar or even scared of death, but the world around him instantly became silent, cold and uninhabitable.

Engulfed by a canopy of silent pain, Albert's vocal chords seemed inoperable as he contemplated the loss of his close friend.

The tears on Albert's face mingled with the droplets of rain as he tried to compose himself.

'I'm so sorry. I don't know what to say. I'm sorry, I'm so sorry.'

Albert reached out and helped Janice to her feet, placing his arm around her as he walked her back to his shed.

Albert turned up the heater and flicked the kettle, fiddling with the mugs and cleaning them with some tissue. He passed Janice a clean tea cloth to dry her drenched hair and face.

'Albert, I looked for your phone number everywhere. Then I popped over to the flat and no one was there. I didn't know what to do.'

Albert ignored the rattle of the kettle and reached down for his bottle of whisky. Pouring two generous measures into the cups, he handed one to Janice as she continued.

'They've taken him away! The ambulance, they've taken him. Told me he'd been dead a few hours. Albert, it was horrible. What am I going to do?'

Albert knelt down and placed his arm around her.

'Don't be afraid. I'll help you sort things out. Don't worry. I'll be here for you.'

Albert swallowed hard as he tried to contain his own feelings.

Janice started to sob again as Albert passed her his handkerchief. Unsure of what to say, Albert wiped his own eyes several times with the sleeve of his coat and poured himself another shot of whisky.

Albert's silence seemed to last an uncomfortable length of time for him, but he was at a loss for words.

'I'll go down to the shop, Janice. Put a sign up, "Closed for a few days". Or do you want me to open it up and man it for today. I can bring some fruit and veg home for you and help you get some dinner on?'

'Albert, I don't care about the shop. I just can't think about that now. It's all too much. I'm sorry, I didn't know where else to go. I don't want to go back to the house on my own Albert. Would you take me to my sister's in Romford?'

'You want me to phone a cab, Janice?'

Reaching for his mobile phone, Albert pressed the power button, to no avail.

'I haven't used this bugger in months.'

'Here Albert, you can use mine. My sister knows I'm coming over and said she'd be in all day.'

Albert opened his wallet, took out the card of a taxi firm, and phoned a cab.

He then passed the phone back to Janice.

'Do you need to go home first and pack a bag or something?'

'Yes, Albert. Will you come in with me? I don't want to be on my own.'

Albert took Janice gently by the hand. 'Of course, love.'

His eyes filled up with tears as the enormity of Stan's death hit him like a wave.

Janice smiled through her tears.

'He loved you. You know that don't you? That's why I had to come and tell you after I called my sister.'

Albert picked up his glass and finished the last few drops of whisky.

'He was my best friend,' Albert said, pausing, trying to regain his composure.

'He was always trying to cheer me up. Told me my glass was half full, not half empty. He always made me laugh.'

'You know Albert. I never begrudged Stan his flutter at the bookies every day. You know why? It was you. You were good for him, always looking out for him. He often shared with me the funny antics you two got up to when he came home from work.'

Albert smiled warmly and wiped his eyes again.

'Do you remember when Stan came to visit me when I was concussed in hospital with cracked ribs and a broken arm? Do you know what really made me laugh? He brought a Bible with him to the hospital and started to read one of the Psalms, loudly. Because of the pain killers I was on, I thought he was giving me my last rites.'

'I know he is in a better place, Albert. He had real faith. I need that strength now. I will miss him so much.'

'We will both miss him, greatly. Before the cab arrives, I want to tell you about what he said to me while I was in hospital. He told me he'd take care of stuff for me while I was recovering. Y'know, the allotment, put a bet on for me, that kind of thing.'

Janice wiped back the tears from her cheeks.

'I remember you breaking your arm. Was that when you fell down the stairs after having one too many?'

'Yes, something like that. Anyway, as you know well, Stan hadn't picked up a spade in his life. He could sell you a sack of spuds, but I'm not sure if his hands ever pulled one up from the ground.'

Albert refilled her glass with another, smaller shot of whisky.

Janice smiled again. 'Well, he was a better salesman than a gardener that was for sure. The number of times folk would come in for a piece of fruit for lunch and leave the shop with a carrier bag full of groceries for the week!'

Albert continued.

'Did you ever hear what happened when he looked after my allotment for a few days? Well, bless him, he noticed that my vegetable patch was very dry, so he connected the hose up, set it to spray and mounted it up through the lip of the shovel handle. Problem was, he went back to the shop and forgot he'd left the hose on!'

Janice looked shocked. 'No, he never told me that!'

Albert continued, 'Well, to make matters worse, it was the Allotment Inspector's patch that was completely ruined and under a pool of water. He'd only gone and watered the wrong plot! Everyone else's was fine. We got away with it, though. The Inspector thought it was vandals who did it.'

Janice laughed as she held Albert's hand.

'Sounds like something my Stan would do.'

The taxi cab beeped at the entrance of the allotment.

'Come on love. Let's go get some things packed for you to visit your sister.'

Five Million Quid

Dave Soddall was now sat up in bed devouring a bucket of popcorn, feverish with a childish excitement.

'You know, honey. Today is a great day,' he garbled.

Sharon sat at the dressing table, brushing the knots out of her long blonde hair.

'Ah, that's nice. Why's that?'

Before Dave had time to respond, the door bell rang, followed by a loud knock.

'Dave, get that love. I'm still in my nightie.'

Dave rolled out of the bed, pulled his pants out of the crack in his bottom and with bucket still in hand, walked down the brown stained carpet to answer the door.

'Alright Sharkie, what ya' doing here so early?' asked Dave.

'I got in touch with your brother Tony, like you asked me to. Ran over some over the facts and figures again, along with the game plan we discussed.'

Dave took Sharkie through to the lounge, brushing off the remains of his breadcrumb chicken marathon the night before.

Sharkie took a handkerchief from his suit pocket and placed it on the sofa before he sat down. Throwing a cushion at Dave, he grimaced.

'Do me a favour. I don't want to bring up my breakfast. Cover up your crotch will you mate.'

'Sure thing, Sharkie. Fancy some popcorn?'

Sharkie cringed. 'I'll pass on the arse flavoured popcorn if you don't mind. Now listen mate, you won't believe the deal I've worked out with your brother.'

Dave looked excited. 'Go on.'

Sharkie opened his laptop. 'Well, the five villas that Tony has are worth about two million quid each. If we sold them on the cheap, even half the price, it stacks up to five million quid. When they bulldoze them, Tony stands to lose his two million for the land plus another two million he spent on bribes, building and furnishing them, so he's looking to get back the four million quid he's put in. This means whether we sell the properties outright or sell a piece of them for timeshare, we've gotta make the numbers add up.'

Dave replied angrily, 'Y'know what? Without my idea he wouldn't be getting anything for 'em, so he ought to be bleedin' happy with whatever he gets.'

'Dave, we both know that he hasn't a chance of selling them, coz everyone in Marbella knows what's gonna happen to them. So here's the proposal: the more we sell, the more we make, right? Well, he wants the money split two ways, him and us. He'll give us 20% commission on whatever we sell. Think of it. If we sell the five villas for only half their value, we reach the magic five million and that's a million quid for us - five hundred grand each.'

Dave stared at Sharkie. Blinking rapidly he let out a deep sigh.

'Bugger me.'

'I'd rather not if you don't mind, but there is something else I need to tell you. You won't like it, but it makes sense. Tony wants you to stay with Kevin and manage things back here.'

'Are you havin' a laugh? You and my crook of a brother aren't going to sideline me or my family.'

Sharkie calmly stroked the palms of his hands against the finely pressed, sheen finish of his suit trousers.

'Dave, trust me, it's not like that. To put it bluntly mate, your brother said you might frighten off the ol' croaks from spending their money, y'know, what with your tattoos and stuff. He did suggest though, that I take your missus with me so that I work the ol' girls and Sharon does the ol' boys. Now that's a plan, eh?'

Dave didn't challenge Sharkie's words. Deep down, he knew it made sense. Truth was, he felt ashamed of how he'd let himself go and would feel more than self conscious amongst folk with money and the dress to match it. Not Sharon, though. If anyone looked a million dollars, it was definitely his missus.

Sharon entered the room, took a cheeky glance at Sharkie and sat down.

'Are you boys talking about me?'

'More than that, love. Sharkie wants to take you on holiday to Marbella.'

Sharon blushed.

'Tony thinks I should stay back with Kev. You know, run things from here. It makes sense luv. You're the pretty face that can make this happen.'

Sharon remarked, 'It'll take more than a pretty face to make this happen, but I understand, love. Hey, rather than starve to death, you'd have to eat take-away food each night. Could you manage that?'

Dave laughed. 'Well, I could murder a Doner or two, for the cause. Team player, me!'

Dave turned to Sharkie, his brow furrowed.

'Next time you speak to my brother, make sure ya tell him it was my suggestion that I stay back here, not his. You understand?'

'No problem, of course Dave. We all have to play our part in making a sack load of cash.'

Sharon smiled at Dave, walked over and sat on his lap, kissing him on the cheek.

'Honey, I know you're doing it for us. Who knows babe, after it's all finished, maybe we can take a holiday in one of Tony's villas.'

'Silly cow! They're being knocked down, aren't they?' mocked Dave.

Sharon replied defensively. 'Yeh, we'll I obviously meant before they're knocked down!'

Sharkie let out a roar of laughter while texting on his mobile phone.

'Maybe both of you should stay at home.'

Sharon stood up from Dave's lap and left for the kitchen to make some drinks.

Young Kevin walked in the lounge with a toastie in his hand.

'Alright Sharkie.'

'How's it going son? Where're we up to now with the website?'

'Just waiting on Tony to email me photos of the villas and it's sorted.'

'Sweet. I'll get the flyers ready with your Dad. Then I suggest we take a trip out to this village we are targeting. Do some leaflet drops and knock on some doors, eh?'

Dave concurred. 'Yep, I've already thought of that one, Sharkie.'

Dave leant over toward Sharkie and whispered:

'You'll be pleased to know that I will be taking a trip away from my trackie bottoms as well, though don't tell the missus. It's a surprise. I'm off to get me some proper jeans and a designer shirt later.'

Sharon brought in a few mugs of tea and rounds of jam on toast.

'Boys, I've been thinking about what people say when flogging stuff on the phone. I made some notes last night while sitting in bed listening to his lordship's snoring and farting. Shall I read it to you?'

Sharkie interrupted. 'I'm not sure they will make much sense after gas poisoning.'

Dave looked over at Sharkie. 'My girl, she's on the ball mate, I tell ya.'

Sharon coughed a little, straightened up on the sofa and began reading.

'Hello, are you the owner of the house? Ah, that's lovely. I'd like to congratulate you (sir/madam) on the wonderful news that you have been selected from our millionaire's list to win a free holiday in Marbella. How does that sound? Ah, lovely. Due to the nature of this wonderful, five star offer, can I confirm that you are indeed a millionaire? Ah that's lovely. I want to reassure you that there are no catches. Your dream holiday is only moments away. Would you like me to send you a brochure? You can also find us on the world-wide web and take a look at your free holiday. Do you have a pen? Ah, lovely. To claim your free holiday go to our website, www.costa Soddalltravel.co.uk and enter your details. We'll be in touch again. Do you have any questions? Ah, that's lovely. Can I take your full name, address, home/mobile number and email address please.'

Dave stretched his arms out to Sharon and beckoned her to come and sit on his knee.

'Y'know what darlin', there's only one thing I can say to that ... ah that's lovely!'

CHAPTER 22

Short & Curlies

With the taxi fiasco now behind her, Gretyl was finally enjoying the ambience of the Curling Me Softly salon.

Sipping from her Will and Kate china teacup, she lounged back, rocking her head from side to side to the warbling voice on her Marilyn Monroe Golden Greats CD.

Two of the stylists, Tina and Shannon, passed each other in the staff kitchen.

'Did you see her dunk that biscuit? Made me feel sick, I tell you. That woman needs a bib.'

Shannon laughed. 'I'm going to change that CD when she falls asleep. Give it ten minutes and she'll be off.'

Tina picked up a few CDs and passed Shannon The Prodigy and Eminem albums.

'This should do it, something more upbeat while Cathy's out. I just want to see the look on the Trollop's face when she wakes up.'

'That would be classic,' remarked Shannon.

Tina looked excited. 'If it weren't for the fact that I've got another two weeks to go here, I'd gladly give her a free face paint while she slept.'

Shannon enquired, 'What face would you paint?'

Tina paused for a moment. 'Thinking about it, I wouldn't touch her face. It's cruel enough to leave it just as it is.'

Kirsty walked into the kitchen with a look of resignation on her face.

'Shannon, I think this wig she's asked me to colour is synthetic?'

Tina butted in. 'You know what, Kirst. Cathy said you should just do what the ol' cow asks you to do, so I wouldn't worry about it. Just match her wig type with the colour chart, mix the bleach powder with peroxide and comb it through like you've done before.'

Kirsty bit her lip nervously.

'Another thing, she wants the wig curled. If I do that, it might take a few inches off the length and I'm worried it'll be half way up her neck.'

Tina laughed. 'She's got a neck?'

'Kirst, I remember the ol' cow lecturing me before, "If only people did as they were told, the world would be a better place." If I were you, I wouldn't worry about the results.'

Kirsty had pinned the wig to the block and returned to comb it through with the dye. She knew the process of changing the colour from black to strawberry blonde might prove a difficult task, but according to the chart it should work.

Within a few minutes of applying the paste, the wig began to give off a foul smell. Kirsty panicked. Not only was the hair lifting out, but after the wig developed an orange tint it was clear that the colour change wasn't happening as planned.

Kirsty walked to the sink and washed off the bleach, ready to add another colour. She grabbed the chart and began to mix the paste to bring the colour back. Now it became worse. The hair was coarse, damaged and coming out in complete clumps now.

The cheap wig was synthetic alright.

Kirsty hurried over to Shannon. 'I can't believe it. It must be synthetic hair. It's ruined. Come take a look.'

Shannon peered over the sink.

'Oh no, Kirsty. It's completely frizzled and patchy.'

Tina laughed. 'Looks more like pubic hair to me.'

Shannon gave Tina the eyeball and nudged her attention toward the visibly upset junior stylist.

'What am I gonna do? I'm more worried about facing that woman than I am facing Cathy,' Kirsty sobbed.

'Sorry Darling', replied Shannon. 'Tell you what. There's a wig shop up the road. I'll give them a call and see if they have the design that Mrs Trollop wanted. I'll sort it with Cathy when she comes back later.'

'I so hope you don't find another wig,' laughed Tina, looking forward to a punch up.

Shannon dialled the 'Hair We Go' salon and asked to speak to Angela the manager. After explaining their situation and Gretyl's difficult disposition, she received some good news.

'Shannon, we have a few wigs that fit the description you've just given me. I'll put them aside for you. On another note, we know your client and to be honest, we'd rather you didn't mention that her new wig came from us. She's been banned from our premises for some time now.'

'What problems did you have with her?' asked Shannon.

'She tried to get a refund on a wig that she didn't even buy from me. I wouldn't mind, but it must have been thirty years old. That was the first time.'

Shannon gawped and shook her head, wondering how else Gretyl had tried to con Angela.

Angela continued. 'The final straw was when she feigned illness at the till, preferring an ambulance to carry her out of the shop, rather than pay us for restyling her wig.'

'Flipping 'eck', replied Shannon. 'I wonder why she's never tried it on with us before?'

Angela laughed. 'It's simple. You're probably the only salon that will give her the time of day.'

'Okay, I'll be with you in five minutes. Thank you and see you soon. Bye.'

Shannon put the phone down, grabbed her car keys and tried in vain to sneak past Gretyl out of the front door.

'Excuse me dear, but what is this atrocious music you've put on? It sounds like a lunatic asylum in here.'

Before Shannon had time to answer, Tina shouted, 'The group is called Prodigy and the song is *Firestarter*. Don't you like this music, Mrs Trollop?'

'Why would I like someone setting fire to my ears? It sounds like something from hell!' Gretyl continued, 'And for the hundredth time, my name is pronounced Trollope but without an 'e' at the end!'

Shannon stared at Tina. 'Weren't you putting the kettle on Tina? I'm popping out in a few minutes so please take care of Mrs Trollop. I'm sure she might like her Marilyn CD back on again?'

Gretyl spotted Kirsty and called her over.

'Young lady, do you have any idea how long I need to be here? I don't have all day.'

Tina rushed over to Kirsty's aid.

'Mrs Troll ... oh, er, you need to allow some time for the colour to take. Then your wig will be blow dried and curled and everything should be ready for you in the next 30 minutes. Kirst, could you go and make her a nice cup of the English Breakfast Tea please.'

Tina handed Gretyl the latest magazine issue of 'Wagawannabe', a magazine dedicated to all things tripe.

Gretyl saw the perfect opportunity to continue her morning sparring session.

'Oh, thank you dear. Is this the stuff young women, unlike yourself, aspire to these days?'

Tina replied, 'What did you aspire to in your day, then?'

As usual, Gretyl was enjoying the sparring session.

'One does not stop aspiring, young lady. As the years move on, so does the successful woman.'

Tina laughed. 'Yeh, they say good things come to those who wait.'

Tina paused before adding her coup de grâce.

'And some have longer to wait than others, eh Mrs Trollop?'

Gretyl smiled. 'What are you dear, late 30's or 40's? Had a hard life, have we? Is that why you're covered in tattoos? And to think, all those men ...'

Before Tina had time to lash out and at the same time terminate her employment, Cathy opened the door.

'Please take care of Gretyl, before I quite literally 'take care of her',' snarled Tina.

Cathy asked Tina to follow her to the kitchen and was told of Shannon's call to Angela at Hair We Go. Cathy then approached Kirsty, asking to see the wig.

Kirsty's bottom lip quivered as they walked over to the wig stand, only to find what looked like road kill hanging out to dry.

'What's happened here, Kirsty?' asked Cathy.

Kirsty began to sob again as she explained the full story to her boss.

Cathy passed her a tissue, put her hand on her shoulder and whispered, 'Sweetheart, it's not your fault. In my book, you did exactly as you were asked and more than that. Both you and Shannon have shown initiative by calling Angela. I'll give her a ring now. Go make yourself a hot chocolate, love. I'll take care of it from here.'

CHAPTER 23

Hair We Go

Kirsty's mobile phone beeped. It was a text message from Shannon: 'Don't worry. Wig sorted. It's a perfect match. Hair We Go!'

Cathy was dialing Angela, the owner of Hair We Go.

'Thanks so much. It's worth the sixty pounds to just keep Mrs Trollop happy. I normally take care of her myself, but I was called out of the shop urgently and regrettably, I had to leave her with my junior stylist. Could you pass the phone onto Shannon for me please?'

Angela passed the phone to Shannon, while Cathy continued.

'Thanks for sorting this Shannon. Do me a favour. Before you come back to the shop, can you pop over to the market for me and pick up our order from Jane. By the time you get back, it'll be the right time to present the new wig to Gretyl.'

Tina heard that the new hairpiece was en-route, so she removed Gretyl's old matted wig from the stand, placed it inside a small cardboard bag and with thick marker pen, wrote on it: 'TROLLOP ROADKILL'.

Twenty five minutes had now passed and Gretyl snapped at Cathy.

'Is my strawberry blonde pixie cut bob ready yet?'

Shannon walked into the salon and offloaded the boxed wig on the counter.

Cathy replied, 'Mrs Trollop, we not only have it ready, but we wanted to present it to you in this lovely decorative box.'

Kirsty walked over in cautious fashion, while Tina leaped from her client to the front door, eager to see the new wig. Shannon watched as Cathy presented the box to Gretyl.

'Mrs Trollop, I think you will find that your wig has been given a wonderful new lease of life,' smiled Cathy.

Cathy opened the box to reveal a giant Afro wig.

'What the bleedin' eck do you call that?' screamed Gretyl.

Cathy looked stunned as she lifted the wig out of the box, wondering if the pixie cut bob was hidden underneath it.

'Excuse me one moment, Mrs Trollop. I'll just ask one of our stylists. We must have picked up the wrong box, erm, wig.'

Gretyl continued, 'If you think I'm gonna wear that monstrosity, you've got another thing coming. This is outrageous. I want my wig.'

Unable to contain herself, Tina laughed as she walked back to her client.

'Sorry for the wait.'

'Oh I wouldn't worry. I've got a front row seat here,' replied the young customer.

Cathy summoned Shannon to the kitchen.

'What's that Afro wig doing in the box?'

'I'm so sorry, Cathy. I must've picked up the wrong one from the counter. Come to think of it, there was a black girl standing next to me in the shop. She must have taken home the strawberry blonde pixie wig.'

'Right then, there's no other choice. I'll have to explain to Gretyl what's happened to her wig. Meanwhile, please make me a very strong black coffee with three sugars.'

Cathy picked up a large box of Thornton's Limited Edition Classics and walked over to Gretyl, with box open wide.

'Would you like one of our luxury chocolates, Mrs Trollop?'

'What I want is the wig I came in with this morning. Where is it? And no to the chocolates, I'm watching my figure. It takes a lot of discipline to maintain this look. It's no wonder that your girls are so fat if they're stuffing their faces with these all day.'

Tina could restrain herself no longer.

'I'm sorry Cathy, but we've had to put up with her crap for long enough ...'

Cathy motioned with her finger for Tina to be quiet and addressed Gretyl.

'Mrs Trollop, you brought in a synthetic wig and asked us to colour and style it. We did as you instructed. Due to the fact that it's not real human hair, the colour has not taken and the roots have come out of the hairpiece. I am sorry, but you were misinformed when you purchased it. Where did you purchase it from?'

Gretyl stood up and furiously summoned for her coat as well as her royal family china teacup, English tea box and Marilyn Monroe CD.

'Where I bought it is none of your business, but I can assure you it cost me a tidy sum, for which I expect to be compensated.'

'Mrs Trollop, I can only apologise. If I had seen the wig before I was called out of the salon, I may have detected it was synthetic, but it isn't always easy to tell. Do you have a receipt?'

'How dare you call in to question the provenance of my designer hair? What I paid for it is of no concern to you. It's what it's worth that really matters.'

Cathy spoke firmly to Gretyl. 'Mrs Trollop, I will not be offering you any compensation, as we did exactly as you instructed us. May I suggest that you take the matter up with the shop you bought the wig from?'

Gretyl snarled at Cathy. 'Where is my wig? I bet there's nothing wrong with it. Maybe the girl has stolen it, wanting it for herself. She's invented the whole thing. I was told the wig was worth a small fortune.'

Tina retrieved the bag with matted wig and handed it to Gretyl.

'There you are, Mrs Trollop. I'm afraid that the wig is totally ruined, but I'm sure you could use it as an alternative beard to the one you've already got, or wear it somewhere else.'

Gretyl swung her handbag across Tina's face, missing it by a few inches.

Tina screamed, 'Get out of here before I do you some harm ... and take your roadkill with you!'

Cathy rebuked Tina and asked her to return to her waiting client.

'This isn't the last you have heard from me,' growled Gretyl.

'I am sorry Mrs Trollop, but I would like you to leave our premises now. You are not only upsetting our staff, but our clients also. You aren't welcome in here anymore.'

Gretyl marched out of the shop and slammed the door.

Cathy turned to her clients.

'I'm very sorry for what has happened here this morning. Can we offer you tea or coffee and one of our luxury chocolates?'

Mrs Thomas who had been sitting under a hairdryer that morning, replied, 'I'm sure I speak for all of us love, when I say that we are glad to see the back of that awful woman. Come to think of it, I hope we never see the front of her again!'

CHAPTER 24

Barley Sugar

It was 5pm and after dropping off Janice at her sister's in Romford, Albert was only a few minutes from home.

Returning by bus had given Albert some time to reflect on the best times he'd enjoyed with Stan. Albert took pen to paper and began to write on his notepad.

'Stan, if you can read this from the Pearly Gates, I want you to know, you were the best mate anyone could hope for. We had so many good times together. You were the only bugger who understood me. You took the time to be my friend and for that I will always be grateful.'

Albert composed himself for a moment and began writing again.

'As I think over the years we enjoyed together, you stood by me through thick and thin and gave me strength in so many ways. I wish you were here mate so I could tell you to your face. I hope you knew I thought the world of you.'

Albert wept. Trying to constrain himself, he wiped back the tears that had now rolled down his red cheeks, gesturing an apology to the young lady who sat beside him.

She handed him a tissue from her pocket and said, 'I'm sorry, I don't wish to be nosey, but are you okay?'

Albert smiled as he looked up.

'Thank you dear, I'll be fine.'

The young woman had already been looking out of the corner of her eye and reading what Albert had written in his small black book.

'Please don't think I'm prying, but I lost my granddad last month. He meant the world to me. Still does. You never really appreciate just how special people are, until they are gone.'

Albert felt a little embarrassed at the direct reply.

'When you're getting on a bit like me, you feel the loss of a friend, very deeply.'

'You must have really cared for them.'

Albert replied with a warm smile and wiped his eyes again with the scented tissue.

'My Nan once said to me, "Jade, there's nothing more special in life, than the privilege you have to love someone."'

Albert nodded his head, grateful for her words.

'Thank you dear.'

Placing his hand in his coat pocket, Albert pulled out a few sweets.

'Can I offer you a rhubarb and custard?'

'Thanks. I've never had one before.'

Albert pulled the paper bag of sweets from his pocket.

'You don't know what you're missing. The oldies are always the best. In here love there are Wine Gums, Humbugs, Barley Sugar, Pear Drops and a few of my favourite toffees.'

Jade laughed. 'Thanks. I'll bear that in mind. It was nice to speak with you. This is my stop now. I hope you feel better soon. Bye.'

Albert smiled and thought, 'How lovely for a young lady to want to talk to an ol' croak like me.'

Flipping open his notebook again, he added some more thoughts before arriving at the bus stop outside his flat.

'I want you to know mate that I'll miss you at the bookies. It won't be the same without you. Actually, I'm not sure if I fancy going on my own. I'd be looking over at the table for your face. Oh, and don't worry. I'll make a habit of putting some of my veg by for your missus. I promised Janice I'd look out for her and I know you'd want that mate. Maybe she can pop along for a brew at the allotment. Be a bit of company for the both of us.'

Albert closed his black book and stepped out of the bus. Now only a few hundred yards from his flat he considered that Gretyl probably wouldn't know about Stan and he didn't feel ready to talk about it.

The door swung open before Albert could place his key into the lock.

'Where've you been? Your dinner's burnt to a crisp. I tried calling your mobile. What's the point in having one if you never bother to turn it on?'

Ignoring the rant, Albert sat down in the armchair, while Gretyl stood in front of Albert.

'Oh, in case you wondered, I've had a terrible day.'

Albert took a deep sigh.

'Sorry to hear that.'

Unimpressed by his indifference, Gretyl threw a cushion at Albert.

'Sorry to hear that? I'll tell you what sorry is. You can make your own dinner.'

Albert muttered under his breath, 'No, sorry would be eating your dinner.'

Closing his eyes for a moment, Albert tried to compose himself.

'Look, I'm not hungry Gretyl, so just leave it will you, please. You're not the only one who's had a bad day, so please, just ... just stop it.'

Gretyl now burst into a full rant.

'Stop it? Stop it? It's alright for you clearing off down the allotment without a care in the world. I've had a nightmare.'

Albert ignored Gretyl and pretended to read the newspaper.

'You've had a bad day? What happened? Tread on a snail? First, some Asian kid picked me up in his filthy car, then the salon ruined my new pixie cut designer wig and if that's not all, they tried to fob me off with some Afro wig as a replacement. Who do they think I am?'

Albert whispered under his breath, 'Boadicea, I'd imagine.'

'Did you hear what I said? You never pay attention or think about my feelings. It's always, "Stan this, allotment that". Why don't you take your bed down to your shed and live there.'

Albert's anger was boiling over. He grabbed a glass of water from the table, threw the contents in Gretyl's face and shouted, 'How dare you! I walk through the front door and get a load of aggro. You ... you have become a miserable, self-centred old cow, acting as if the world has to revolve around you all the time.'

Albert held back the tears and sat down in the chair again.

Gretyl looked stunned and picked up a tea cloth to wipe her face.

'Albert Trollop ... you don't know how to make a woman like me happy.'

'You're right, I have no idea how to make someone like you happy. I'm sick to the back teeth of hearing how I never do this or that for you. Do you want the truth? You embarrass me.'

Gretyl walked over to the sink and started to rinse out the cups.

'What poison has Stan been putting in your head? I told you before, he's a bad influence.'

Albert threw his newspaper on the floor and shouted again.

'You insensitive cow. He won't be much of an influence now ... he's dead.'

Gretyl put the cups down and turned to Albert.

'What do you mean, he's dead?'

Albert placed his head inside his hands and rubbed his forehead.

'He's dead. He died in his sleep last night.'

'I'm sorry, but how am I supposed to know stuff when you never talk to me?'

Albert began to weep, as he contemplated again the loss of his dear friend.

'Janice came to the allotment first thing this morning to tell me. I've been with her all day. Helped her collect some things from the flat and took her to the sister's in Romford. That's why I was late for your rotten dinner.'

Albert continued to sob in the armchair. He had hoped to visit the allotment and deal with his grief there, before the reality of Stan's death hit home.

Gretyl put her arm on Albert's shoulder as he walked past her, but he shrugged her offer of sympathy away and slammed the bathroom door.

Gretyl knew she'd gone too far this time.

CHAPTER 25

Naughty Apron

Sharon had very little sleep that night and woke up again to Dave's snoring. Since her head landed on the pillow, her mind was filled with thoughts of her trip to Marbella with Sharkie. Feeling an occasional sense of disloyalty to her husband, Sharon tried to put the thoughts aside, but they were soon flowing stronger than ever.

Dave had let himself go these days. Though Sharon loved him, she knew he didn't make her feel, well, sexy. He had tried to bridge the lack of excitement in bed with the odd compliment, but Sharon regarded her marriage as a mostly amiable, if a little dull, affair that lacked any real comfort or ambition.

Sharkie had now unleashed feelings inside Sharon that frightened her and she now worried that her marital faithfulness would not stand the repetitive onslaught of such lustful, devoted attention. Coupled with the thought of a blue sea, golden beach, Sangria and endless sunshine in Marbella, she was sipping a dangerous concoction.

On the bedside table, Sharon's pay as you go mobile phone was now beeping at 7.35am. She stretched across Dave's huge Chewbacca chest to reach it.

Sharon opened the text message:

'Alright Sharon. Glad we can be a team. I'll do the talking, you do the tanning. Here's to the famous 3 S's.'

Knowing that Sharkie's advances would make the trip difficult, Sharon sent a dousing text.

'Actually, I've got my own 3 S's for Marbella – SELL, SELL and SELL!'

Sharkie was due to pick the Soddalls up the following morning for their trip to Poncey Bridge and Sharon was motivated and ready. She had already written a questionnaire to gather the villagers' information and felt confident about their plan. Sharon was particularly looking forward to wearing her pin-striped blue suit, complete with a white blouse and red high heels.

Dave was up early, ready to face the challenge of finding a new pair of jeans and a decent shirt. Eager to surprise Sharon, he kept it quiet.

Ten minutes had passed and Sharon could hear the shower in the bathroom and was puzzled why Dave was up so early.

'You alright love?' asked Sharon.

'Yeh. I fancy going out for an early walk this morning.'

'Going for a walk?' she replied, rather puzzled.

The last time Sharon could remember Dave going for a walk was when he rushed out to help Mohammed (the delivery driver of the local takeaway), who had broken down.

Sharon saw the driver a few weeks later and asked, 'Mohammed, did my Dave manage to get your car started the other day?'

Mohammed replied, 'The only thing Dave tried to start was his kebab, chips and garlic bread.'

Sharon's memory was interrupted by the sound of several thuds on the bathroom door.

'Dad, open the door, I need a pee,' pleaded Kevin.

'What on earth's going on?' wondered Sharon.

It was enough of a shock to see Dave up so early, but Kev? There were only twelve hours to his day and they always started in the afternoon.

The night before, Dave had offered his son a fiver if he'd go with him into town and help him choose his trousers and shirt.

Kev replied, 'A fiver for getting up that early? Are you kidding? That'll cost you a tenner, or I'll tell you what dad - call it five quid and we go in the afternoon?'

Dave aptly reminded his son, 'With the serious dosh we'll be making soon, you won't be bickering over a fiver. Until then and while you live under my roof, you'll do as you're told and help your old man out. We have to plan for our success.'

'What do you know about success?' Kev wondered and conceded, setting his alarm for the early rise.

Sharon spoke through the toilet door to Kevin.

'What're you and your dad up to this morning?'

'I'm popping into town with dad.'

Dave glared at him while towelling himself off from his shower.

'Yeh, we're going to look at some holiday brochures and dad wants to get a travel guide on the Costa Del Sol while we're there.'

Dave dropped his towel and gave Kev the thumbs up. Kev looked away in disgust and gave his dad the thumbs down.

Sharon frowned. 'That doesn't explain why you're both leaving so early?'

Dave butted in. 'I figured, love, that after town, me and the boy could go eat out somewhere and look over the travel book 'n' stuff.'

'So why didn't you invite me? When was the last time you took me out to town for a meal?'

Dave explained as politely as he could that shopping with his wife was the last thing that would help him prepare for the challenge ahead. He needed to focus and do things his way for a change.

Sharon seemed impressed at the initiative shown by her man and wondered if after all these years, he'd finally got some get up 'n' go?

Dave opened the bathroom door and pranced over to Sharon, rubbing her shoulders.

'Oh, another thing, darling. When we get back from town, I want us all to watch the documentary that I recorded, 'Posh Tarts, Rich Farts.' There's a bloke in that village that seems to pull all the strings. If we can reel him in, we'll be laughing all the way out of our council house.'

Sharon giggled.

'Mr Soddall, this new drive is rather, erm, sexy. I'll tell you what love. I'll make some of my lovely home-made chocolate cookies for when you get back. Otherwise, you could send Kev out for the brochures and I'll put my special little apron on for you.'

Sharon wondered that if she could satisfy herself with Dave, then maybe, just maybe, the distraction of Sharkie wouldn't be so appealing.

Dave couldn't believe what he had just heard.

'Are all my lucky numbers coming up at once?' he thought.

Seductive images of Sharon, minus her apron, were flashing through Dave's head. He hadn't felt this excited since his favourite football dream when he scored a hat-trick in the first three minutes of the World Cup Final against Germany. Obviously, England won 3-0.

Over the last few years, Dave had begged Sharon to wear that apron. Truth was he couldn't remember the last time he saw her wearing very little, let alone nothing under the nurse's apron. Along with the rest of Sharon's saucy underwear, the apron had been tucked away in the wardrobe for some time. For Dave, it wasn't the only thing that had been tucked away.

Dave walked over to Kevin and whispered in his ear.

'Tell you what son, go get your dad a super large, white collared shirt and same size jeans and there's an extra fiver in it for you. I've got a large belt if the jeans are too big. Then pop into Smiths and get a travel book for the Costa Del Sol. If they've got one just for Marbella, that's even better.'

'Not much chance of the jeans being too big,' Kevin mocked.

Kev really didn't want to be in the house if the parents were going to be gross and the idea of shopping with his dad was torturous enough.

'I'll do it. Give me the tenner first. That's the fiver plus the five we agreed earlier.'

Dave passed the wrapped up notes to Kevin and bid him farewell, shoving Kevin towards the door.

'See you later, son.'

Dizzy euphoria passed over Dave as he realised he needed to grab the opportunity before him, quite literally, with both hands.

Dave had decided to play it cool, though - especially having recently watched a documentary about an over-sexed man who died as a result of an embolism, possibly brought on by too much excitement.

Walking up to the bathroom, he replaced his old, hole-ridden underpants with a pair of clean Rudolph the reindeer boxer shorts he had received for Christmas.

'Sharon, the boy's gone to town for me. I'll go downstairs and fetch your apron.'

Dave leapt down the stairs like a gazelle, the loud thuds reminding him of the huge increase in weight he'd gained over the last five years.

In no time at all, Dave returned to the bedroom panting, holding an apron in one hand and his overgrown belly up in the other.

Sharon burst out laughing.

'Dave, you silly ol' sod. What you wearing them for? It's not Christmas, dear.'

Dave handed the apron to Sharon.

'It is to me!'

Standing upright in his Rudolph boxers and with gyrating hips, Dave sang his own cheesy version of *Rudolph The Red-Nosed Reindeer*.

Sharon laughed and kissed Dave on his lips, tasting the fresh minty mouth wash that for a moment reminded her of their younger days. Dave was just as randy then, but he had the physique, energy and charm to back it up.

Sharon felt comfortable undressing in front of Dave. For the first time in ages, she wanted him to see her naked body.

Confident in her appearance, she'd managed to keep a fantastic figure, only changing one dress size in fifteen years. Now sexually excited, she wondered if these feelings were a result of Sharkie's attention. Regardless of the origin, she wanted to share herself with her husband and share she did.

The radio alarm clock buzzed. It was 10am and Dave had forgotten to turn his normal alarm call off. He rolled over the pillow, stretching across Sharon and pressed the button.

'Shaz, you still haven't put that apron on for me.'

Sharon pinched his cheek with her thumb and finger.

'You cheeky sod. You never gave me time to get into it.'

Sharon had released the full measure of her repressed desire upon Dave and he really didn't know what'd hit him. The last thirty minutes had been the most passionate he could remember and it left him feeling somewhat emotional.

Dave's eyes were wet.

'Shaz, I want to say something to you, but I don't want you to laugh at me ... I really do love you.'

Sharon ran her fingers over his hairless scalp.

'I know you do love. Are you going all soppy on me?'

Dave continued, 'I know I've let myself go. I don't blame you for not wanting to wear that apron again. Truth is luv, I feel bad about stuff. I want to be someone who excites you again.'

'Babe, when we first met, we were very much in love. We still love each other now and we've still got a little spark, but if you want things to heat up, I guess you just have to put your wood in my fire a bit more often.'

Dave smiled. 'I've got another surprise for you later.'

'Twice in one day?'

Dave winked. 'Well, you'll have to wait and see.'

Dave wanted to get his notes ready for the afternoon family meeting, so he popped downstairs and picked up his pad, keen to take special note of the way in which the village of Poncey Bridge operated.

Made infamous by a TV documentary for being nuts, eccentric, bizarre and even cultish, Poncey Bridge seemed to be governed by whatever the village Committee said - or, more accurately, what the Chairman said.

In addition to Dave's own scribbled ideas, Kev had gathered his own research from website forums and printed off his notes for his dad.

1. The committee is made of generations of the same families. No one else gets in.
2. There is no reported crime in the area, as the committee in their own words, sort it.
3. Unemployment is virtually unheard of in the village.
4. There is no more than one of every service in Poncey Bridge. I.e. one bank, one school, one solicitor, one decorator - quite literally one of everything, apart from an Estate Agent. There was no need for one of those.
5. The villagers rarely put their properties up for sale, because they're not allowed to sell outside of the families that already live there.
6. Poncey Bridge only has one public road running through the village and there is nowhere to stop on it. The other roads are private.

7. The villagers don't like to mix with outsiders.
8. They seem to follow a number of old laws from the Middle Ages, saying that they aren't governed by the state if they had not entered into their contract (or something like it).
9. The village committee was held responsible for sending sacks of hate mail to a variety of outside groups and causes that opposed their way of life.
10. The Chairman seems to control the money and any major spending in the village.

    A cold chill ran down Dave's spine. He had thought the folk in Poncey Bridge were just a bit eccentric when he first saw the documentary, but now this final point shook him to the core.

11. There is little evidence of any significant financial transactions taking place outside of Poncey Bridge.

'What stays in the village, gets paid in the village,' was one popular quote from a resident.

After reading the notes, Dave began to wonder if he had targeted the wrong village and prayed that their plan for a scam in Marbella wouldn't fail.

'Surely these are just technicalities?' he hoped.

Dave pictured himself at the Grand National jumping all the fences with his racehorse, only to fall at the last hurdle.

'I'm not giving up,' Dave muttered to himself. 'I can't. We can't. We've come too far. We have to make this happen.'

CHAPTER 26

Will Power

Albert set off to the allotment early in the morning and spent his time thumbing through the large collection of photos that were kept inside his wooden chest.

Finding some of Stan, he removed a few of the Korea photos from their frames, preferring his best friend in them. Stan would now take pride of place in the centre of the shelf.

A white envelope addressed to Stan Jones also stood beside his favourite photo. Stan stood upright to attention, with his famous bushy moustache, carrot (pistol) in belt, onions hanging like grenades around his neck, an overturned hanging basket for a helmet, twig shaped like a pipe in mouth, whilst holding one of Albert's giant leeks, pretending it was a rifle. This always made Albert smile, especially as the leek was also pointing at Mr Singh, the loathed Allotment Inspector.

The envelope contained Albert's thoughts that he had started on the bus journey and finished later the previous evening. If Janice had planned a cremation, he wanted it to be placed inside Stan's coffin, or in the grave if it were a burial.

Albert had charged his mobile phone and made his first call to Janice. Enquiring as to her current state, he also offered to sort all of Stan's shop stock with Pete, who had a fruit and veg stall at the local market. Sadly, at least a quarter of the stock would need to be thrown, with most of the soft fruit perishing. Pete had volunteered to sell the potatoes, carrots, onions, bananas and apples that were left over and give the proceeds to Janice.

Albert placed his photos back in the wooden chest and locked the front door of his shed. He had arranged to drop the shop key off with Pete and though Albert was keen to help, he wasn't ready to step foot in Stan's shop just yet.

Pete could be trusted to sort the shop out, so Albert set off and with the key in an envelope he popped it through Pete's front door.

As he left, Albert felt a strange, vibrating sensation in his pocket along with a loud beep emitting from his trousers.

'Blimey, it's me phone,' he figured.

Not quite sure of how to answer it, he pressed all the buttons until the ringing stopped.

'Hello? Who is it?'

Gretyl was sobbing on the phone.

'Albert, you need to come home, quickly, please.'

Albert was in no mood for one of Gretyl's crises and told her so.

'No, you don't understand. I'm so happy,' said Gretyl.

Albert mocked, 'I'm pleased for you dear. What is it? The shopping channel has one of your bags in a different colour?'

Gretyl snapped. 'I can't wait to see your face when I tell you the news, you miserable ol' sod.'

'Miserable ol' sod. My best friend has just died and you phone me up like some delirious lottery winner.'

Gretyl paused. 'You're right Albert, sorry. But it's better than winning the lottery. You need to come home, quick. Please.'

Albert turned his phone off, puzzled at what on earth had made his wife so happy.

In the distance, Albert could see the shutters down on Stan's shop, so he decided to cut across the grass lawn, back to the flat for his lunch and of course, the surprise that Gretyl had in store for him.

Gretyl was looking out of the window, eagerly awaiting Albert's arrival. Seeing him approach the flats, she left the front door open and sat down in the kitchen, with a letter in hand and a hot brew on the table for both of them.

Albert arrived, parked his bicycle in the hall and sat down in the kitchen.

'What's been making you so deliriously happy then?'

Gretyl passed him the handwritten letter.

'You won't believe what's in this.'

Albert proceeded to read the letter aloud.

'Hello Gretyl. I'm quite sure that you are unaware of my existence. My name is Ms. Victoria Hamilton-Smythe and I am your father's half sister ...'

Albert paused for a moment. Gretyl had no living family that he was aware of. She had mentioned to Albert on several occasions that as a child she had heard about French royal nobility in her family history, but she knew nothing more of it.

Gretyl hurried Albert.

'Keep reading, keep reading. It's wonderful news.'

Albert was certainly surprised. 'Goodness me, now you can really find out about your family, eh?'

'Albert, it's more wonderful than that.'

He continued reading. 'My father had a liaison with a young woman in our family service during The Great War. Your father was born as a result. As was the right and proper thing to do, the woman was asked to leave and my father never spoke of his illegitimate son (your father) or mistress. I learned this myself after his death when I discovered a letter addressed to this woman. The family secret has remained for nearly 80 years, but as I am close to death, I decided to write this letter and inform you of a number of things.

'As you are quite aware, I'm sure, illegitimate children have no right to inheritance and as such you have no natural born right to any of my property or its belongings. However, you are the last and only relative and though merely a half-blood, I had a decision to make: either I share my fortune with the cat sanctuary, or yourself. I despise cats, so seeing as you are family of sorts, I have decided that you will be both the executor of my will and the sole beneficiary of my estate, which is currently valued at a little over fourteen million pounds.'

Albert coughed loudly several times and then started to wheeze. Turning to Gretyl, he shook his head, astonished at what he had just read.

'Is this a wind up?'

Gretyl replied, 'It's for real. On the second page she gives the name and address of her solicitor, along with a name and telephone number of her maid, who has a key to the house. I've been on the phone to both of them and I'm getting a train there tomorrow.'

Albert couldn't take in the enormity of what he had just read.

'I am sure it will be interesting to learn about your extended family,' he said.

'Sod the family. I want the keys to the house. And Albert, you won't believe where the house is. It's my dream. Finally, I'm back where I belong. Read the rest of the letter.'

Albert picked up the letter again.

'I am absolutely sure that you will fit into village life, quite wonderfully. Upon my death, I would recommend you visit your next door neighbours, Neil and Elizabeth Rochester at 62, Codgers Lane. I am sure they will be very happy to welcome you to Poncey Bridge.'

Albert passed the letter back to Gretyl.

'Well dear, you've always wanted a holiday home, so there you are, you've got it.'

Albert was pleased for Gretyl, but felt it had little bearing on himself. To be honest, the only two things he enjoyed in retirement were a little flutter at Bet Paddy and his daily pilgrimage to the allotment. No amount of money was going to change that.

'Are you having me on, Albert? Holiday home, my royal behind! I can't wait to move out of this pokey flat. Oh, think of all the space, all the wall space. The frogs will have a new home, lots of new friends and you my dear, you can have a room all to yourself, even your own toilet. You can stay in there for as long as you want.'

The room fell silent. Gretyl waited for a response but none was forthcoming.

'Did you hear what I said? Your own room, TV, even your own maid should you want one.'

'Gretyl, I couldn't move out. This is my home and I wouldn't give up my allotment. Especially now, since Stan has died.'

Gretyl stood up and remonstrated.

'Are you havin' a laugh, Albert Trollop? You prefer that pockey hut to a mansion? We can do so much with this money. I'm sure they've got a big enough garden for you to bury yourself in.'

'The only place I want to be buried is here and if you carry on, it'll be sooner rather than later!'

CHAPTER 27

Lock Down in Poncey Bridge

Neil Rochester had excelled in his role as the Chairman of the Poncey Bridge Committee for over 25 years. Starting with his great, great grandfather, the Rochester family had enjoyed the privilege of this position since the late 18th century when they bought the hundred hectare land.

In the past 25 years, the remaining land had been sold off to the inhabitants of the village, with Neil Rochester making over £13.8 million.

Not only was the family name known for its wealth, but Neil had enjoyed considerable sporting success over the years, being a part of the Great Britain Rowing team, as well as a keenly competitive polo player. However, his sporting days were at an end and he was now approaching the age of retirement.

Patricia Rochester had been married to Neil for over 30 years and was a faithful wife. Now in her late 50s, her days were spent quietly reading and knitting for her daughter's little girl and decorating dolls houses for a local charity outside of the village. Happy with a simple life, it was also an antidote to her frequent bouts of depression and loneliness.

'You're home early. A quiet day at the office?' asked Patricia.

Neil replied, 'Not much doing at the fort, dear. I must go and sort the agenda for the Committee meeting tomorrow. I'll vanquish the damn thing now.'

'Super. Do you think you could raise the question of a house sale?'

Neil's demeanor changed.

'I've told you before, it isn't going to happen. You know full well that we have a restrictive covenant on this property. That means no one can apply for a mortgage on this land. We've sent a message out for decades that visitors are not welcome. For goodness sake, my family has lived here in this very house for over two hundred years. I'd be the scorn of the village if I walked now.'

Patricia sat quietly, rocking in her chair as she worked the woollen ball with her knitting needle.

Neil continued, 'We've gone over this so many times now. We can't simply up and leave. I have big responsibilities here. The village needs me. My business needs me. Do you understand? These people need me.'

Head down, Patricia carried on knitting and mumbled under her breath, 'The only thing I understand Neil, is that you don't need me.'

Neil was unimpressed. 'Here you go again. It's all about you and what you want. You haven't fared badly out of the life I've given you. All I ask for in return is that you make sure my shirts are washed and ironed and that my dinner is ready.'

Patricia ignored the comment.

'For cryin' out loud, why the sour face? It's not like you have to lift a finger in this house. I even pay for that to be taken care of.'

Over the years Patricia had watched her husband become a crude, insensitive man who, not only bored with his marriage, openly despised it. Neil had made it clear on a number of occasions that Patricia could never match up to his mother, belittling her at every opportunity.

It was five years since their only child, Jenny, moved out of the home, due in most part to the tension and awful atmosphere that filled most days.

Following Jenny's departure, Patricia had suffered a nervous breakdown. Her depression was now only managed by a medley of tablets that the village doctor prescribed. Neil had insisted that absolutely no one was to hear of what he called 'the wildly exaggerated and entirely unnecessary episode'.

Neil retreated to the study after giving his wife instructions for dinner later that evening. He needed a solid hour to write the monthly committee agenda and booted up the desktop PC, loading last month's agenda. Neil renamed it for the month of JULY and scrolled down to remove the following items:

8. Request for the Women's Institute to hold monthly meetings in the village.

11. Dog fouling fines.

12. Location of the best bloom summer extravaganza.

The three new items to be included were:

1. New signs for private roads with graphic warnings depicting consequences to trespassers.

2. Dispute between Mrs Blowhorn and Ms. Kingsley-Thatcher.

3. Ms. Hamilton-Smythe – deceased and a deeply concerning new development.

Neil couldn't continue after typing point three. After the many encounters with Gretyl's half-aunt, Victoria, he was glad to see the back of her. However, what was causing him no end of grief was the discovery only days ago from her cleaner that Victoria had indeed left a will and that the entire estate and property would be given to an outsider from London.

Neil had been exasperated; it had been a firmly held policy of the village that in no circumstances was any property to be sold without permission from the village committee, or be left to a person resident outside Poncey Bridge.

The checks and balances that were normally in place to stop this disaster happening were clearly no match for the cunning Victoria Hamilton-Smythe. The thought of an outsider, with the attendant possibility of contamination by a lower class of society, seemed a far worse and pressing concern for Neil.

Neil thumbed through his diary and found the number of a woman called Tracey. She was the cleaner who had first broken the news of her employer's death.

'Tracey, its Rochester, Neil Rochester. How are you, my dear?'

'I'm fine, Mr Rochester. How may I help you?'

'Tracey, the reason I'm calling is that we have our monthly village meeting tomorrow evening and I'm putting the minutes together. I have a few questions about your old employer, Ms. Hamilton-Smythe, if that's ok?'

'Mr Rochester, I'm not quite sure how I can help you,' Tracey replied cautiously.

Neil continued. 'First things first, I would love for us to get off on the right foot. I know that I had my fair share of conflict with your previous employer and I am quite sure that you have only heard things from one side of the fence, so to speak. Please believe me when I say that I was supportive of you working in the village. I have no problem associating with professional people and I will do my best over the coming months to express this in the village meetings.'

Victoria had made it very clear to Tracey that she despised Neil, not his wife Patricia, whom she described as a pleasant woman who had been reduced to a mixture of hypochondria and compulsive anxiety by her marriage. Agoraphobic, no doubt a result of her husband's abusive behaviour, she would never be seen venturing out beyond the boundaries of her own property.

'Mr Rochester, I really don't want to get involved ...'

Neil rudely interrupted.

'Please listen carefully. When we spoke outside the house, you informed me that there is a benefactor of the will and that 'this woman' lived in London. I'm sure you know that it's my duty to protect the village from any potential threat to our ... ahem, its way of life. You may also know that our village has 'laws'. These were established hundreds of years ago and we proudly uphold these today. As a result, it's simply not possible for an outsider to force their way in. Only blood relatives are allowed to inherit properties in the village and I'm quite sure Victoria had no children or living relatives, so who the hell is she? The deeds make it very clear that the property and its land cannot entertain a mortgage and can only be purchased by one of the original families who already live here. What is this woman's name? Where does she live? I need to speak with her right now, before the village is up in arms.'

Tracey replied angrily. 'I am not at liberty to discuss this with you. Now, please don't call me again.'

Tracey slammed the phone down while Neil threw his against the wall. He stood up and kicked out against the door, driving his heel through the small glass pane of his French doors.

Neil's shin was now wedged tight in the door. Unable to wriggle free due to a glass dagger that had penetrated his skin and bone, Neil fell to the floor, screaming in pain.

'Argh. I'll make the cow pay for this.'

Patricia heard a large bang upstairs and locked herself in the kitchen, terrified once again by one of her husband's violent outbursts.

'Patricia. Come here quickly,' he yelled.

Reluctantly, she opened the door and walked up the stairs, finding Neil lying down with his leg twisted on the floor in a small pool of blood.

'Goodness me, what have you done?' asked Patricia.

'What took you so long? Didn't you hear me? I'm lying here in pain. Where were you? You're useless. Get the phone and call an ambulance.'

Patricia hurried nervously to pick up the pieces of the cordless phone.

'Neil, it's broken.'

'Why are you so thick? I can see that for myself. I threw the damn thing. Go call from the other phone in the bedroom, you idiot.'

Patricia was shaking now. She hurried to the bedroom and dialled 999. The ambulance was only minutes away and though the bleeding didn't appear severe, she was instructed by the emergency services to keep Neil talking and make sure he remained conscious.

Patricia handed a handkerchief to Neil.

'They will be here in a matter of minutes. Told me to talk to you and make sure you are fully conscious for when they arrive. Are you ok? Would you like a cup of tea?'

Neil lifted his arms up in the air in protest.

'Oh, I've never been better. Nothing that a good cup of tea can't cure! Come to think of it, why not get your best china out and we can have a cup of Earl Grey together ... and while you're at it, fetch me some Madeira cake, chocolate truffles and my best bottle of brandy. For goodness sake woman, what planet are you on?'

'Sorry Neil. I don't understand. Would you like a cup of tea?'

Neil picked up his slipper from the floor and threw it at his wife, narrowly missing her head. He continued, 'What's this handkerchief for?'

Patricia blushed and took a few steps back.

'Er, you looked uncomfortable and I thought you might want to wipe your brow?'

'Why of course ... please fetch me the crossword for today as well. I tell you what ... if my leg is still stuck here in ten minutes time, go fetch the washing and I'll fold it for you.'

Patricia rushed towards the door to make her exit.

'Okay, I'll get the kettle on. Was it one slice of Madeira or two?'

CHAPTER 28

Hawaii 5-0

Dave Soddall, having barely slept a wink, had managed to keep his new jeans and shirt a surprise from Sharon.

Dave wasn't too sure about the stone washed look of the jeans, with their 'fashionable' rips, or the Hawaii beach shirt with dolphins that Kevin had chosen. The significance of the outfit was clear though. Dave wanted to be a new man.

Not only would Sharon wake up to Tom Selleck (without the moustache, hair or medallion), but a hugely improved version of her husband. What's more, Dave had planned to surprise Sharon with his first attempt at cooking an English breakfast. After all, they had a huge day ahead of them.

Dave cracked the eggs over a bowl and removed some of the shell from the yolk. Placing on the grill what he thought was a frying pan he poured in the leftover oil from the chip fryer. Cooking had never been Dave's strong point. In fact, Dave had never made a point of cooking at all, but this new found hope and desire for a better life had not only given his large frame some energy. His brain was now tingling with new thoughts and ideas.

Devoid of a recipe, Dave had decided to use eight frozen sausages and ten rashers of bacon. He threw them into the hot pan and swished it around in the inch deep olive oil with three runny eggs.

Unsure of the cooking time, he decided that the darker the breakfast the better, so he stirred the contents together for about five minutes. The egg was most certainly cooked and stuck to the meat, and if brown meant well done, it was certainly over-ready. The bacon and sausages were also charred in appearance, so Dave named his first attempt at breakfast, 'Smoked meat with crispy pan fried bird'.

With toast at the ready, he rummaged through the fridge and found some chopped tomatoes, along with some onions, lettuce, HP sauce, coleslaw and olives. Dave served it up on their best and unused china plates.

The food on the plate now swam in a lake of oil. Unsure of the appearance, Dave added lemon juice to try and mask the smell, adding more ketchup and mustard to break up the food into small islands on the plate.

'It may not look like the perfect breakfast, but it's the perfect start to a perfect day,' Dave thought.

Dave lifted the sofa cushion and removed his new shirt and jeans he'd hidden from Sharon, only to discover the cushions had an unpleasant odour to them. Investigating further, he found that remnants of fried chicken, cold chips, popcorn, crisps and onion rings had welded to the furniture and in turn, to his shirt.

Housework and cleaning were not the Soddall family's strong point. At first glance, the house looked like an old fashioned and tired terraced property. However, beneath a thin veneer of decency, there lurked a world devoid of cleanliness.

Dave fetched some of his cheap aftershave from the shelf and sprayed the shirt and trousers from top to bottom. He inserted his hairy, white legs into the jeans and was relieved that the button and the hole were able to make contact. Like a matador, he grabbed the shirt collar and whisked it around his large frame.

'Shaz will be in for a shock now.'

He snuck out of the front door barefoot and tiptoed to the neighbour's rose bed.

Crouching beneath the front window ledge and safely out of view, he picked two blooms from her rose bush and ran back inside. The breakfast was now adorned with two roses on his discoloured and tea stained Homer Simpson tray.

Sharon rolled across the pillow as she heard Dave's loud entrance and moaned.

'I can't believe I had a whole bottle of that cheap Lambrini and on an empty stomach as well. I haven't overslept in years. What time is it?'

Dave placed the tray on Sharon's lap as she sat up in bed.

'Five to ten. I need to get ready. Sharkie will be here in less than a couple of hours to pick us all up. Dave, what's that sickly smell?'

Dave moved his eyebrows up and down in the direction of his shirt and jeans.

'Love, haven't you noticed something?'

'Dave, are you wearing fancy dress?'

Dave looked sternly at Sharon.

'I'm trying to make an effort and all you do is take the pee. That smell is the aftershave Aunt Hilda bought me and that lovely cooked breakfast on your lap is what I've just made you with my very own hands.'

Sharon puckered her lips and blew a kiss in Dave's direction.

'Aw, I'm sorry honey ... but your aunt has been dead for ten years and she bought that aftershave at a car boot, already opened. I only keep it on the shelf to tip down the sink when it needs unblocking.'

Dave sat on the edge of the bed and tried to divert her attention toward his burnt offering.

Sharon smiled and looked down at her breakfast. She was touched at Dave's effort and desperate to see him become the new man he was trying to be. She wanted to encourage him, but eating this might prove a bridge too far, even if the bacon smelt decent enough.

Sharon detected an unpleasant smell.

'Honey, did you turn the gas off?'

Dave leapt from the bed and threw himself down the stairs after realising he'd left the pan on in the kitchen. Choking on the smoke, he tried to open the window but it hadn't been opened in years and was jammed shut.

'Now I definitely need to change the battery in the smoke alarm,' he muttered.

Dave opened the front door and with a tea towel tried to waft the smoke out. He then walked up the stairs and sat on Sharon's bed.

'Was it the gas, love?'

Dave panicked and ran down the stairs for a second time. The kitchen had quickly filled with smoke again, so he turned off the gas stove and tried to chase the smoke out of the front door.

Much to Dave's surprise, Sharon was halfway through her breakfast.

'Flippin' eck love. Did you really enjoy my smoked meat with crispy pan fried bird?'

Sharon tried hard not to gag after inserting an olive into her mouth and attempted to conceal the remaining food in the serviette.

'Enjoy, well that's not quite how I'd put it. It's definitely the best breakfast you've cooked before, but then it's the only one you've cooked too.'

Grumbling and rumbles escaped from under the covers as Sharon tried hard to muffle the sound of her digestive tract processing Dave's culinary delights.

Sharon burped.

'Excuse me. Y'know what's funny though, love. I recently read a story in my girlie magazine 'Hot Flush' that said a fry-up was the best cure for a hangover. I'm not sure about that now.'

Dave joked, 'Well, our trip to Poncey Bridge will sort you out love. All that fresh air will do you the world of good. You can let off a bit o' gas and everyone will think it's the cows.'

'Mr Soddall, one minute you're trying to dine the lady and the next you're making crude remarks. Anyway, since when did you decide to join the cast of Hawaii 5-0?'

Dave stood by the bed with his son's large black sunglasses perched on his bald head. His untucked shirt hung over his new jeans, creating the false impression that he was more streamlined than he really was.

Sharon pointed to the grey, curly chest hair that was forcing its way out of Dave's open shirt.

'Honey, do your shirt up. That dolphin looks like it's got a perm from the 80s with your chest hair all over it.'

Dave raised one of his arms and kissed his left, saggy bicep.

'What's it like to have a new man around?'

'Let me know when he turns up,' teased Sharon.

Dave's flabby biceps were covered with faded green tattoos that extended to slightly firmer forearms. His upper left arm displayed a Union Jack with 'God Save the Queen' wrapped around it, while his right arm proudly showcased the West Ham United FC logo with, 'I'm Forever Blowing Bubbles'. Unfortunately, the letter 'n' had faded so that it read 'Queer', while the capital 'B' for 'Bubbles' earned him the name, 'Monkey Love' with his mates down the pub.

The birthday gift of a Michael Jackson T-shirt with Dave's nickname printed on the back received plenty of laughs as well. One of Dave's spectacled friends called 'The Brain' sent a card that said, 'Dear Monkey Love, Happy Birthday! It's time to go 'Ape' with your 'priMATES!"

These words had gone straight over Dave's head.

Dave sat down on the end of the bed.

'Shaz, I read that Marbella is a millionaire's dream and billionaire's playground. From what I can tell, we can offer the villagers everything they could want in a holiday home. The fact that Tony's villas are set outside the main town in the hills will give them the sheltered life they already have in Poncey Bridge. Today, we can have a look at these folks, hand out flyers, take phone numbers and get this show on the road.'

Sharon replied, 'What does Sharkie think of our chances?'

'I've known him for years. He's a ruthless bloke. He wouldn't be in this if he didn't think he'd make a serious wad of cash. He's as bent as they come. That posh BMW that he drives must have cost him over fifty grand.'

Sharon felt butterflies in her stomach. It wasn't Sharkie's money that impressed her. It was the fact that this guy who earns a small fortune each year was playing a key role in their Marbella scam.

'You know what, Dave. With Sharkie in our corner and Tony desperate to get out of one, I can't see how we can fail. For the first time in our lives, we have a plan that makes sense and we're working it.'

CHAPTER 29

Majestic Heights

The Trollops had barely managed a few hours of sleep. Gretyl lay awake, anticipating a good rummage through her half-aunt's belongings later that day. Wanting to make an impression, she had been up since 4am and even baked a vanilla sponge later that morning for the cleaner who held the keys to her new home.

Albert had spent most of the night thinking about the death of his friend. Stan's untimely departure had left a lasting and gaping hole in his life and he knew he would have some painful adjustments to make.

Albert had also been thinking that he would very happily support Gretyl's move to her new home - on a permanent basis.

'They say money can't buy you happiness, but I hope it does something for Gretyl,' he mused. 'But as for me, I just want to be on my own now.'

An old fashioned sense of loyalty and convenience had kept his marriage together over the years, but now Gretyl had the means to up and leave, everything was changing.

A voice in Albert's head whispered, 'Maybe Gretyl's happiness is the key to my own.'

Albert finished his small lunch of tinned sardines with crackers and carried his plate to the sink. Gretyl finished wrapping the vanilla sponge she had just baked for Victoria Hamilton-Smythe's cleaner and pecked Albert on the cheek as she walked towards the door.

'Albert, I'm leaving.'

Albert extended a conciliatory smile.

'I understand. I'm sure it's for the best.'

Gretyl frowned.

'What are you talking about? Ah, nice. You want me gone for good? You'll not get rid of me that easily, Albert Trollop. I'm only off to meet the cleaner who has the keys for the house.'

'Of course, love. I mean, you're leaving to get the full story from the woman about your aunt, 'n' stuff.'

'Albert, I know you said you won't leave your allotment, but I won't let that come between us and our dream. You can have your own vegetable patch, green house, everything, when we move. The cleaner said that the rear garden is over an acre. Think of it Albert, our very own garden.'

Albert replied, 'You've never shown an interest in gardening before? What about your phobia of creepy crawlies?'

Gretyl checked her mascara in the mirror.

'Sod the insects. Where else could I top up my tan in the summer? Come to think of it, I'd love some decking and we could afford to pay someone to take care of it. No more green fingers for you, Albert Trollop.'

Albert snapped. 'I love my green fingers and trust me, there's plenty of folk who'd deck you for free.'

'This is no joking matter, Albert. Don't think for a minute that I'm going to budge on this. Oh, and another thing. Open the windows. I can't bear the stink of your fish.'

Albert remained silent. It would only be a few minutes before she'd be out of the door, so he grabbed the newspaper and locked himself in the toilet.

Gretyl picked up the handset from the telephone seat in the hallway and dialled 'Quicky Cab'.

'Ah, yes. I expect your best vehicle, suitably polished at the entrance of Majestic Heights, by the grass lawn in five minutes.'

The operator identified Gretyl's voice. 'Which side of the estate, dear? Is it the high rise flats by the burnt out cars or the Spa end with the smashed windows?'

Gretyl was unimpressed by the description.

'At the main entrance, of course. I'm meeting some very important people today. You'll recognise me, Gretyl Trollop, by my wide-brimmed orange chapeau, with matching dress.'

The operator whispered under her breath:

'I can think of plenty other things you're known by.'

Gretyl pressed her ear closer to the phone.

'Sorry dear, I don't think I got that?'

The girl asked, 'And where's the cab going to?'

'I shall inform the driver of my destination when he arrives. You people never communicate with each other and I won't repeat myself, twice.'

'Our driver will be with you in a few minutes.'

The operator ended the call abruptly.

Gretyl picked up her case and left the flat. Pressing the lift button, she was horrified to read, 'LIFT OUT OF ORDER.'

Gretyl began walking down the twelve flights of stairs, grumbling as she went. The thud of her high heels echoed down the passage as the driver outside honked his horn. Removing her heels, she hurried bare foot down the steps, shoes in one hand, her small red case bouncing on its plastic wheels in the other.

By the time Gretyl was half way down to the sixth floor, the car was still honking insistently. Gretyl stopped, withdrew her embroidered handkerchief from her bosom and wiped her sweat-drenched brow.

The fur coat had to come off so she threw it over her shoulder like a fireman's lift, panting heavily down the staircase until she reached the ground floor and ran out to the car.

'It may not appear so but I am a lady of years and your common honking is quite distasteful! How is a lady to remain composed when harassed by such an ignorant cab driver like yourself? Another thing ... is it you or the car that stinks to high heaven?'

The heavy-set and bulky driver turned around and glared at Gretyl. As he puffed on a long, rolled-up joint it appeared to Gretyl that he was not all there.

Gretyl stared at the two teardrop tattoos below his eyes, her gaze following the line of the scar that ran down his left cheek to his chin.

'Woman, listen to me very, very carefully. The last person who dared to diss me was shot in da face. Now you look like someone's already done that to you, so I'm gonna' give you two options.'

The irate driver slowly flicked his tattooed fingers in the air as he counted.

'One, apologise very nicely, get that pig ugly face out of my car and go wait for your cab. Two, close your eyes and start praying.'

'I'm very sorry,' Gretyl yelped as she leapt out of the back door and scampered back to the foyer of the flats.

The loud horn sounded again as a young man carrying a number of small bags barged past Gretyl and knocked her to the floor.

Shocked by her encounter, Gretyl remained silent and tried to compose herself as she sat up and looked out of the window. The car, with its blacked out windows, was now moving out of sight.

Gretyl noticed what looked like talcum powder on her dress. Stirring her finger into it, she sniffed to see what it was. Having suffered with sinus problems for ten years, Gretyl struggled to smell anything at all so she dipped her finger in the white powder again and snorted it violently.

'Hmm, doesn't smell like talc to me. It doesn't smell like anything at all for that matter. Maybe it's the flour from my baking.'

Gretyl now sucked the remaining powder from her fingers.

'Ew, tastes bitter. Hope it's not rat poison!'

And then the penny dropped.

'Oh my God!' Gretyl cried, uttering the closest thing to a prayer in years.

Gretyl panicked.

'I know what this is! The lad who ran into me must've spilled it on my dress.'

Gretyl looked down and noticed more of the white powder scattered on the floor. She bent down to pick up a small half-filled polythene bag. Gretyl was now sure that she had just unwittingly taken drugs.

As she sought to calm her nerves, Gretyl heard a postman delivering the mail into the letter boxes.

'Alright, love. Lovely day today, don't you think?'

Gretyl made no answer but quickly hid the powdered sachet inside her handbag.

She could feel her heart rate increasing.

A strange numbness was now spreading over her tongue and a wave of euphoria, accompanied by a hot flush, was engulfing her entire being.

She brushed off the rest of the powder from her dress, strolled outside and listened with a newly found attentiveness to the pleasant melody of birds singing.

The warm sunshine and cool breeze caressed her like a cherished childhood memory.

Even the broken windows of the vandalised shop across the courtyard glistened like crystal.

'How strange?' she thought.

The feelings of dread only moments ago were quickly replaced by waves of bliss.

She tilted her head back and smiled at the sky, sketching the clouds with her finger.

Gretyl flopped onto the grass and propped herself up against the hard suitcase, her dress and pointy heels sprawled across the pavement. Looking down the road, she watched as a Vauxhall Astra parked up alongside her.

Rashid, a young driver from the taxi rank, opened his window.

'You order a taxi?' he shouted.

At that moment he recognised Gretyl from the recent trip to the hairdressers. He tried to pull away, but she had already opened the front passenger door.

'Clapham Junction station please. Be a sweetheart and fetch my luggage, would you?'

Rashid kept quiet and stepped out of the cab to retrieve the bags.

'If only all young men were as courteous as you. Why, I could wish I was in my teens all over again.'

Rashid stared at the beads that hung over the rear view mirror and offered up a silent prayer.

Gretyl smiled at him while her bulbous eyes fixed on Rashid's impressive nose.

'Oh my, you are very handsome aren't you? Your nose is like a strong tower. Reminds me of ...'

Rashid hurriedly looked down at the screen on his PDA which displayed the job information.

'Trollop, Majestic Heights,' he said loudly.

Gretyl's head wobbled to the right as she began to slur.

'Has anyone told you that you look like Omar Sharif? I know he's not my colour, but don't tell anyone – he sure does tickle my fancy.'

Gretyl withdrew her pocket mirror from her handbag.

'Goodness me! My eyes look big.' Gretyl screeched. 'That's what made in China gets you these days, flaming mirror.'

Rashid sighed and pulled away from the curb. A few uncomfortable minutes later he was parking in the taxi bay at the station.

'That'll be £3.60 please.'

Gretyl leaned toward Rashid from the passenger seat, her face twitching spasmodically.

'Is that all that you want, dear?'

Rashid cringed.

Gretyl opened her handbag and searched through her sticky sweet-encrusted coins for the correct change. Aware that the meter was still running and giddy from the white powder her hands fumbled awkwardly.

'Sod it!' she mumbled.

Some of Gretyl's cash had stuck to the bottom lining of the bag so she tipped it upside down and began to shake it violently.

Rashid leapt in his seat as the open pouch of cocaine emptied itself over the front of the car.

'What are you doing? What is that crap on my lap? Lady, don't even tell me that's what I think it is?'

Gretyl laughed.

'Why is there a rabbit sitting on your head? That's a very clever trick.'

Rashid's face suddenly lost much of its colour. He rushed to the rear of the car and collected Gretyl's small case. He marched to the passenger door and beckoned to her to step out of his vehicle.

Gretyl refused to budge.

'Young man, there's really no need to be so rude. I'm certainly not. Though I do think I should get a discount on the fare. You never told me I'd be sharing this taxi with a naked man.'

'You are hallucinating! I'd be ashamed if my grandmother was a drug addict like you. Now please, get your coke arse out of my car.'

Gretyl tried to compose herself before stepping out of the vehicle.

'Young man, you'll regret speaking to a lady like that,' she said as she wandered off.

Rashid ran to the back of his car and buried his head in the boot, franticly searching for his mini vac to hoover up the contents. After a few moments, he discovered it inside the compartment of the spare wheel. Desperate to be on his way, he returned to the front seats and was relieved when the powerful suction slowly began to remove the traces of white powder.

But his relief was short lived.

The next moment his temporary peace was shattered by the sound of an approaching siren.

'This is the police! Put your hands on your head and step away from the car, now.'

Rashid immediately obeyed.

A police officer strode towards Rashid and cuffed him.

'We have received a complaint from an elderly passenger that you offered drugs to her, while a naked man in the rear of the vehicle tried to accost her.'

'You gotta be kidding me. That ol' cow was as high as a kite and emptied a bag of cocaine in my taxi! She was the one snorting it. She was the one hallucinating. Couldn't you tell?'

'I put it to you sir that the elderly passenger challenged you and knocked the bag of drugs away. You fought back, the bag split and you tried to hoover up the evidence. We're now going to search your vehicle under the 'Misuse of Drugs Act'.'

Rashid protested.

'I'm telling you the truth officer, honest. I know it sounds crazy, but that woman is one nasty ol' witch. She even ran off without paying for her fare.'

The officer placed the mini vac inside an evidence bag.

''Ran off' you say. I would suggest she had good reason to. I am now arresting you on suspicion of possessing controlled substances.'

The officer cautioned Rashid and put him in the back of the police van.

Gretyl watched from a distance, grinning as the van drove off. She turned to a lady standing at the station entrance and remonstrated.

'Imposter! How dare he impersonate Omar Shariff? I hope the rabbit's okay and they catch the naked man!'

CHAPTER 30

Moving On

The previous night an ambulance had been seen arriving at the Rochester's home to take Neil to hospital. In the Accident and Emergency Department a nurse had removed the tiny glass fragments from his leg and bandaged him up before discharging him to return home.

Neil had slept well that night after insisting that Patricia sleep in the spare bedroom - on account of his wound. He consumed half a bottle of sherry to numb the pain. Having mixed a few painkillers with the alcohol, Neil became almost comatose, wrapped in the silk sheets of Patricia's bed. He slept in until late morning.

When he eventually woke up, Neil sat up and gazed at the small bandage around his shin. Feeling completely hung over and woefully sorry for himself, he yelled:

'Patricia, Patricia. I'm up. Come and help me out of bed before I pee myself.'

Patricia promptly arrived carrying a tray of toasted Paninis, fresh ham and cheese, orange juice and a pot of tea. She carefully placed it on the bedside table and arranged the cutlery and cloth serviette, pouring the Earl Grey tea into a china cup.

'Forget the damn breakfast woman, it's my bladder! Now help me up will you.'

Neil stood up and adjusted most of his weight on one leg, placing his arm around Patricia's shoulder. She couldn't remember the last time Neil had touched her in a way that was comfortable.

It was nearly midday and aided by his wife, Neil managed to walk to the bathroom.

'Can you go to the PC and print off my notes and agenda for the committee meeting this evening?' Neil asked. 'I need about 40 copies of the minutes to hand out. If I have to hobble to the meeting, I will.'

Neil sat on the toilet and put his head in his hands, wondering where he could turn for help. He had only one person whom he regarded as a friend in the world, an old school acquaintance who worked in the stock market in Lloyd's of London. His name was Gerard.

From time to time, Gerard and Neil had shared information which had been mutually and financially beneficial. To the more discerning eye it would be classed as insider trading. Their early partnership had led to the setting up of a hedge fund. This had failed spectacularly.

Unable to fund some of Gerard's latest ideas, the drinks after work soon stopped, along with the phone calls. Neil deeply resented his friend's recent lack of concern, especially since he was now facing financial ruin.

The phone in the lounge rang and Patricia politely answered.

'Good afternoon Mrs Rochester, James Windsor here. I would like to speak to your husband please.'

Mr Windsor was by far the richest man known to the Rochester family. After some soliciting from Gerard and Neil, Mr Windsor had made an investment of over ten million pounds into their private equity hedge fund. The high risk fund collapsed and now there was little hope of Mr Windsor or anyone else investing with the pair ever again.

Running up the stairs, Patricia gently knocked on the door and covered the mouthpiece of the phone with the palm of her hand.

'Neil, I have Mr Windsor for you.'

Neil spun the toilet roll and pulled the sheets.

'Speak up, woman! I can't hear you.'

Patricia lifted her hand from the mouthpiece and summoned Neil again.

'I'm sorry dear, but Mr Windsor is on the phone.'

Neil pulled his pyjama bottoms up, bellowing through the door.

'For crying out loud, woman! Can't a man take a crap without being interrupted?'

Neil unbolted the lock.

'Who the hell is it Patricia?'

Patricia whispered in Neil's ear.

'I was trying to tell you discreetly that it's Mr Windsor on the telephone.'

Neil blushed before taking the handset.

'Rochester here. How may I help you?'

A voice snorted sarcastically down the phone.

'James Windsor here. Would you like to finish in the bathroom before I continue?'

Neil cringed.

'Oh, I do apologise, Mr Windsor. I was just having some friendly repartee with my wife. Please do continue.'

'Listen, I have some very bad news for you,' Windsor said with his customary abruptness.

Neil shuffled nervously.

'What news?'

'Rochester, I wanted to inform you that Gerard Holmes has been suspended by the FSA this morning and is being investigated by the Serious Fraud Office. Your name has also been implicated.'

Neil's face blanched.

'It was bad enough losing my investment in your failed hedge fund,' Windsor continued, 'but to be associated in any way with criminal activities is not something I am prepared to tolerate. I'm going to sue you for every penny you have. Do you hear me?'

Neil froze.

In that brief moment, Windsor's words hung over him like a judge's verdict. Neil had already been under investigation with the Serious Fraud Office and Financial Services Authority over five years ago, but the case - involving an illegal use of Euro bonds - had been dropped due to an untraceable paper trail.

Windsor now closed in for the kill.

'Rochester, this is far more serious than money. If this goes to trial, the judge could find you in breach of your fiduciary duty to your clients and that carries a hefty prison sentence. Heard about prison, Rochester? Made any plans to retire there, have we?'

Neil erupted with rage.

Throwing his phone against the wall - shattering it instantly - he shouted:

'Right, that's it. I've had enough of this business and this place. Patricia, it's time for us to sell up. I'll announce it to the committee tonight. Cash sale only. The village will buy it and even if we have to take a hit on the value of the house, so be it. We need to move on.'

Patricia's hands began to tremble visibly.

'Neil, what is it? What's happened?'

'Don't ask so many questions. I'm sick and tired of all the bureaucracy here. You and I can make a fresh start somewhere new. Let's go abroad, somewhere with plenty of sunshine.'

'Neil, we hardly see our daughter or our grandchild as it is. Wouldn't this cut us off from them even more?'

'We can send for the family to come and visit. It will be like an extended holiday for the length of our retirement.'

Patricia picked up Neil's untouched breakfast tray.

The two of them walked downstairs to the kitchen.

There Neil continued with his hard sell.

'Let's take a flight over. We can have a good look at what's available. What do you say? The Costa Del Sol looks a beautiful place.'

The microwave beeped and Patricia served Neil the hot Panini at the breakfast table, her hands still shaking.

Neil sat down and tried to work out the possible ramifications of Gerard's arrest and his own involvement. Having been under investigation with the SFO and FSA before, Neil had little doubt he was now cornered.

In all of Poncey Bridge's history, there hadn't been any significant hardship amongst the villagers and certainly never the threat of a bailiff's visit. Now Neil faced the prospect of both terrors, aware that his name in his business and private world would soon be in tatters.

'I need to turn my assets into cash before the creditors are called in,' Neil mused.

For the next few minutes, Neil was deep in thought.

He surmised that he needed to liquidate his businesses and declare bankruptcy very soon, but not before the quick cash-in-hand sale of his house and assets had gone through. He figured that a drastically reduced cash price for the house would be more than enough incentive for a local buyer.

Neil tallied up the assets he could sell fairly quickly with a modest reserve at auction. These included:

- Rolls Royce classic car, £60,000
- Four antique paintings, £100,000
- Wine cellar contents, £20,000
- Antique ornaments, £20,000
- Antique jewellery, £50,000

Totalling up, Neil figured that there should be at least £250,000 from the list and with the house valued at £1,500,000 a quick cash sale would definitely raise at least half of that.

However, these calculations brought little comfort to Neil.

'One million. One poxy million! That's all I've got to walk away with?' he thought. 'This paltry sum won't fund the lifestyle I was expecting in my retirement.'

Patricia had taped the phone back together and tested the line. Apart from a slight crackle, the dial tone seemed clear enough. Neil snatched the phone from her.

'I want to get rid of some of our stuff quickly. Get me the number for Harvey Spicer, the auctioneer at Bonds. He's an old crook, but he'll sell our things fast if I make it worth his while.'

Patricia took a deep breath.

'Neil, what's made you change your mind so quickly? Why the sudden rush?'

Neil reached out across the table, gently stroking her hand.

'Darling, I know I've not been the best husband. I haven't always listened to you or stood up for what you want, but now I want to change. You deserve it. It's all about you, honey. It's about our retirement. We deserve to be happy.'

Patricia withdrew her arm from Neil's hand and walked away.

Opening a cupboard with her back to him, she slipped two anti-depressant pills into her mouth.

She poured a glass of water, closed her eyes, and gulped down the double dose.

CHAPTER 31

Grassy Verge

Sharkie pulled over in his BMW to answer his Blackberry phone. It was Carl, a colleague from whom he'd earned some big commissions over the past decade.

'How's it going wide boy?' Carl asked.

Sharkie adjusted his black Ray-Ban sunglasses in the mirror.

'Sweet Carl, sweet. You got some news for me, bro?'

'Well I've looked into this chair-bloke for you in Poncey Bridge and asked some questions. Turns out he's a hedge fund manager who's blown his wad. My mate calls him 'Ponzi Bridge' after the guy got greedy and blew his investor's cash. Apparently, he's trying to tap people up for money wherever he can.'

'That's just the news I was hoping for, Carl,' Sharkie interrupted. Carl continued.

'Be careful though, mate. Nobody trusts him in the game. Word is he's a total knob. He's been suspended before by the FSA, and investigated by the Fraud Office.'

Sharkie clenched his fist, punching the air in delight.

'That's pukka news mate. I owe you a good drink. Mum's the word. Catch you later.'

Sharkie began an Internet search on his smart phone for Neil's business number. Finding Rochester Investment Services based in Poncey Bridge, he selected the number and dialled.

'Good afternoon. May I speak with Neil Rochester please? My name is Peter Lovitt.'

Patricia passed the phone to Neil.

'Rochester speaking.'

'Good afternoon Mr Rochester, I'm Peter Lovitt. I'm a director and entrepreneur of several businesses. Your name has been passed to me as someone who knows the financial markets and can maximise a client's investments. Am I correct?'

Neil sat back in his Parker Knoll recliner.

'Well Mr Lovitt, I've been in the business for over thirty years and I'm as keen to make money as I've ever been. What is your proposal?'

'I represent a wealthy developer and owner of five luxury villas in Marbella. My client has other business interests he wishes to pursue and as a result he's looking for the prompt sale of his luxury properties at a substantial saving for the buyer. We are talking upwards of half of their market value.'

Neil licked his lips before answering.

'I could be interested in property abroad, at the right price, of course. In fact, you may have called me at the right time. Marbella is of particular interest to me.'

Sharkie looked at himself in the mirror and relaxed in his leather seat.

'Great. I happen to be visiting a client in an hour at the Michelin bistro, which I believe is only a few miles from you. Are you free later this afternoon?'

'I can be, Mr Lovitt. Shall we say 3.30pm at the Marquis Brasserie in the village, just over the bridge? It's a private road and if anyone stops you, tell them you have an appointment with me.'

'Fantastic. I look forward to seeing you then, with my assistant, Miss Souddalle. Goodbye.'

Sharkie began to develop his business plan at lightning speed as he drove off to the Soddalls' home.

On arrival, Sharkie opened the rusty black gate and walked down the uneven path, careful to avoid the feline excrement making contact with his Italian loafers.

The butterflies fluttered in Sharon's stomach as the doorbell rang. Dressed in her blue pin-striped trouser suit, white silk blouse and red high heels, Sharon rushed eagerly down the stairs.

When Sharon opened the door, Sharkie took a few steps back, and looked her up and down.

'Perfect, absolutely perfect Sharon.'

Sharon blushed. 'Oh, thanks. I'm glad I can still fit into this little number.'

Dave Soddall walked down the stairs and greeted Sharkie in the hall, complimenting his guest.

'Looking dapper as ever, I see?'

Sharkie laughed, taunting Dave.

'Wish I could say the same, pops. That shirt looks like a fairground ride. I'm glad I brought my Ray-Bans. What's going on with those jeans?'

'Less of the cheek, or you'll get a slap,' replied Dave.

Sharon kissed Dave on the cheek.

'Don't worry, love. I like your jeans and I love the effort. Come on, let's go.'

Leaving the house, Sharkie escorted Sharon to the front passenger seat but she chose to sit in the back, behind Dave - who had leapt into the front.

Sharkie opened the electronic sunroof, switched on his in-dash satellite navigation system and punched in the address of the Michelin Star restaurant.

'I hope you guys are hungry. I'm taking you to the best restaurant you've ever seen.'

Sharon cringed.

Dave replied, 'As long as they do a nice bit of steak, I'm always up for that.'

Sharon pressed the electric window button down and inhaled the fresh air.

'I hope this trip isn't too long, I'm not feeling too good,' she said.

'We should be there in an hour or so. Make yourselves comfortable,' replied Sharkie.

Sharkie spoke up above the mellow sounds of the jazz music from his CD player.

'I've got a surprise for you guys. I was going to wait until the restaurant, but I guess now's as good a time as ever.'

Dave laughed.

'Don't tell me. You're joining the monastery after we've finished?'

'Nope.'

'You've started paying child maintenance to half the single mothers in London?'

Sharkie laughed out loud.

'Fat chance of that.'

'Think how many kids could be walking around in pin-stripe suits, just like their dad?' Sharon added.

Sharkie's voice took on a serious tone.

'I think we've cracked the village before we even need to get on the phones or hand out leaflets.'

Sharkie went on to relate how he had managed to persuade Rochester to meet him that very afternoon.

Dave sat in the front seat with his mouth open wide, while Sharon's heart raced at the thought of their plan taking another giant leap forward.

'That ... is ... amazing,' gulped Dave. 'Are you telling me this guy's already on board to buy a villa?'

'It's much better than that,' smiled Sharkie. 'I've been told that he manages Poncey Bridge's investments, so if we can persuade him to purchase all the villas as one development, he can make a fat profit for himself and we'll make our own fortune - all in one hit. No surveys, timeshares or different buyers!'

The news proved too much for Dave who farted loudly in his excitement.

'Ooh, sorry 'bout that. You may wanna roll down your windows,' said Dave.

Sharon held her hand over her mouth and nose.

'Dave, you pig. I already feel like I'm gonna vomit and I'm sitting right behind your arse.'

Sharkie had reached the M25 motorway and was playfully weaving in and out of the traffic.

Sharon belched loudly and shifted uncomfortably in the back seat.

'Sharkie, please slow down. I think I'm gonna be sick. I think you need to pull over.'

Sharkie panicked at the wheel.

'Do you think you can hang on a few minutes, Sharon? There's just four miles to the Services.'

Sharon reached hurriedly for the carrier bag and retched violently onto the Costa Soddall Travel leaflets and flyers.

Sharon vomited again, depositing the remains of Dave's breakfast over Sharkie's leather seats.

'I'm so sorry,' Sharon said, wiping the sick from her chin.

Looking desperately for somewhere to pull over, Sharkie spotted a small lay-by and manoeuvered the car skilfully between two lanes, reducing his speed drastically as he brought it to a stop.

Grabbing her handbag, Sharon made her way up a grassy slope and hid behind a large row of bushes.

Sharkie grabbed his pack of wipes from the door pocket and circled round to the back door.

'How am I gonna get the smell out of this car? I'm out tonight. I'm not getting any action in this, am I?'

Dave walked toward the back door.

'It's only a car! Give me the wipes and I'll sort it,' he said firmly.

'Only a car? Do you know how much this baby's worth? You don't have a clue, do you mate.'

Sharkie flung the hand wipes at Dave.

Dave now enraged, grabbed Sharkie by his suit collar, pulled the jacket over his head and threw him violently to the floor.

Sharkie was now sprawled out in the dirt.

'You broke my nose!' he shouted, clutching his bleeding nostrils.

Dave leaned over Sharkie.

'You arrogant git. I didn't touch your nose.'

Sharon stepped down the hill and returning to the car, saw Sharkie holding his face.

'Oh no. What's happened? Dave, what have you done?'

Sharkie picked himself up from the floor and walked toward the driver's door.

'You can both go back to your pokey little council house. We're done,' he snapped.

Sharkie locked the doors and started the engine, while Dave tried to get back in the car. But Sharkie put his foot down on the accelerator and sped off, leaving both of them by the side of the motorway.

As he drove, Sharkie lowered the windows in his car, concerned that the smell would never leave. He looked at his reflection in the rear view mirror and noticed some swelling and bruising around his right eye.

'A trip to ACE valeting and Boom Mens Emporium is what I need,' he thought.

As a frequent patron to both, he speed dialled the telephone numbers.

Meanwhile, Sharon stood at the roadside, venting her anger at Dave.

'If you hadn't cooked that tripe this morning, this wouldn't have happened. Then you fart in the car which nearly knocked me unconscious and if that's not enough, you go and chin the only bloke who can get us out of our mess.'

Dave looked hurt by Sharon's words.

'I make an effort with myself 'n' cook breakfast for you and what do you do? Throw it back in my face. It tasted fine to me. I didn't ask you to puke up, did I?'

Sharon screamed. 'I'm so angry! What have we done? It's another balls up, isn't it? It's all ruined; story of our lives.'

Dave put his arms around Sharon and held her close as they stood by the roadside. He gently hushed in her ear, trying to calm her.

Sharon's words broke up as she sobbed.

'Dave ... I'm sorry. I ... just ... feel so flippin' ... angry and ... embarrassed.'

Dave cupped her head in his hands and kissed her softly on her forehead.

'It's okay, love. It's not your fault. I know you're upset. And the vomit thing - that could have happened to anyone.'

Dave wiped away Sharon's tears with his stubby thumbs, as Sharon rested her head on Dave's shoulder.

'Where do we go from here?' asked Sharon.

'I'll ask Fat Pete from the club to pick us up. Don't worry darling.'

'No, I don't mean that. I mean our dream. Poncey Bridge. Marbella. No more dream house. Is it really over? How can we do this without Sharkie?'

'We'll bounce back. We always do. Something will come up. I'll get us out of that house. I'll think of something love, don't you worry.'

CHAPTER 32

Mind the Gap

Gretyl's voice sounded muffled on the phone.

'Albert, I wanted you to know where I'm up to.'

Albert couldn't quite recognise the voice.

'Is that you, Janice?'

'Who's Janice? Put Albert Trollop on the phone. This is his wife, Gretyl.'

'Love, this is your husband. Why are you calling me on my mobile?'

Gretyl was coming down from her cocaine high but paranoia was still coming and going in waves.

'Oh, Albert, it is you! Don't leave me. I'll let you grow your vegetables. I'll sell my wigs. I'll leave the frogs in the lock up. Whatever makes you happy?'

Albert was worried now. He hadn't heard Gretyl this puddled for years.

'I thought you'd be on a train by now? Are you ok? What are you on about a lock up?'

'I'm on the platform and I'm scared, Albert. There are women with black sheets over their heads and the men have backpacks strapped to them. Everyone's staring at me and I don't like London anymore.'

Albert spent a few minutes trying to calm Gretyl down and encouraged her to buy a cup of coffee before she boarded the train. Seeming agreeable, she ended the call and stepped off the platform towards the opening doors.

Gretyl was now on the train, sweating profusely, wedged in the centre of a crowd of standing passengers. With no room to remove her fur coat, her heart was beating rapidly while her anxiety and paranoia reached a new height of desperation.

Gretyl turned to the young woman beside her and snapped.

'Being crowded on a train is one thing, but making an acquaintance with your armpit is quite another.'

Gretyl was further aggravated by the amplified smacking noise of gum being chomped and a loud American voice booming into the offending chewer's phone.

'Another thing, do you really have to sound like a pig when you chew?'

The woman, dressed in a leather baseball jacket, cap and skin tight jeans was holding her map in front of Gretyl's face as she finished her call.

'My, there's no beatin' about the bush with you folks, is there? I love the way you're so frank. I was just asking a friend where I should be going while in London. We Americans visit more places than McDonalds, y'know.'

Gretyl was unimpressed.

'I tell you where you should go ... back home ... eating your cheap, crappy burgers. Go supersize yourself there.'

The American stepped away.

'Well, I hope I don't meet any more Brits like you.'

'I'm one of a kind, love, one of a kind.'

Gretyl closed her eyes.

After a few moments she opened them again and began to gawp at a woman in a hijab standing nearby.

'Where are you from? Bangradeshi? Well, this train 'aint going far enough for the likes of your lot.'

The woman in the hijab gasped before squeezing down the carriage, while a West Indian man sucked his teeth loudly and turned toward her.

'Ooman, what kine bakra behaviour dis? Shut your ugly face.'

Scared by the man's demeanour, Gretyl turned to notice an Asian boy fiddling suspiciously inside his rucksack.

Gretyl's paranoia now reached fever pitch.

Inhaling short, fast breaths, Gretyl's wide eyes fixed onto the young man who was now making his way toward the door. Their eyes locked briefly.

Gretyl froze.

The boy looked nervously away and reached inside his jacket pocket to retrieve his mobile phone, desperate to avoid eye contact with Gretyl.

'My God!' she thought to herself. 'He's got a bomb.'

Gretyl screamed at the top of her voice.

'He's Al-keheed-er, he's got a bomb!'

Pouncing on the lad, she knocked him to the floor as she tried to grab the mobile phone from his hand. But the boy resisted and managed with one huge heave to roll Gretyl's bulk off his chest.

The passengers helped the young spectacled lad to his feet.

'Someone needs to report this racist cow,' murmured a harassed mother, with two kids clinging onto her leg.

Gretyl pulled herself up against a seat, grabbing hold of her suitcase as she did.

'You can all blow up together then. I'm getting off this train.'

Even through his cracked lenses, it was obvious that the young boy's eyes were welling up with tears.

An elderly gentleman stood up, offering the young man his seat.

'Fella, what's your name?'

'Michael.'

'Listen Michael, don't take it personally. The woman's clearly mentally ill and she doesn't speak for the rest of us.'

'I know,' the boy replied.

The passenger continued.

'It doesn't matter what you look like. It matters who you are.'

A few of the passengers nodded approvingly.

'Thank you. My parents are from India and were proud to move here. They started from nothing and have worked hard all their lives.'

The elderly man continued.

'I fought alongside some of the finest troops from India in the last war.'

Michael dried his eyes with his sleeve.

The old gentleman put his hand inside his suit jacket and withdrew a leather wallet.

'Here, young man.'

Unfolding what looked like a number of twenty pound notes, he handed them to Michael.

'I hope this helps sort your glasses out.'

As Gretyl listened, it began to dawn on her that she'd made a terrible mistake.

'It's not my fault,' she thought.

Gretyl now realised that the drugs had made her delusional. She looked down at the floor, avoiding eye contact with everyone.

The Jamaican who had told Gretyl to 'shut her face', approached Michael.

'She cyaan get wey wid dis! I'm off at nex station. Duh yuh wah mi to find someone fram de Transport Police?'

A young mother butted in.

'We should make a citizen's arrest.'

Michael calmly replied. 'Thanks, but I just want to go home.'

The young mother turned to Gretyl.

'You ought to be ashamed of yourself. He's someone's son. It should be you that's paying for his glasses. Your words were disgusting and everyone else here thought the same.'

Gretyl looked up at her.

'It's not my fault. I've had a terrible day! First, I got in a drug dealer's car by accident and then there was loads of white stuff all over me. Then I sniffed and licked it and now I feel terrible.'

The Jamaican laughed.

'At least it wus nah ah date rape drug then.'

Gretyl was parched. She opened her suitcase and reached for her bottled water only to find that the cake box had tipped open and the contents had spilled inside.

'De ooman wus baking ah cocaine cake. Dat is naasy.'

Gretyl was indignant.

'How dare you! Do I look like the kind of woman who would make a cocaine cake? It's a fresh vanilla sponge I made for a friend.'

The sound of passengers sniggering moved like a Mexican wave through the carriage.

The door opened and the carriage emptied itself of all but the kind, elderly gentleman and a few folk down the opposite end.

Gretyl breathed a sigh of relief. She tilted her head back and took in several deep breaths, before swigging from her water bottle.

'If there is anything dodgy in my system, I'd better wash it out', she thought.

Gretyl spoke to the smartly dressed gentleman:

'Excuse me. Would you keep an eye on my suitcase while I visit the ladies toilet?'

He agreed, adding that he would be getting off the train in approximately ten minutes.

'I'll be back before then.'

Locked in the toilet, Gretyl's mobile phone rang out.

'Are you okay, Gretyl? Where are you now?' asked Albert.

'Oh Albert, it's been so horrible.'

Gretyl sobbed, making no attempt to keep her voice down.

'Albert, people have been absolutely horrid to me. Anyway, I can't talk now, gotta' hover and shake. No bleedin' toilet paper. I'll phone you when I'm at the cleaners. Bye.'

Gretyl exited the toilet and sat clutching her suit case.

It had been a trying day but she brightened her mood with the welcome thought that within a matter of moments she would be taking possession of the keys to her dream home at 60 Codgers Lane, Poncey Bridge.

CHAPTER 33

Towel Down

Glowing from his facial at the men's emporium, Sharkie gazed at his pampered reflection, admiring the gleaming finish of his newly waxed car and glistening face.

'How can she resist this?' he thought, admiring his features.

Sharkie wanted a piece of the action with Dave's wife and though she was certainly older than the girls he usually slept with, there was something about Sharon that really excited him.

'Sharon needs me. She can't be getting any satisfaction with Telly Tubby Dave?' he thought. 'She needs a man who can make her feel like a real woman.'

Aroused by the thought of Sharon feeling indebted to him, he dialled her mobile number.

Sharon stepped out of the bathroom and rushed down the stairs, wrapped in a small towel.

The phone displayed Sharkie's name as it rang in the hall.

'Sharon, love, I need you to hear me. It's really important,' Sharkie said.

Sharon said nothing.

'I should have never left you by the roadside. It was bang out of order and I'm really sorry, but Dave assaulted me and I just flipped a lid. Did you get home okay?'

'Yeh, Dave rang Fat Pete from the club to pick us up and I've just got out of the shower.'

'Listen, about the sick thing ... don't worry, I've had the beamer cleaned out and it's as good as new.'

'Is your car all that you care about?' Sharon asked indignantly.

'Sorry, that came out wrong. What I meant was, don't feel bad about it. We've all chucked up in our time. Only last weekend, it happened to me after I'd had a few too many at Chicago's in town.'

Both Dave and Kev were out of the house, so Sharon removed the small towel from her waist and wrapped it around her dripping hair. She switched to speaker phone.

'Look Sharkie, all that matters to me is the deal in Marbella. That's all I care about. What are we going to do about it?'

'Well, I'm here aren't I, standing outside your front door!'

Sharon panicked as she spotted Sharkie's face peering through the glass window into the hallway.

'Flippin' eck, Sharkie, wait there a minute. Let me get some clothes on.'

Sharkie laughed.

'Don't mind me. I gotta say, you're a very beautiful woman.'

Sharon rushed up the stairs, while Sharkie waited at the door, refreshing his mouth with a peppermint spray.

A few minutes passed before Sharon answered the door, wearing jeans and a sweatshirt. Sharkie followed her into the hallway, still gawping.

'I bet you could wear a bin liner and still look hot,' he said.

'Good job I've used up all the bin liners in my wardrobe then,' she joked.

'You're too much of a tease Sharon. That's what makes you so irresistible.'

In the past Sharon had enjoyed the odd innocent flirt, but this time it was far from innocent. Sharkie had just seen Sharon naked in her hallway and he was simmering with lust.

'Not a word of what you saw to anyone, Sharkie. I'm serious now.'

Sharkie stepped towards Sharon and gently placed his hands upon her shoulders.

'I respect you too much to say anything. Besides, I don't kiss and tell. It's our little secret.'

Sharon felt awkward and tried to step back as his hands began to move down from her shoulders.

Sharkie leaned over and kissed her softly on the cheek.

Sharon's body tingled. 'Oh, erm, I haven't offered you a drink. What do you fancy?'

Cocksure, Sharkie replied, 'I'll have a stiff one, if you're offering.'

Sharon ignored the innuendo and tried to ward off the rising sense of desire in the pit of her stomach.

Turning to the mirror, Sharon realised she wasn't wearing any makeup.

'He really seems to fancy me. Maybe I still look good compared to the young birds he dates,' she thought.

Sharon couldn't stop thinking about the adoring gaze of his deep blue eyes and how it made her feel. She was amazed that he could desire her with no makeup - and after vomiting on his leather seats.

Sharkie was shallow alright but Sharon began to wonder if there was a decent and attractive side to him that no one had nurtured.

Walking back into the lounge, Sharon placed two mugs of tea on the side table and sat down opposite him.

'Let's be straight with each other,' she said.

'Sure, love. You know you can talk to me about anything,' replied Sharkie.

'It's all about doing the business for me. I'm not playing around. You're very flattering, but I'm not about to do something I'll regret later. We nearly scuppered this deal on the motorway and I'm not compromising that again. Do we understand each other?'

Sharkie replied respectfully.

'I don't want to play around with you Sharon. You're a classy woman and I'd never take advantage of that.'

'It's just that sometimes things get a little too close for comfort between us,' Sharon interrupted.

Sharkie nodded his head, acknowledging her words.

'I can't deny that I'm attracted to you and I won't pretend that I haven't thought of you, somewhere sunny, enjoying life away from the stresses and strains of making ends meet. You deserve better Sharon. No. You deserve the best.'

Sharon's heart began to race.

'Look, let's keep the main thing, the main thing,' she said. 'Help yourself to Dave's TV remote. I'm going upstairs to get dressed. Can you give me a few minutes?'

Sharkie smiled and put his feet up on the side table.

'For you Sharon, I'd give you all the time in the world.'

Dave had taken Kevin out to KFC for lunch and noticed Sharkie's BMW outside on his return.

Sharon heard the squeak of the gate outside and looked through her bedroom window. She could see Dave and Kev walking down the path to the front door, having what looked like a heated discussion.

Sharon opened the top window and listened in.

'He'd better behave himself when I get in, or I tell you, he'll be getting a serious slap,' said Dave.

Kev grabbed his dad's arm before he placed the key in the door.

'Remember what mum said. It's just about the money. Find a way to get on with him, dad. You're not the only one who has put a lot of time into this. Don't hit him.'

Dave looked at his son and took a deep breath. He opened the front door and found Sharkie with his feet up, watching Sky Sports.

Sharon opened her bedroom door, keen to listen in on the conversation downstairs while she dressed.

'Making yourself at home then, are you?' said Dave.

Sharkie knocked his tea on the floor.

'Look Dave, I don't want any more trouble. I'm here to give you a second chance. I mean y'know, take your missus to Poncey Bridge for the meet. Are you alright with that?'

'Second chance? Sharkie, just remember that I invited you into this. I introduced you to Tony and I'll decide whether my wife is getting involved. Do you understand?'

Sharkie looked uncomfortable.

'Look Dave, no offence intended. I'm just saying that if there's any bad blood between us, we can get over it and still make this happen. We can still get rich on this, every one of us. Don't you want a piece of that?'

At that moment, Sharon re-entered the room.

'Look, both of you. Behave yourselves. We don't have to like each other to make this work, but we do have to work together,' she said firmly.

'I just want him to remember his place,' answered Dave. 'This is my house and I won't be disrespected in it.'

Sharkie stood up. 'Look, maybe I've made a mistake coming back here.'

Sharon picked up her handbag from the chair and grabbed Sharkie by the arm.

'Come on, we're going. I'm not gonna kiss this opportunity away because you're both having a dick measuring contest.'

Dave walked over to Sharon and kissed her cheek.

'You're right love. You look a million dollars. Go knock 'em dead.'

Kev looked up from his laptop. 'Don't forget to show him the website. He'll know we mean business then.'

Walking over to Kev, Sharon ruffled his hair.

'I'm doing this for all of us. We've put a lot of time and effort into this idea and we won't fail, will we Sharkie?'

'Not a chance,' replied Sharkie. 'If he's as crooked 'n' skint as I've been told, this Rochester bloke's not gonna turn down such a huge pay day.'

Sharon left the house and prepared to climb into Sharkie's shiny BMW.

Before she did, she turned to look at her husband.

She remembered the words Dave had whispered in her ear before leaving the house.

'If he as much as tries anything on, he's a dead man.'

Sharon knew that this wasn't a veiled, empty threat.

'Honey, don't worry. I'm a big girl and I can look after myself,' she had whispered back.

As Sharon melted into Sharkie's car she glowed inside as she thought about Dave's words.

'After all these years, he still gets jealous and wants to protect me,' she thought.

'That's really kind of hot.'

CHAPTER 34

The Rendezvous

Tracey lived just a few miles outside Poncey Bridge and had first met Victoria Hamilton-Smythe over ten years ago at a craft fair.

Both Victoria and Tracey had simultaneously spotted a beautiful antique figurine ballerina and wanted to pounce on the sale, eager to beat any competition.

Victoria studied the print underneath the vase while Tracey enquired about the price. Wanting the figurine for her mantelpiece in the study, Victoria tried to throw Tracey off the scent.

'I'm afraid it's a fake, my dear. It's not worth a fifth of the price,' she bluffed.

Tracey thanked her and pushed back with a bluff of her own.

'I'm not much interested in its value. I just think it looks beautiful. That's all I'm looking for.'

Victoria smiled. 'How true, my dear. How charmingly put. Are you a collector?'

'No. I used to dust down hundreds of lovely porcelain ornaments. My employer was very particular how each item was to be cleaned. You could say my expertise was making sure the fine bone china was in pristine condition and never collected dust.'

Victoria, having recently lost her home help, seized the moment.

'That's interesting. My maid of thirty years has just retired and she enjoyed a similar role, cleaning my large collection of china wall plates and antiques. Do you still provide cleaning services?'

Tracey needed the extra hours so enquired about Victoria's location.

'I'm only a few miles away in Codgers Lane, Poncey Bridge,' Victoria said.

Tracey was surprised that anyone from Poncey Bridge would consider employing a person who lived outside the village. However, the offer of £15 per hour was nearly twice her usual rate and had in the end proved the perfect incentive. The arrangement had turned out mutually beneficial; Victoria acquired a new cleaner and Tracey an old ballerina.

Tracey was just finishing dusting this very same ballerina when she heard the squeaky wheels of Gretyl's suitcase as it wobbled down the pathway towards the door.

'I'm Tracey and I'm pleased to meet you,' she said, opening her home.

Gretyl thrust her arm out and shook Tracey's hand.

'I'm Mrs Trollop, but you can call me Gretyl if you wish. Would you take my case?'

Tracey was shocked by the uncanny resemblance between Gretyl and Ms. Hamilton-Smythe. Both in appearance and mannerisms, she looked every bit a close relative rather than a distant one.

Gretyl handed her heavy fur coat and suitcase to Tracey.

'Thank you, dear. Now if you don't mind, I'll have a black coffee with three sugars. I've had a terrible journey.'

'I'm sorry to hear about the journey. Problem with the trains?' replied Tracey boiling a kettle.

Kicking her shoes off, Gretyl arched her back and stretched out her legs onto the leather pouffe, her toe nails piercing her tights.

'Oh my dear, you wouldn't believe me if I told you,' Gretyl replied.

Gretyl told the story of the entire journey barely coming up for air as she did. She described the broken lift, the drug dealer's car, the mishap with what she thought was baking powder, the abusive cab driver and the threatening people on the train.

She continued to narrate the story of her life, yapping away about her singing days and giving wildly embellished accounts of her romantic liaisons.

In spite of some of the tedious details, Tracey couldn't help finding Gretyl highly amusing.

'Right my dear. You've heard enough of me for now and we have plenty of time to get to know each other, so if you don't mind, let's pop into the village and then straight to the house.'

Tracey nodded politely, surprised that Gretyl had not asked any questions about the relative who'd left her a vast fortune.

Gretyl rose from the sofa and reached for her fur coat.

'Tracey, my dear, I've enjoyed the services of a cleaner back in London. Would you continue your hours at the house with me?'

'I'd have to think about it, if you don't mind. I've had several run-ins with your next door neighbour and to be honest, I really don't feel I fit in the village.'

'There'll be plenty to talk about,' Gretyl replied. 'I'll need a good ally in the village. You look like the perfect person.'

CHAPTER 35

An Indecent Proposal

Sharkie was only a few minutes away from their destination and followed the road signs to Poncey Bridge.

'I'm glad we're doing this together.' he said to Sharon. 'No disrespect to Dave, but I think you really shine when you're out of that house.'

Sharon didn't answer.

Sharkie kept glancing at Sharon, watching her as she stared at the array of quaint roadside cottages along the road. Sharkie wondered if the aroma of summer flowers and the palette of their vivid colours might be evoking some childhood memories in Sharon, as it was doing for him.

Sharkie pulled over to a small garage forecourt and stepped out of the car to use the toilet.

Sharon closed her eyes and took several deep breaths as she kicked off her shoes, resting her perfectly manicured pink, painted toes on the dashboard.

Sharkie returned to the car. Noticing that Sharon was dozing, he took care not to wake her.

As she lay there, Sharkie studied her cute freckles on her nose and especially her soft, inviting and bewitching lips.

Sharkie leaned closer, wanting to feel her breath upon his face, but pulled away, worried that the fragrance of his aftershave might warn Sharon that he was very close.

Sharkie imagined her lips moving to the words, 'Just kiss me.' He hoped that he would find the courage to gently place his lips upon hers, but he hesitated and sat back into his seat.

Sharon opened her eyes as Sharkie pulled away.

Sharkie wondered in this cat and mouse game, if Sharon could also bear the suspense any longer.

'Sorry, Sharkie, I must have had a quick nap.'

'Don't be sorry. You look beautiful when you are sleeping.'

Sharon took a long stretch in the seat and raising her arms in the air, let out a noisy yawn.

'Sharkie, after what happened today, I can't believe how relaxed I feel with you. I think I need a good spoiling from time to time.'

'You know me, Sharon. I've been a player and worse than that, but I respect you and I just want to see you happy.'

The BMW rolled off the forecourt, only a mile away from Poncey Bridge now.

'I hope she thinks I'm treating her like a lady,' he thought.

Sharkie pulled himself together.

'Back to business, as you would say, Sharon. Now a quick recap - the Intel we've got on this guy tells us he's got access to serious wads of the village's money and we are talking, millions. If he's keen to get out of the UK, it could be the perfect time for him to do this deal. If he's going bust, he'll want to get his hands on as much money as he can. It's perfect.'

'I can't believe we're so close to making real money,' Sharon replied excitedly. 'When we first had the idea, we thought we'd just be selling timeshare, but if this guy could buy the lot, it would be amazing.'

The lane leading into Poncey Bridge was lined with long hedgerows, ancient trees, electric gates and high fences. It was nigh-on impossible to see the village without crossing the small bridge next to the sign that read, 'Private - Residents Only'.

Sharkie drove over the bridge and stopped at what appeared to be a level crossing.

'Where's the train track?' Sharon asked.

Sharkie eyeballed a white-haired gatekeeper who approached his car.

'Can I ask what business you have in the village?'

Sharkie removed his sunglasses.

'My name is Peter Lovitt and I have an appointment with Neil Rochester.'

The old gatekeeper, dressed like a lollipop man, withdrew a mobile phone and dialled.

'Mr Rochester, I have what appears to be a travelling salesman asking for you, by the name of Peter Lovitt. He is with a lady that looks like she's his secretary.'

'They are associates of mine from London,' replied Neil. 'Direct them to the Marquis Brasserie please.'

'Very well, sir.'

The gatekeeper raised the barrier and beckoned with his fingers for Sharkie to pull up alongside him.

'Your appointment has been confirmed. Proceed approximately 800 yards and the restaurant is on your right.'

A few moments later, the BMW was parked outside the Brasserie and Sharkie was shaking the hands of his new business partner.

'Good afternoon Mr Rochester. I'm Peter Lovitt and this is my partner, Sharon Souddalle.'

'I'm delighted to meet you Mr Lovitt and of course, you too, beautiful lady. Please take a seat and I will ask the staff to arrange refreshments for us.'

Sharkie looked at the oak-panelled walls of the Brasserie which were decorated with a variety of brass ornaments and paintings that reflected village life for the past five hundred years.

He also studied the wine list and baulked at the exorbitant prices of the vintage selection.

'Only the super rich dine here,' he thought.

Sharkie moved his hand discreetly under the table, gently squeezing Sharon's thigh.

'Are you okay?' he whispered.

Sharon quickly shifted her position away from Sharkie's touch.

'I'm fine. It's all rather exciting. I feel like a Bond girl about to meet the villain,' she replied softly.

Sharkie flashed a cheeky grin.

'Does that make me 007, then?'

'It might do, James.'

Sharkie laughed.

'Thank you, Moneypenny.'

Neil returned to the table.

'I hope you don't mind, but I've taken the liberty to order a decanter of the finest cider brandy. It's quite spectacular and one that's been secretly made in this village for centuries.'

Taking a cigar from his top pocket, he cut above the cap line and lit it with a gold and platinum engraved lighter.

'We don't tolerate cigarettes but we like the pedigree of cigars here,' Neil gloated.

Sharkie laughed.

'I'm partial to a nice little Cuban, myself.'

'Really? Hmm, well, any man who loves a cigar is welcome here, despite what you may or may not have heard.'

Neil looked at Sharon and took a deep draw on his long, thick shaft.

'Do tell me about yourself, Miss Souddalle.'

'What would you like to know, Mr Rochester?'

'Oh my dear, more than you'd be willing to tell, I'm quite sure.'

Sharkie interrupted.

'Sharon has worked with me for some time now. She's been instrumental in networking our business with some very exclusive clients, Mr Rochester.'

'I'm sure you take care of your clients very well, Miss Souddalle,' Neil replied.

Neil poured some brandy from the decanter into three crystal glasses and passed them around.

Sharkie continued.

'As I mentioned on the telephone, I represent a wealthy and successful client based in Marbella. He has a very attractive business opportunity for the right professional investor.'

'Do go on. You have my full attention, Mr Lovitt.'

Sharkie passed the brochure of the villas to Neil, grateful that Tony had appointed a professional photographer to capture the decadence and luxury of the finished properties.

'Well, they certainly look impressive. Do tell me again why I should be interested?' Neil asked.

'The current valuation of the villas stands between ten to twelve million pounds,' Sharkie said. 'Due to other opportunities which my client wishes to pursue, he's willing to consider offers over five million for the five luxury properties. This not only represents some of the best prime property in Marbella. For the shrewd investor, should they wish to sell the development on, the profit to be made will be in the millions.'

Sharon leaned forward to speak and Neil repositioned himself to get a better view of her cleavage as she did.

'These villas represent the very best Marbella has to offer. Tucked away just a few miles from the old town with easy access to every pleasure, these newly built villas have swimming pools, Jacuzzis, large marbled verandas and outdoor patios. The gardens are beautiful and each property is separated by at least one hundred metres from the other, giving more privacy.'

'Miss Soudalle, they sound hard to resist, rather like yourself,' Neil responded.

'For those who work hard, it's important to play hard, don't you think, Mr Rochester?' Sharon concluded.

Neil sipped his brandy while his lecherous eyes explored Sharon's body.

'You know what they say, Miss Souddalle. All work and no play, makes Jack a very ... dull ... boy.'

CHAPTER 36

Horse Duvets

Only a few streets away, Gretyl approached the village in Tracey's car. En-route to the house via a stop for lunch in the village, Tracey lowered her window and met the familiar and unwelcome face of the gatekeeper.

'What brings you back here?' said the old man, puffing his chest out like a determined Dad's Army sentinel.

'Actually, we have business here, so please open the gate,' Tracey answered firmly.

'If you want to get in, it's my business to know your business. You weren't welcome here before and you're certainly not welcome now. Goodbye.'

Gretyl, thrilled at the conflict, opened the passenger door and walked toward the scrawny little man.

'Now listen here. I am the sole beneficiary of 60 Codgers Lane and will be moving in very soon. So step aside and raise the barrier before I teach you a lesson.'

Undaunted, the gatekeeper took his mobile phone from his pocket. Before he had a chance to speak, Gretyl had swung her rhinestone-studded, crocodile skin handbag across the man's head.

'Now raise the gate like a good boy,' she scolded.

The bewildered gatekeeper stumbled back to the barrier and teetered for a moment, before waving the vehicle through with a frantic motion of his shaking arm.

Travelling along the High Street, Gretyl pointed at the Marquis Brasserie.

'This looks good. Let's eat here. It's my treat love.'

Tracey looked for a parking space outside while Gretyl walked into the Brasserie.

'Garcon, Garcon. I'd like your best table for two, please.'

At the sound of her voice, Neil Rochester turned and approached Gretyl.

'I'm sorry, but we are closed. Should you require a snack, the Farrell Public House is open. It's just a few miles away from our village.'

'Well, it says 'open' on the door! Is this your café?' snapped Gretyl.

'It's not a café,' scoffed Neil, adding, 'May I ask how you managed to enter the village?'

'Ask your decrepit lollipop man,' replied Gretyl contemptuously as she sat firmly and resolutely in a seat.

At that moment Tracey walked in and joined Gretyl at the table. Seeing her with Gretyl, Neil withdrew for a moment with a look of confusion and surprise.

Gretyl scanned the menu for the largest starter she could find.

'Look at this menu, Tracey. They ain't too smart here, are they? They can't even write in English.'

Gretyl laughed as she placed her order with the waiter.

'For my horse duvets, I'd like the a-parrot-ive soup with plenty of those crunchy things ... cretins please.'

Tracey didn't know whether to laugh or cry.

'I'll have the same please. They're famous for serving cretins here,' Tracey said.

Looking up from her menu, Gretyl saw Neil approaching once again, this time looking disdainfully at her brown fur coat, green striped tights and red high heels.

'Madam, the village does not entertain visitors without appointment and as the Chairman of Poncey Bridge, I know you don't have one, so I'd like you to leave please.'

Gretyl stood up and glared at Neil, her eyes piercing into the back of his skull.

'Listen sonny Jim. I'm not a visitor and I don't need an appointment. Ms. Hamilton-Smythe's estate has been bequeathed to me. Now go sit down like a good boy.'

Neil gawped at Gretyl.

'I don't have time for this,' he snapped.

Neil backed off and returned to his table.

''Ere, Tracey, you stay put love.'

Eager to eavesdrop on Neil's conversation, Gretyl stood up and walked furtively towards where he was sitting and crouched behind a fish tank. She peered through the glass at Neil's table, her swollen eyes as bulbous as a nocturnal Tarsier.

Neil continued after his interruption.

'Sorry about that. Back to business: if the numbers add up, I'd happily manage the Marbella properties myself.'

Gretyl grinned as she watched Sharkie take the bait and press in for the kill.

'I understand you manage investments for some high profile clients. Can you bring together the kind of funds we are talking about?'

'Mr Lovitt, I'm in the business of raising millions and I've done precisely this sort of thing before. I manage all the investments for the village and have access to very large sums of money - for the right opportunities, of course.'

Sharkie could hardly contain his excitement.

Gretyl shook her head sideways at Tracey and gawped in shock at what she was hearing.

Tracey winked at Gretyl, enjoying every moment of the drama.

Sharkie replied, 'This, Mr Rochester, is why I've approached you. My client needs the transaction to happen very quickly. All the paperwork is in place for the right buyer. The offer price of five million pounds includes the notary, registry, solicitor and other fees.'

Sharkie leaned forward and continued.

'Mr Rochester, we would add your fee to the purchase price which, typically, is in the region of 25%. Your fee would be one and a quarter million pounds.'

As Neil smiled greedily, Gretyl shuddered.

'I flamin' knew it,' she thought.

Sharon added, 'If you're looking to live abroad, you could live in one of the luxury properties and manage the villas. It's a win-win situation for everyone, don't you think, Mr Rochester?'

'Yes, it's a no-brainer. As long as my fee is built into the purchase price, that would make it £6,250,000. The village committee would never approve the investment if they thought I was profiting from it in any way. Mr Lovitt, Miss Soudalle, I believe we have a sale.'

Neil stretched his hand out to cement the deal.

Sharon looked almost giddy as she took his hand.

'Mr Rochester, We would like you to accompany us to the villas and see for yourself just how stunning they are. All expenses paid, of course,' she said.

'I think I could force myself to do that,' he replied. 'One thing though. My window for making this happen is very tight. If the village is to approve such a large investment quickly, I'd need to bring a small group from the committee over to Marbella with us. Would that be a problem?'

'We'd expect nothing less,' replied Sharkie. 'Let's just say we'd put things in place to deliver the wow factor. Could you provide us with profiles of the guests you are bringing? The information would of course be strictly confidential between us, but it would enable us to put together a very personal experience for each of them.'

Neil agreed and then leaned in closer and said quietly, 'I cannot emphasise enough that what we discuss together must remain highly confidential. The village does not take kindly to guests and they would be very suspicious of any talk concerning our project together.'

Neil's brow unfurrowed and he smiled.

'The good news is that tonight I am chairing our monthly meeting and I can raise this project with the committee. Exciting times lay ahead, I'm quite sure of that.'

The waiter stepped out from the kitchen and spotted Gretyl leaning down in front of the fish tank.

Gretyl saw the man approaching and hurried back to her table.

'If madame enjoys fish, maybe she would like some carp for lunch?'

'The only thing that's fishy in here is sitting over there,' said Gretyl pointing to Neil's table.

Gretyl turned her back on the waiter and whispered to Tracey. 'You oughta hear the shite he's talking. Is this the pillock that I'm moving next door to?'

The waiter raised his eyebrows and walked away.

Tracey smiled and motioned with her finger, 'Not too loud, Gretyl.'

'The nasty git is proper dodgy. I smell a giant rat, dear!'

'You do read people quickly,' said Tracey. 'He's a slippery customer. Nothing would surprise me with Mr Rochester.'

Gretyl grinned.

'I tell you what, Tracey. I've no doubt that exciting times lay ahead ... starting with that committee meeting tonight!'

CHAPTER 37

Captain Mainwaring

Several days had passed since Gretyl arrived at the village and Albert had resisted Gretyl's repeated requests to join her at the new home.

Keen to help Janice with any practical jobs, Albert also collected Stan's personal effects from the shop, sorted the post and made any necessary phone calls to the relevant authorities and distributors.

Stan's cremation was only a day away and Albert was en-route to the Funeral Directors, after arranging to meet Janice outside.

Instructions had been left for Stan to be dressed in his wedding suit, along with a haircut and tidy shave. Stan had been in very good shape until his last few years, where his lungs suffered a number of illnesses that finally led to a pulmonary embolism and sudden death.

Janice wanted to know that Stan was at peace and though a little frightened to see him again, knew that with Albert's help, she'd get through the day.

'Good afternoon. Mrs Jones and I have come to visit her husband,' said Albert.

Albert held Janice's hand as they were led into a small magnolia coloured room where the casket was laid open.

Janice panicked, holding her hand over her mouth.

'Albert, where's his moustache?'

Albert rushed out of the room, looking to question the funeral director.

'I'm sorry. We were left clear instructions for his face to be shaved,' the director said.

'His face, yes. Not his moustache. He's had that thing since his early 20's. He looks totally different now.'

The funeral director summoned a member of staff to hurry and offer Janice a hot drink.

'Mr Trollop. I am deeply sorry. There clearly has been some kind of mix up. I will come immediately and apologise to Mrs Jones.'

Much to Albert's surprise, they returned to find Janice smiling.

'He used to make fun of my uncle's bushy moustache and swore dead he'd never grow one. He said, "When you've got a boat race as pretty as mine, why cover it with hair?"'

Albert replied, 'Good for you darling. Good for you. I must admit, he does look a darn sight better without Captain Mainwaring's moustache.'

'But do you know why he grew one, Albert? It was a bet with my uncle. He told Stan that he could never grow one until he was a real man. Well, Stan won the bet and bought me flowers with his winnings.'

As the tears ran down her cheek, Janice leant over the casket and kissed Stan.

Albert stepped aside. 'I'll give you a few moments. Just give me a shout when you're ready.'

Walking up and down the corridor, Albert didn't feel ready to say his last goodbye to his friend just yet. No, he'd wait for the funeral tomorrow, read a poem during the service and say his farewell there.

Stan had always been a joker and Albert wouldn't have been surprised if the disappearing moustache was mentioned in his will along with a few other surprises.

Albert's phone rang and recognising Gretyl's number, he stepped outside to take the call.

'Yes, what is it?' Albert answered, irritated.

'Well, that's a fine way to greet your wife.'

'I'm sorry, but I'm at the funeral home at the moment. What's up?'

'Nothing's up. I just wanted to tell you about the house. It's amazing.'

Since Gretyl had left London for her new home, she'd phoned Albert every few hours or so, prattling on with news of her latest discoveries.

'Did I tell you Albert - there are hundreds of wall plates in the lounge and the cabinets are full of porcelain figurines? They're expensive, too.'

'Flamin Nora,' Albert snapped. 'You live in a mansion and you still have to find wall space for your frogs and all the other rubbish?'

'There's no need for that, Albert Trollop ... anyway, I haven't finished yet. There are huge walk-in wardrobes and six en-suite bathrooms with enough shoes and clothes to fill a dozen shops. And guess what? They're all my size!'

'Your relative sounds like an identical twin,' mocked Albert.

Before Gretyl could reply, Albert cut her short. 'I've got to go. The funeral director's waiting for me. And don't push me with the house stuff. We don't have to sort it all now.'

'That's easy for you to say. There's plenty of work to be done and we need to move stuff over from the flat. I won't let you waste your life away in that hole any longer.'

Albert's blood began to boil.

'You don't understand,' he said. 'It's not the flat. It's my whole life and you can't just pack that away. I haven't even buried Stan yet and once again you're just thinking about yourself. You want me to trade what I've loved for somewhere I don't even know. I really have to go now.'

Gretyl retaliated. 'I thought you loved me? Sounds like I'm the one being traded in here. Here I am, trying to get us a better life that I've always dreamed of and you'd rather sit in your tin-pot shed. Well, I won't have it, Albert Trollop.'

Albert ended the call and turned his phone off.

At that moment Janice walked out of the funeral home.

'Would you like to go back in?' she asked.

'Thanks, but I'd rather say my goodbyes tomorrow, if that's okay?'

With a reassuring smile she took hold of Albert's arm.

'Come on love, let's go and get a cup of tea and some of your favourite Banoffee pie.'

CHAPTER 38

The Agenda

Neil Rochester arrived at the Poncey Bridge village hall, ready for their monthly meeting. Last month's gathering had proved quite uneventful, as usual. Dog fouling fines would be increased by 200%. Photos of the offenders would be printed on a public community warning, framed in hazard tape.

Neil entered the ancient doorway of the hall, having heard the last minute reports of a brawl between Ms. Kingsley-Thatcher and Mrs Blowhorn.

The two matriarchs had bickered over whose garden would be crowned 'Bush of the Year', the spat ending with both women sprawled out, tangled and bloodied in Mrs Blowhorn's rose bushes.

Neil couldn't stand the women anyway and as the Chairman, he would gladly call for their expulsion from the competition for the next five years.

Further items for the night included:

(1) The commissioning of various new signs with graphic warnings for trespassers.
(2) Troublesome new developments regarding Ms Hamilton-Smythe's estate.

Neil banged on the table with the Rochester engraved gavel and called the meeting to order.

'Please take your seats. We've a lot to get through tonight. Order, please, order.'

Neil stood at the front table, staring down at the insubordinates still to take their seats.

'Ladies and gentleman, I'm sure you'll wish to be home at a reasonable hour this evening so please allow me to amend the agenda.'

Neil waited for silence before he continued.

'Not wishing to miss a fantastic opportunity for the village, we have a late and nonetheless, important item to discuss. Please add to your agenda, item 1 – Investment opportunity for luxury villas.'

Alistair Plant glared at Neil.

Long established rivals, Alistair frequently challenged Neil's domination over village life and deplored the age-old ruling that kept the Rochester family chairing the village meetings.

'I'd like to state for the record that we haven't agreed the minutes of the last meeting,' Alistair complained.

'You're quite right, Alistair. I take it that everyone else has read the last meeting's minutes? If so, there's no need to read them again. There's plenty to address with tonight's agenda.'

Neil's comments were met with silence, prompting Alistair to stand up.

'Well, as I said ... I haven't read it yet!'

'You've been a part of these meetings for over thirty years now and you've forgotten that we arrive for 7pm, read the notes and are ready to approve for 7.30pm? Now, for your benefit, would you like to read out the minutes to us all so we can be sure you're ready to move on?'

Everyone glared at Alistair, while his wife Jacqueline pulled his jacket so hard he fell back into the chair. She wanted to be home by nine o'clock to watch her favourite murder mystery on TV.

'Great. If everybody's happy to move on, let's do so, shall we?' said Neil.

Alistair doubled up on the chair and yelped in pain as his attempt at a second protest was interrupted by Jacqueline's firm grip on his member.

Neil continued.

'Tonight, I'd like to share with you a fantastic opportunity for our village. As you're aware, working in the financial services industry has introduced me to some of the most wealthy and successful people in the world. As a result, I've been privy to information that has benefitted my clients for decades. Today, we have an investment opportunity that is quite simply one of the best I've seen in my long career.'

Neil looked for approval, found none, and so pressed on.

'As you know, I've managed the investments for the village very successfully and for no personal gain ...'

Neil smiled, expecting a loud burst of applause. Again, nothing was forthcoming.

'We've been approached with an offer of five luxury villas set on the most prestigious and desirable land in the world. With more millionaires per square mile than anywhere else, we have been offered an investment that will cost us in the region of six and a quarter million pounds. These properties together have a current valuation of between ten to twelve million.'

Jack Hodges stood to his feet. He was a progressive entrepreneur, managing director of several businesses and a vocal supporter of change in the village.

'Neil, I know I speak for a few of us here. We can't live in the dark ages. Poncey Bridge has to move on as well. Maybe it is high time we extended our portfolio beyond the UK.'

Neil nodded approvingly.

'Well, some change is for the best, I agree Jack. I've seen the portfolio for the Marbella villas and I recommend we keep them for our own use and watch their value increase. I'd happily manage it and we could all enjoy the health benefits of a warm, dry and arthritis free climate.'

Alistair stepped away from his chair and more importantly, from his wife's grip, pointing his forefinger in the air.

'I'd like it to be noted for the record that ...'

Yet again, Jacqueline's interruption had an instant effect on Alistair's flow, this time waving a sheaf of papers in his direction.

Alistair cringed, knowing exactly what Jacqueline was threatening and had been doing so for the last few months.

Jacqueline was waving her divorce petition.

CHAPTER 39

Gloves Off

After drinking Victoria's vintage brandy for the best part of the day, Gretyl had decided to go out for an evening stroll. Waltzing along with her imaginary friend Wayne Sleep, she glided along the path, arms outstretched and moving with all the grace of a mini-tornado.

Gretyl's blonde Gracie Allen wig was now twisted sideways, the flowery dress from Victoria's wardrobe strangling her bulbous frame and perilously close to ripping.

Far too sozzled to care or notice, Gretyl's dancing matched the rhythm of her tone deaf singing until a stiletto gave way, causing her to fall down the kerb. Gretyl lay sprawled out on the ground like the corpse at a crime scene.

Slowly picking herself up, Gretyl's attention was drawn to a white building barely one hundred metres away, the soft glow of the outdoor lighting showing off the immaculately landscaped garden. With broken stiletto in hand, she made her way toward the beckoning lights, entered the door of the village hall and observed the proceedings unnoticed.

Hidden from Neil's gaze, Gretyl watched him scan his audience, carefully honing in on the individuals who would be his most loyal supporters.

'I can see from your faces that the investment is a popular choice. Anticipating your response, I've already approached five of you who represent different aspects of our community to accompany me on a fact-finding trip for three days to Marbella. We can then report back our own, first hand experiences of these amazing properties at the next meeting. Now, let's see a show of hands. All those who support this proposal, please raise your hands now.'

No more than a third of the hands were raised.

'That's great. We have a majority vote. I'll prepare the paperwork and get everything underway.'

Neil was halted again by Alistair, now undeterred by the threats of his wife.

'Excuse me! Before we move forward, I have a number of questions.'

Neil tried not to lose his cool as he answered.

'I'm happy to answer you, Alistair. Does anyone else have any points they wish to raise before we all listen to him?'

The room was silent.

'Alistair, it seems like you're the only person holding up the agenda again.'

Alistair stood to his feet to protest.

'Are we to trust your instinct on what is deemed to be a good investment? Rumour has it that your radar's been a bit off these last few years?'

Neil snapped.

'That's the pot calling the kettle black, don't you think? I heard that you lost the family savings on the horses!'

'You've gone too far this time, Rochester. I think we should take this outside.'

'Very well. Excuse me, ladies and gentleman. I'd like to speak with Alistair privately. We will continue this public meeting in just a few moments.'

As soon as the two men stepped outside, Neil locked the front door.

Gretyl had already shifted her location and was now following events behind a large bush.

'Now Alistair, you and I need to get a few things straight. If you don't -'

Alistair interrupted Neil with a wild swing of his fist. Completely missing Neil's face, his arm was promptly seized and twisted behind his back. Neil then moved around his antagonist and tightened his arm around his neck, dragging him away from the view of anyone who might look out of the window.

'Now listen, Alistair. We both know you can't stand the position I have in the village, so here's the deal and everyone's a winner, especially you.'

Alistair's face began to change colour as he motioned with his arms for Neil to release him.

'You're quite right, sorry.'

Neil released his grip.

'Now listen carefully to what I'm about to tell you. If you repeat any of this your wife will hear about your addiction to tarts and I'm not talking about the baked variety. I know all about the late night visits to Miss Double D's cake shop.'

The face that had turned blue now turned red.

'Go on ...' he stammered.

Neil continued.

'I'm planning to move out of the village. Patricia's agoraphobic and needs to be somewhere else. The doctors have also confirmed that she suffers from SAD syndrome and needs to be in the sunshine more often. I need to make this change for my wife and it's time for you to step up to the role, Alistair. You'll be the next Chairman.'

Alistair looked stunned.

'Your family has chaired for generations,' he stuttered. 'What else do you want out of this?'

'I want to manage the development in Marbella and this is how you'll get to see the back of me. The village will buy the properties and I'll move abroad to manage them.'

Neil now played his ace.

'For a quick cash sale, I am prepared to sell my property to one lucky cash buyer for half of its value. Is that something you might be interested in?'

Alistair's face lit up.

'I won't pretend. I'd gladly accept the challenge to chair the committee,' he said. 'I've always believed my plans for the community would be in the best interests of others. As for your property, I'd be interested at ... say... half a million in cash.'

'Alistair, the house and role of Chairman can be yours, but I'll not sell my home for a penny less than £750k. I know you've been desperate to buy in the village, so let's agree. I can have my solicitor draw up the documents within a week.'

Alistair paused for a moment, trying to play it cool.

Neil continued his aggressive pitch.

'Look, I know you've been looking to buy a property for your son's wedding present and I also know that you've been looking 'outside of the village' to spend over a million.'

'Okay, point taken,' replied Alistair.

'Three things I need from you Alistair. First, I want you to shake my hand now on the house and the Marbella investment in full sight of the prying eyes at the window. Second, I need you to publicly approve my managerial role and my move to Marbella. Finally, I want in writing - and in the presence of my solicitor - an agreement that guarantees me rent free accommodation in the villa for the duration of my lifetime. Can you do this?'

After a moment of reluctance, Alistair stretched out his hand to shake on it, making sure that the gesture was in full view of those looking through the windows of the village hall.

The two men walked to the entrance of the hall, opened the door and returned to their seats inside.

As all eyes were gazing at the two men at the front, Gretyl secretly hopped back to her observation post just inside the doorway.

'Ladies and gentleman, both Alistair and I have resolved our disagreements. In fact, with his own pedigree as an investor, he'll gladly support and facilitate the exciting opportunity before us. Isn't that right, Alistair?'

Alistair stood up.

'I can confirm that having discussed this with Neil, all the checks and balances seem to be in place. More than that, I'd highly recommend that we have a person on the ground to manage the development. I for one, wholeheartedly support the idea of a cash purchase, with Neil managing the site and bookings for our luxury holidays. Now let's see a show of hands again, so we can get this approved and move on this evening. All those in favour of moving forward with this investment please raise your hands.'

Alistair smiled as the majority of the room raised their hands.

'Thank you Alistair,' Neil said. 'Now let us move on quickly to a very important matter of discussion, point 2 on your agenda - the estate of Victoria Hamilton-Smythe and troublesome new developments.'

At this Gretyl's ears pricked.

'Today, I have had the misfortune of seeing the woman who is the sole heir. To describe her as a woman would be unfair to women. All I can say is this: we've never tolerated perversions in the village and we don't intend to now.'

Neil paused for some audience participation.

'Hear, hear!' someone shouted. 'We don't want old prostitutes in the village.'

Neil smiled.

'As you're all aware, it's been our dearly held policy that under no circumstances should any property be sold or left to an outsider. Well, our deceased neighbour has brought a curse upon our village. I'm afraid she does have a living relative, who not only looks like her but shares the same wicked defiance. She's not welcome here and we must do our utmost to drive her out.'

At this, shouts began to fill the hall.

'She'll contaminate our way of life.'

'Let's poison the old bag.'

'We could cement her inside her house.'

'Throw her in the lake. If she floats, she's a witch. If she drowns, she's a witch.'

Gretyl stood listening behind the folds of a large red curtain. She could contain herself no longer. Half drunk on her benefactor's brandy, she stumbled to the front of the hall, ruffling an old lady's hair on her way as she sought to steady herself.

Those present stared incredulously.

Others held their noses.

Arriving at the podium, Gretyl addressed the group.

'Hello, my lovelies. I bet you're pleased to meet me! I'm Mrs Trollop, the heiress of erm, what's-er-name's estate and I'm your new neighbour.'

At this Neil jumped from the platform and raised his voice angrily.

'This meeting is for members only and you are not welcome here. I'll order a taxi to take you back to the station.'

'Aw, what's your problem, dear? Feel threatened by a real woman? Am I just too much for you to handle?'

Gretyl wiggled her hips as she spoke.

Alistair stood to his feet and joined Neil in marching Gretyl's corpulent and odorous frame to the front door, accompanied by the applause of their fellow villagers.

As Neil flung Gretyl out of the entrance, she turned to him and spoke with a wide grin on her face.

'I heard your speech to the faithful this evening. Very persuasive, I must say. Though I wonder what they'd think if they knew about your deal with oompa loompa here.'

Alistair's face turned beetroot red while his mouth spat venomously.

'You old trout!'

Gretyl laughed.

'You dwarf!'

Alistair lunged forward at Gretyl.

'If you were a man, I'd kill you right where you stand!'

'If you were a man, I'd do likewise,' retorted Gretyl.

At this Neil stepped in.

'Listen very carefully, Mrs Trollop,' he said. 'For your own health, I suggest that you keep your mouth shut. A false accusation would bring you a world of pain. I can assure you of that. There's nothing for you here. You need to move out before you're carried out!'

Gretyl pouted her lips.

'If I were you, I'd be very careful how you speak to me. Had a profitable meeting in the posh cafe today, did we?'

Gretyl's impertinent tone riled Neil and her use of the word 'profitable' shook him visibly.

'Look, maybe we've got off on the wrong foot and misunderstood each other,' he said with a smooth parsonical lilt. 'You have to understand, it's been our policy that property only changes hands between villagers. Victoria was a deeply unpopular resident while she was alive, always challenging our authority. We don't need any complications. If you were considering selling the property, I'm sure the village would make more than a generous offer to compensate you.'

Gretyl, keen to play the game, went along with Neil's suggestion.

'I've no desire to move, but if you want to make me a generous offer, put it in writing,' she said. 'After all, it makes no difference to you whether I stay or leave, but it's gonna cost you if I keep my mouth shut. For a start, I want that free trip to Marbella, all expenses covered.'

Neil replied assertively.

'Mrs Trollop. I'll talk to you tomorrow about this. Goodnight.'

The two men returned to the hall.

Back at the podium, Neil addressed the members.

'In light of today's events, I'd like to make a suggestion that I'm quite sure will be agreeable to you all. We postpone the rest of the agenda for the evening, except for one point. Let's finish this evening with a plan of action regarding the aptly named Mrs Trollop. All those in favour, please raise your hands.'

It was soon agreed (in three minutes to be precise) that out of the village investment funds (£17.4 million pounds) Mrs Trollop would be offered the sum of £2.6 million for her property, being approximately 30% more than the estimated value. The property would then be sold at a later date to the highest bidder in the village, with the additional profits going back into the investment fund.

Neil returned home, thrilled at having bagged the deal for the villas in Marbella and with Alistair's support, his move abroad seemed closer than ever. However, 'the fly in the ointment' still had to be removed.

Neil wrote down the substantial offer for the house on headed paper and factored into the agreement £2500 cash for her trip to Marbella. Though it pained him to make any concessions for Gretyl, the cash gift was a very small price to pay for her silence.

Neil picked up the phone in his lounge and dialed Sharkie.

'Mr Lovitt. It's Neil Rochester here. I've got some very good news for you.'

Twenty minutes into the conversation and they had made substantial progress - from the travel itinerary, excursions, meals and accommodation including live entertainment for the guests.

With so much at stake, Neil sat for the next hour contemplating Gretyl's threat and his strategic response. If she'd really heard in the

Brasserie about his cut in the deal, it would destroy his last chance to make serious money before the looming threat of bankruptcy.

Opening the draw, Neil retrieved his leather binder, filled with hundreds of business cards. Searching through, he found the card he was looking for filed under 'Disaster Relief'. The white card was crammed full with text on the front and telephone number on the back.

'Need to ELIMINATE weeds? Then take ACTION! REMOVAL's our speciality! We do the DIRTY work and never leave a MESS! We're always HITTING TARGETS and always AIM to please! SATISFACTION guaranteed! ANYTIME, ANYWHERE!

Call Arti Chokes, Mown Down Solutions.'

Neil's thumb hovered over the dial button while he considered his next step. After all, Gretyl's request for a holiday could prove the perfect backdrop for her demise.

'Now that would suit my plans, quite wonderfully,' he thought to himself.

'Time to make a killing,' he added, with a sinister grin.

CHAPTER 40

Distant Memories

It was Friday morning and Albert was smartly dressed for the funeral. Wearing a black suit, white shirt and black tie, he stared at his reflection in the mirror.

The bags under his eyes looked purple, creased with large, dark ripples while the cracks on his nose had weathered over the years, each line like the ring of an oak tree.

'Life is a priceless gift. You only truly appreciate it when it's been taken away,' he pondered.

Albert began reflecting on his marriage. He knew he and Gretyl had grown apart over the years so it was much to his relief that she hadn't offered to attend the funeral. This was Stan's day, it was precious and Janice would need his support away from the prying, jealous eyes of his wife.

A black limousine pulled up outside, waiting at the entrance of Majestic Heights. Albert locked the front door of his apartment and walked to the lift. He pressed the button and heard the cables moving up the shaft. The doors opened and he entered, barely noticing the customary stench.

The chauffeur from the funeral directors opened the car door for Albert. Janice was sitting in the back waiting for him, her face covered by a black net veil.

Albert gently squeezed her hand.

'Good morning, love. You okay?'

'I think so. I'm not sure, Albert. I just need to get through today.'

Albert nodded.

'You know what I find hard, Albert? I don't know what I'm supposed to feel today. Always the joker, I know he'd want us to be happy. Why then do I feel so guilty for feeling so sad?'

'I understand. I had mixed emotions writing a word for him. I think he'd want us to be ourselves though, don't you Janice?'

169

Janice nodded. 'I know he'd want a simple funeral. That's why I've chosen one hymn and his favourite song for the way out.'

'Well done, love,' Albert whispered. 'Stan would be very proud.'

Arriving at the crematorium, Janice and Albert noticed that a large queue of people had formed just outside the front entrance.

Janice squeezed Albert's hand.

'Just look how many people have come to remember my Stan.'

The funeral bearer opened the door and Albert helped Janice to her feet. It was nearly 10.30am and the funeral party was ready to enter the chapel.

The priest welcomed the family and friends and motioned for them to take their seats.

'We are here today, to honour and celebrate the memory of Stanley Archibald Jones. Let us bow our heads together for a moment, in silence and respect.'

The congregation dutifully bowed their heads.

'Would you please stand with me to sing the hymn, Amazing Grace.'

After the hymn had finished, Albert stood up and approached the microphone to share his tribute.

'To the friends and family gathered here today, please forgive me if my words seem short. I'm just not sure if I could adequately share how much I loved Stan.'

Albert spent the next five minutes talking about their strong friendship which had lasted for over sixty years. Wiping away the tears, he walked back to the aisle, to be greeted by a kiss on the cheek from Janice.

'Thank you so much, Albert. What you said meant the world to me.'

'And you meant the world to him, Janice.'

After a short sermon, Father O'Connor made a closing reference to Stan's character.

'There's a famous saying, "If you don't stand for something, you'll fall for anything." Well, everybody knew what Stan stood for. His life was a letter, written by the Holy Spirit, for all to see. We experienced his love, benefited from his care and were always humoured by his famous wit. Who could forget when, for our harvest festival, he carved John 3:16 out of his fruit and vegetables.'

The priest paused.

'Stanley Archibald Jones was a truthful man, never afraid to say what he thought. I know he visited a number of us in hospital. He was a man of integrity, a man of his word and a husband and friend who will be sorely missed by us all.'

Closing with prayer, the congregation stood as the rollers on the plinth moved the coffin beyond the curtains of the crematorium.

Janice held on tightly to Albert's arm.

'This song is for you and Stan. He told me you often sang it together and out of tune.'

The priest pressed the button on the pulpit to play a CD of the old wartime song:

'Pack up your troubles in your old kit-bag,

And smile, smile, smile,

While you've a lucifer to light your fag,

Smile, boys, that's the style.

What's the use of worrying?

It never was worthwhile, so

Pack up your troubles in your old kit-bag,

And smile, smile, smile.'

By the time the last chorus came round almost everyone was either singing along or whistling the tune.

From the crematorium the congregation made its way to a buffet arranged by Janice at the Dog and Duck. For two hours the mourners mingled, telling their favourite stories of Stan, toasting his memory. It was nearly four o'clock in the afternoon before the hall was cleared of its several hundred guests.

When the room was empty, Albert dialled for a cab.

Janice walked over.

'Albert, I need to ask a favour of you. I hope you don't mind.'

'Of course you can,' replied Albert.

'Would you mind if I stayed at yours tonight? I don't want to impose on my sister again. If your couch is free, that's fine. I just feel a little scared going back on my own tonight.'

Albert was in a quandary. Janice had already been a huge source of comfort for him, but the last thing he needed was to complicate his feelings.

'Erm, of course you can. The couch is plenty comfy. I'll take that and you can have the bed.'

'You're too kind, Albert. You really are.'

Albert patted Janice on the shoulder.

On their way to Majestic Heights, Albert waited in the taxi while Janice collected a few things in a small suitcase from her house.

When they arrived, Albert apologised for the smell in the lift and held her suitcase off the grimy floor until the tell-tale sound of the bell announced that they were nearly home.

Approaching the front door, Albert could see a note taped over the lock.

'Please call me. It's very urgent! My number is under your front door – Sajan.'

Tearing the note away, Albert opened the door and retrieved the number from the floor.

'Is everything okay?' Janice asked.

'I'm not sure. Sajan's a friend from the allotment. Maybe he's got himself into trouble? I'll call him straight away. Come in, make yourself at home and flick the kettle on.'

Albert picked up his telephone and dialled the landline number.

'This is Albert Trollop. May I speak with Sajan, please?'

'Why of course, Mr Trollop. I'm very sorry to hear your news. If I can help in any way, please do let me know.'

'That's very kind of you. It's never easy losing a friend,' Albert replied.

Sajan's father gasped.

'My goodness!' he cried. 'Did someone die in the fire?'

Albert's heart began to race. 'Fire, what fire? I'm sorry, I don't understand.'

'Please, let me get my son for you. One moment please.'

Sajan came to the telephone.

'Albert, I'm very sorry, but it's your allotment.'

'What's happened, son? Has there been a fire?'

Sajan tried to compose himself before answering.

'I don't know how to say this, but ... your shed was set on fire.'

'How? When? What happened?'

Sajan paused for a moment.

'I'm sorry but there's little left. I've been there and tried to salvage what I could from your wooden chest in the shed but the fire was too strong. By the time it was put out, it was too late. I left a note on your door because I knew you were at your friend's funeral today.'

Albert sat down at the kitchen table and covered his face with his hands.

'Albert, what's happened?' Janice whispered.

Albert looked toward the window, his tired and pale face etched with pain.

'I don't need much,' he sobbed. 'I've always been grateful for what I have ... but my memories ... all of them ... they were in that shed.'

Janice sat down next to Albert and gently stroked his arm while he explained about his wooden chest that kept all his old letters and photos, including photos of Stan.

As Albert continued to describe the contents of his shed, the doorbell rang.

It was Sajan.

He had dashed over to Albert's flat to offer him some support.

'Thank you for coming over,' Albert said.

'You're welcome, Albert. I just thought you might like it if I came with you to your allotment. I didn't like the thought of you going on your own.'

I'll come too,' Janice said.

'Strength in numbers,' Sajan added.

CHAPTER 41

Door Step Diva

Gretyl had run several errands since early in the morning and having been out of the house for most of the day she had just woken with a start from her late afternoon siesta.

It was now 6pm on Friday evening and Neil stood at the door, ready to deliver a written offer for Gretyl's property. He had also enclosed a personal cheque for £2500 with a sticky note attached that read: 'Holiday Fund'.

Gretyl answered the door in her comfy Cher wig and fire engine red satin and lace dressing gown.

'Is that something for me?' she asked rudely, annoyed that her sleep had been interrupted.

Neil was taken aback but replied calmly.

'The village has agreed to offer you substantially more for your property. How does £2.6 million pounds sound?'

Gretyl laughed.

'It would sound a lot of money if I didn't have at least four times that amount coming to me in the next few months.'

Neil threw the letter angrily at Gretyl.

'Let me be clear. I'll personally make your life a misery if you decide to stay. If I have to spend all I have to see you removed from the village, I'll do it. You really have no idea what I could do to you.'

Gretyl smiled and picked up the letter.

Opening it, she noticed the cheque.

Gretyl fluffed her Cher-like wig for attention.

'From what I heard in the café yesterday, you haven't got long anyway - that is, if I agree to keep quiet about your little fiddle.'

With that, Gretyl began to warble her own muddled version of a Cher number.

'I'm not sad that you're leavin, it's high time you believe it ... cos after all is said and done, you're going to be out on your bum, Oh Oh.'

Neil raised his eyebrows.

'You really are mentally ill,' he said.

Gretyl laughed as she finished her song and then looked Neil straight in the eye.

'I'm going to make myself clear, you cranky little man. It's not like I want to live next door to you either. You'll sell your house to me and on the cheap if you want to buy my silence.'

Realising he was cornered, Neil sighed.

'You're a cunning woman, Mrs Trollop. Okay, we have a deal. Once I confirm that the sale in Marbella is complete, you may buy my property. That is, if you can keep your mouth shut!'

Gretyl immediately retorted.

'Listen to me carefully. If you as much as fairy puff in the wrong direction, I'll have you! The village will be against you, there'll be no big pay cheque, no holidays in the sun and you'll be stuck with me every day for the rest of your pathetic life. Understand? Now be a good boy and get off my doorstep. I'm not missing my shopping channels for you.'

Neil stormed back to his home.

He withdrew Arti Chokes' business card from his pocket and dialled the number from his house phone.

'Mown Down Solutions, Arti Chokes speaking.'

Arti took the mobile phone and walked into his office, closing the door.

Neil held his hand over the mouthpiece of the phone.

'Is this a secure line?'

'Who's asking?' replied Arti.

'My name is erm, you can call me Mr 'X'. I need a professional to take care of my dirty work and I hear that you're a hit with your clients?'

Arti replied with an almost funereal tone.

'We always aim to please. If you need a job doing that you can't do yourself, you have dialled the right number.'

'There's a troublesome new development in our village and I need you to remove a very stubborn weed.'

'Do you wish to meet up and discuss your proposal?' replied Arti.

Neil's heart beat began to accelerate.

'It needs to be soon. Can you meet me tomorrow evening?'

'One moment, Mr 'X', I need to check my schedule.'

Arti pulled the phone away from his mouth and placed it down on the table. One at a time, he cracked his fingers and took note of Poncey Bridge's area code from the readout of his mobile before returning to the call.

'Yes, we can meet at 7pm. I have your location.'

Neil suggested they meet outside his village.

'That's affirmative. At this time tomorrow, precisely 7pm, I'd like you to take a look in the window of your local post office and you will see a note for 'Mown Down Solutions'. There you will receive instructions of our meeting point. Due to the highly specialised nature of our work, we require a cash deposit of £5000 upon our first meeting. You will place the unmarked bank notes in an envelope and hand it to the gentleman you meet. He'll be wearing a white baseball cap.'

Neil's heart was now racing.

'The man wearing the white cap, will that be you?'

'Erm ... yes,' replied Arti. 'No more questions over the phone. We are on a 24 bit secure line, but with the Secret Service, you can never be too sure. We'll discuss the dirt that needs removing tomorrow. Goodnight, Mr X.'

CHAPTER 42

Deadly Comforts

Arti's wife Doris walked into the office with a hot chocolate.

'Business call, my dear?' she said softly.

'Yes, kitten. I might be away for a few days, if I get the job.'

Ten years the senior of her husband Arti, the miniature frame of 74 year old Doris resembled Miss Marple only frailer and shorter.

Despite moving home sixteen times, Doris and Arti had enjoyed a steady state of marital contentment for over forty years. Doris had never raised an objection to the relocations; she put it down to the travelling demands of her husband's work and an apparent phobia on his part of living in one place for any length of time. Doris had always been very supportive of her husband's work, especially one that had paid so handsomely - although she had on occasions expressed to Arti her surprise at how lucrative a gardening business could be.

Arti looked out of the window at his customised vehicle. Every inch in his side-loading transit van was perfectly ordered, from the purpose built shelving through to fixtures and fittings along the back wall. The only similarity with his actual trade and the gardening cover were the tools that were useful for digging graves. The van wasn't sign-written so he never entertained any genuine gardening enquiries.

The blacked out windows also hid everything from sight, along with the specialist equipment concealed under the counter and operated by a secret button beneath one of the wooden panels in the floor.

The gadgetry consisted of watches (with hidden cameras), various enhanced pens (poisonous, scanners, audio recorders and powerful lasers), sunglasses (that transmitted images to the lenses from the rear), remote monitoring, surveillance equipment, cellular jammers, GPS trackers and a dozen small weapons.

Doris seemed completely oblivious of her husband's alternate livelihood and never asked where the money was coming from, preferring to enjoy at least four lengthy sun filled holidays each year.

At home, Arti could be mistaken for a comfortable, retired accountant, a pipe and slippers man who sported the latest offering from Doris' hand knitted jumpers.

His four bed detached house included a loft conversion dedicated to his love of war documentaries, crime fiction and spy dramas. Hundreds of DVDs and video cassettes occupied the shelves from wall to wall, while crime novels filled much of the floor space, packed neatly in cardboard boxes and fastidiously labelled with a laminated sheet, by Title, Author and Year.

Now sitting at a desk in the loft, Arti switched on his laptop and placed his thumb on top of a fingerprint reader on the screen.

Once he had accessed his secret database, he clicked on a poster icon and began to type a few lines of text for his advertisement for 'Mr X'.

'Mown Down Solutions - The Farrell Pub – Saturday - 7pm - membership fee to be paid upon arrival - Arti, white cap.'

Scrambling his Internet search through a gateway that hid the computer's IP address, Arti searched for the post office details. Looking at the information associated with the property, he scanned the Internet for data related to the Shagpile family, the owners of the post office.

Arti picked up his phone and dialed the number of the post office.

'I'd like to place an ad in the gardening services section of your window please,' he said.

Arti was not expecting the uncooperative reply that followed.

'We're closed and in any case we're only open to people in the village. You're not from 'round here are you?'

'I'm aware of the policy,' replied Arti forcefully, 'but my request involves clients in your village who wish to remain anonymous. I require a simple message notifying them of our next appointment. Would you like me to inform them of your reluctance to help, or should I just simply pay you the fifty pound fee I always set aside for small window ads?'

Mrs Shagpile was defiant. 'Why don't you just phone them yourself?'

'I require a public notice for all of my appointments, Mrs Shagpile.'

'How do you know my name?' she replied suspiciously.

'In my profession, Mrs Evelyn Shagpile of 32 Royal Avenue, I am privy to a wealth of information. You attended the Croft Manor school, take medication for hypertension, have two children, a dog called Jeeves and if I am correct, like to shop out of town yourself?'

'How dare you! I don't know who you are, but you can go and get stuffed.'

Arti replied calmly, 'If you won't assist me, I cannot be held responsible if your husband's guilty pleasures are made public. It would be simply awful for family and friends, don't you think?'

Arti had run a number of searches on the Shagpile family and obtained the IP address of their home. Hacking into their personal records, his key logging software discovered a number of monthly payments going out from her husband's bank account to a variety of hardcore websites.

Evelyn froze. She knew of her husband's 'secret interests' but she had chosen to ignore them.

Arti read out the single lined advert and asked her to repeat it back, and confirm that the announcement would be in place for tomorrow.

Mrs Shagpile replied in a conciliatory tone.

'Er, yes. It's only a few lines. I'll put it in the window in the morning. Goodbye.'

Arti smiled as he ended the call.

He sat back and looked around the luxurious loft, reflecting upon the fruits of his labours.

Another 'gardening' job had just been secured and the rewards would be much appreciated - not least by his unquestioning and credulous wife.

CHAPTER 43

Costly Silence

Neil Rochester ran back to the house and within an hour of visiting Gretyl Trollop he had already put the paperwork together for the trip to Marbella.

Neil used his credit card to purchase the group's flight tickets online, after agreeing with Sharkie that this sum would be reimbursed after the trip. Arti's ticket was also booked and he would fly out separately, Monday evening.

Eager to confirm Gretyl's departure, Neil had booked her flight from London Gatwick to Malaga and printed her boarding pass.

Neil walked over to her house and rang the doorbell.

'Mrs Trollop. I'm sorry we got off on the wrong foot earlier. Here is your free flight ticket to Marbella, ready to depart with us in three days on Monday. I've also arranged for you to stay in one of the luxury villas.'

Gretyl snatched the boarding pass and print out, only to notice there was no return date.

'Mr Rochester, do you intend for me to stay in Marbella? I'm not reading a return date here?'

'I thought you might like to choose the length of your stay. On Monday, I'll introduce you to Sharon Souddalle, my associate. She'll take care of your return flight, when you're ready.'

Gretyl saw through her neighbour's tactics immediately.

'He's desperate for my silence and I'll make him pay for that,' she thought.

Gretyl raised her eyebrows at Neil.

'It all sounds good and dandy, but I don't have a passport yet, so that's you stuffed. What's Mr High and Mighty going to do about that then?'

Neil stared at Gretyl, floored by her admission.

'You don't ... what? But you asked me to get you on the trip and that's what I've done.'

Neil paused, searching for a reply while Gretyl stood by the front door smirking.

'Umm ... Give me a moment ...'

Neil walked away from the door and safely out of earshot he dialled Arti's mobile number.

'I've got a real problem. I need you take care of things for me overseas on Monday, but the old bag that needs removing doesn't have a passport.'

Arti replied confidently.

'All I need from you is a photo of the weed you want removing. Please send the image to this secure phone and I will have the necessary documents ready for you tomorrow evening. This will incur an additional fee of five thousand pounds, payable tomorrow evening. That makes ten. Please ensure that you bring the funds with you.'

Neil ended his call and walked back to Gretyl.

'Step back to the wall, please.'

Gretyl ran her fingers through her wig.

'What kind of woman do you think I am? I hope you have pure motives Mr Rochester, because I really don't think you're strong enough ...'

'I need to take your photo for the passport,' Neil replied indifferently. 'I have influential friends who will arrange to have it ready for Monday.'

'Mr Rochester, why are you going to all this trouble?'

Neil had to think on his feet. Gretyl proved a real and present threat to his plans and it was essential that she meet her fate while in Marbella, before she could blow the whistle on him.

'Look, I won't pretend - this deal is important to me, Mrs Trollop. If you're happy, then we are both happy.'

Gretyl stood back to the wall, while Neil used the camera in his phone to take the shot.

'Could you, just erm, move the hair around slightly ... so I can see your eyes? That's it, all done.'

'Another thing,' Gretyl added. 'This cheque you handed me is post dated. If you want me to go, I need £2500 in cash for Monday.'

Neil clicked on the image and sent the photo to Arti.

'That's no problem. I'll have your passport and cash. Can you be ready for me, say 11am, Monday morning?'

'The question is, Mr Rochester. Will you be ready for me?'

With a swish of her satin dressing gown, Gretyl Trollop, the new prima donna of Poncey Bridge, slammed the front door in her neighbour's face.

CHAPTER 44

Out of the Ashes

Albert, Sajan and Janice circled the plot where the shed had once stood. They had searched through the charred remains for the last hour, poking the embers with a stick and hoping to find something that survived the intense flames. The Fire Service said that the wooden outbuilding had burned for too long before they could help.

Sajan had managed to recover some photos from the scorched wooden chest. It had offered some protection against the flames but the prints were discoloured and curled up under the smoke and heat. Albert carefully placed the only surviving images in his top pocket, desperate to preserve whatever memories he had left.

Albert's mind was racing with questions.

'How could this happen? Everything I loved was in there. Who would do this to me? Why was it that only my shed was targeted?'

Scanning the debris and the surrounding land, Albert spotted a tell-tale fuel can in the grass.

'Who would ever hate me enough to burn my shed and destroy my memories?' he said wearily to himself.

Albert sat on the ground, unable to think clearly, until suddenly he began to hear a familiar voice in his mind.

'Albert, I know you said you won't leave your allotment, but I won't let that come between us and our dream ... don't think for a minute I'm going to budge on this ... no more green fingers for you, Albert Trollop.'

The words seemed to play over and over again, as if on a continuous loop.

'Gretyl's the only one person that could have done this,' he thought.

Albert was incensed and stood up from the blackened grass.

'The vindictive old cow! I bet she paid someone to do this to my shed.'

Sajan and Janice flinched.

'If she thinks she can smoke me out and force me to move, it'll take more than petrol to do that!'

Amidst all his shouting, Albert hadn't noticed his phone was buzzing. Calming down, he felt the vibration of an incoming call and put the handset to his ear.

'Hello, dear, it's your beautiful but lonely wife. How are you?'

Before Albert had time to reply, she continued.

'It's marvellous up here! Oh and on Monday, I'm going on a free holiday! I won it at the prize raffle in the community hall. I'm so excited, fired up and ready to go. Now listen, I need you to come back here tomorrow. There are a few things I need to go over with you, before I leave.'

Albert sat back down again on the grass with his head bowed, taking deep breaths.

'Are you alright? Come on down, get your bags packed and come visit your poor ol' wife.'

'You bitch! I buried my friend today ... and my allotment shed burned down as well. Know anything about that?'

'Albert, why are you talking to me like that?' Gretyl stuttered, stunned at the violence of her husband's outburst. 'What do you mean your shed's burned down? What's happened?'

Albert began to weep.

'Albert, please talk to me. What's happened?'

'You ... you should have been ... here with me,' Albert sobbed. 'My best friend ... Stan ... he died. Where were you? All you could talk about ... talk about was yourself. You're one vindictive ... nasty woman. I don't know what ... what I ever saw in you. Whatever it was ... it's not there anymore. You're ... you're not there anymore.'

'Albert, I'm so sorry. You're right, I am a self centred old bag ... but I love you, Albert Trollop. Please believe me. Forgive me Albert ...'

'Forgive you,' Albert retorted. 'Forgive you for desecrating my memories? You've got a nerve.'

Suddenly Albert dropped his phone and grabbed hold of his chest.

Sajan, who had walked away for a few minutes to give Albert some space, quickly ran over to his friend.

'Albert. Are you okay? Shall I call an ambulance?'

Gretyl heard Sajan's voice in the background and panicked.

'Albert my love, are you okay? Pick up the phone. Please ... pick up the phone!'

Albert switched off his phone and asked Sajan to help him to his feet.

'I think I'm okay, son.'

Sajan was not so sure, however. He called his father, who was a doctor, on his mobile phone. He was told to call an ambulance. Albert refused, so Sajan's father offered to pick them up from the allotment and give Albert a quick check up.

Back at the flat, Dr Panesar asked Albert a number of questions regarding his medical history and gave him a physical examination. He concluded that the tightening of the chest was most probably an angina attack. This had abated within a few minutes once Albert had used his medication spray.

Janice stood over the kitchen chair where Albert was recovering and gently rubbed his shoulders.

'I'm so sorry,' she said to Albert. 'But at least we've got each other to lean on.'

For a moment Albert leaned back and enjoyed the caring and soothing touch of his friend's hands. He could not deny that her tender companionship made him feel wanted, warm and alive.

For a moment Albert wondered if he should phone Gretyl. But this thought soon passed as Janice's fingers relaxed him even more.

Albert stood up from the chair and wandered over to the couch.

Janice dimmed the lights and took his shoes off, propping his head up with a soft pillow and laying a blanket over him as he rested.

Within minutes, Albert had fallen asleep and Sajan quietly departed.

It was now almost 10pm and Albert had been sleeping deeply.

He was rudely awakened by the fumbling of keys and a loud banging at the front door of the flat.

Janice opened the door slightly, leaving the latch still on.

'Hello. Can I help you?' asked Janice.

'Who the flaming 'eck are you? Let me in my house, now,' barked Gretyl.

185

Barging past Janice into the front room, Gretyl hovered menacingly over Albert who was just beginning to sit up on the sofa, rubbing his eyes.

Gretyl pointed at Janice.

'Who is this woman?' Gretyl fumed. 'Why is this scrubber wearing a dressing gown in my house?'

'I'm sorry,' Janice stammered. 'I just stepped out of the shower. Let me go and turn the kettle on.'

'That had better be the only thing you've been turning on in here,' Gretyl exclaimed.

Albert shot Gretyl a stern look.

'Shut up, Gretyl. This is Stan's wife, Janice. She came home for a cuppa after the funeral.'

'It's not the only thing she came home for, is it? Whose suitcase is that in the bedroom?'

'You've got the wrong end of the stick as usual,' Albert said angrily. 'I told Janice she was welcome to stay here for a few days because she didn't feel ready to go back to her home after Stan's funeral. That's why my bed is made up on the couch. What are you doing here?'

Gretyl, sizing up the situation and alarmed by her husband's rising rage, backed down.

'I was worried about you. All I heard on the phone was a kid asking if you needed an ambulance. I couldn't stay at the house after hearing that. That's why I ordered a cab straight here.'

'Well, you wouldn't want my death on your conscience, would you?' Albert replied.

At that moment Janice walked into the room with a tray of biscuits and hot drinks.

'Albert, would it be easier if I left?' she asked.

'Darn right, it would. My husband's had enough drama for today,' Gretyl snapped.

Albert turned to Janice.

'Please stay, Janice. You are always welcome here. If anyone's leaving, it's you, Gretyl.'

Gretyl looked stunned.

'I'm your wife and this is my home. Why are you doing this to me, Albert?'

Janice, visibly upset, interrupted.

'Albert, I think it's best that I leave out of respect for your wife. I'll be okay at the house tonight.'

Janice walked through to the bedroom and began repacking her suitcase.

Albert leaned closer toward Gretyl's face.

'You left me at the hardest time of my life! You destroyed the only thing I loved and then you repeatedly humiliate my best friend's wife. What do you expect me to say ... welcome home love, nice to see you?'

Gretyl tried to hold Albert's hand, but he forcefully removed it.

'I'm sorry Albert, you're right. I should have been there for you, but I'm here now. And the allotment – I would never set fire to your shed, never. I would never try to hurt you.'

Albert turned away in disdain and walked back to the bedroom to talk with Janice.

'You don't have to do this, Janice. It's not your fault.'

'Albert, I think you need some space and time to talk with your wife,' Janice replied. 'It's not right if I stay.'

Albert could hear Gretyl crying in the lounge but felt nothing. He sat quietly on the bed while Janice finished her packing.

Gretyl walked into the bedroom.

'Janice. I'm sorry. I'm a silly ol' cow at the best of times. I just misunderstood why you were here. I thought you were after my husband.'

At this, Janice simply walked over to Gretyl and kissed her on the cheek.

'I understand. It was an easy mistake to make, but it's important that you both have time and space to talk. Marriage is precious. I know that all too well, after today. I miss my Stan.'

Albert stood up from the bed and helped Janice to the door with her suitcase.

'Janice, if you need anything, just give me a call. I'm sorry about this evening.'

'Albert, you've given me such strength today. I only wish I was able to leave you with some too. We'll speak soon. Thank you again. Bye.'

Albert shut the front door and returned to the lounge, where Gretyl was still crying.

'Gretyl, I want you to leave. I need my space to think. I've had one of the hardest days of my life and I'm not ready to talk now.'

Gretyl looked up from the floor, trying to make eye contact with Albert.

'Please Albert, I've got nowhere to go tonight and I'm tired from all the travelling.'

But Albert was implacable.

'There's a hotel just past the bookies, at the end of the high street. I'll call a taxi and you can stay there tonight. Do you have money on you?'

Gretyl had never seen Albert like this before.

'Albert, please don't put me out of the house. I'll sleep on the couch if you like. Hey, in the morning, how about I make you one of those cooked breakfasts I love?'

'Gretyl, if you care anything for my feelings, then go. When I'm ready, I'll call you.'

Gretyl sat in silence, while Albert ordered a taxi.

'Yes, I'd like a taxi from Majestic Heights to the Hunters Inn hotel.'

Gretyl walked out into the hall to interrupt Albert's call.

'Albert, do you remember our wedding day? You said you'd spend your whole life trying to make me happy.'

'Well, I never thought I'd live this long. Believe me Gretyl, my life is spent.'

CHAPTER 45

The Makeover

Sharon Soddall had spent her Friday night enjoying a full beauty treatment from her friend, Caroline. From the quick tan, facial, ritual wax, manicure and pedicure Sharon was positively glowing and felt ten years younger.

Having expressed concern about her wardrobe for the short trip, Sharkie had taken care of things, surprising Sharon that evening with a card containing £1000 in cash for her wardrobe and holiday expenses.

It was now Saturday morning and Sharon was up early, ready for her shopping break. Sharon told Dave she'd be spending the best part of the day in London, looking for her Marbella outfits. What she had failed to mention, however, was the small matter of the grand she had to spend.

Sharkie was now waiting outside the house, ready to impress by taking her to the best boutiques and clothes shops in London, followed by a big slap-up lunch in the West End.

Sharkie had planned the itinerary with Sharon in mind. One of his friends had given him the keypad code to a private parking space just off High Street Kensington. With Harrods nearby and easy access to cabs, they could travel a short ride to Oxford Street later that morning.

Sharon tiptoed down the stairs, stilettos in hand, and turned the door lock quietly, careful not to wake her sleeping beauties upstairs.

'Morning, Shaz. You look gorgeous.'

Sharkie leaned over and gave her a small, respectful peck on her cheek.

'Off we go then. I'm so excited. I really don't know what to say about what you gave me last night,' said Sharon.

Sharkie grinned, interpreting her words quite differently.

'I'd be happy to do it every night,' he winked.

Sharon blushed.

'You cheeky bugger.'

Deciding to play it cool the entire day, Sharkie wanted to earn Sharon's respect and ultimately, her affection. He knew the chemistry was already there and didn't want to rush anything. He anticipated that the perfect moment in Marbella would present itself. He intended to make his move then.

An Ibiza anthem blasted from Sharkie's Blackberry phone, its ringtone prompting a cheesy grin.

'Mr Lovitt, Neil Rochester here. How are you this morning?'

'Very well thank you, Mr Rochester.'

Sharkie winked at Sharon while pressing the speakerphone key.

'Good, well it's just a quick call to say everything is in order and we look forward to meeting you in the airport lounge. There's just one concern that I need to brief you about.'

'Go ahead.'

'Well, the woman I had an altercation with at the Brasserie ... it appears she was eavesdropping on our conversation. She's just moved into the village and threatened to blow the lid on our deal unless she gets a free trip with us to Marbella, but I've sorted it - bribed the old witch with a ticket and some spending money.'

'Does this woman pose a problem?'

'No, Mr Lovitt. She's as rough as they come and cheaper than a pound store. We just have to entertain her until we've signed the paperwork and I've transferred the money from the village investment fund. She can say what she wants after that, because I'll be gone, you'll have your money and we'll all be happy.'

Sharon leaned forward to join in the conversation.

'Hello Mr Rochester, Sharon Souddalle here. I'd be more than happy to befriend her on the trip, if you think it might help?'

'That's an excellent idea, Miss Souddalle. In fact, if you wouldn't mind, it might be wise if you share a villa with her. You know, keep an eye on her.'

'Mr Rochester, if it means we can all sign off on the deal, I'd be more than happy to.'

'That's excellent news. Oh, and she has a one way ticket. I hope it's not a problem with the seller in Marbella if she needs to extend her stay. I told Mrs Trollop that you'd be more than happy to arrange her return trip to the UK when she's ready.'

Sharkie interrupted.

'That's fine Mr Rochester. We've also arranged a few little extras on the flight out, with complimentary luxury chocolates, champagne and a free duty gift of perfume or aftershave for the guests.'

'That's wonderful, Mr Lovitt. I look forward to the trip. See you Monday. Goodbye.'

Sharon turned to Sharkie.

'That's a nice touch. You think of everything, don't you?' she said warmly.

'To be honest Sharon, I've only been thinking about taking care of you on the trip, but you have to think on your feet. Anyway, Tony wired me some money for expenses and stuff, so it's all sorted.'

Sharon looked concerned.

'Hang on a minute. I can't have Tony buying my outfits.'

Sharkie put his hand on Sharon's shoulder.

'Darling, that grand I gave you is from my pocket, not his. I know it's only a short break, but I wanted to make it a bit special for you.'

Sharon looked eagerly into Sharkie's piercing blue eyes.

'Thank you,' she said coyly. 'I'm not used to such thoughtfulness or such generosity.'

'You ain't seen nothing yet,' Sharkie replied.

CHAPTER 46

Domestic Upheaval

After making a call to Harvey the auctioneer, Neil Rochester had spent the weekend gathering various personal items together for the sale.

Neil figured that his estimated wealth had increased significantly with the prospect of his house sale, not to mention the Marbella investment. Unwilling to remove Patricia's jewellery from the sale, Neil had boxed up her prized collection and hidden it under their bed.

'She won't miss it,' he convinced himself. 'She never wears it or leaves the house anyway!'

Neil walked over to his wife to break the news.

'Patricia, Alistair has agreed to buy our house for £750,000 cash. I think we'll make a quarter of a million from the auction sale with Harvey and the Marbella portfolio will earn £1.25 million if we are willing to manage any bookings and retire there. We can live rent free in the sunshine.'

Patricia shifted awkwardly on her chair.

'I don't know what to say Neil. I've wanted out of the village for years, but I don't want to be so far away from our daughter and beautiful Beatrice. She's only two years old and I couldn't bear to miss her growing up.'

Neil had already anticipated this response.

'I understand, but this is really a once in a lifetime opportunity. Who wouldn't want to live in a beautiful villa in sunny Marbella? Let's take the risk. If you don't like it, you can always come back.'

'Neil, I need to think about it. This is all happening too fast for me.'

Unable to control his anger, Neil retaliated.

'When was the last time you saw her anyway?' he snapped threateningly. 'You only knit stupid jumpers for her and you can do that anywhere.'

'Don't bully me, Neil. The reason we haven't seen our granddaughter for a while is because you refuse to drive me there and Jenny is too upset when she comes here.'

Neil seized a handful of the Marbella brochures and hurled them at Patricia.

'After all the years you've pestered me to leave and now you're dragging your feet!'

'I don't trust you Neil. I don't know what you're up to. You've only ever done things for yourself.'

'Well, whether you like it or not, we're moving house. If you don't like it, go live with that daughter of yours and her spoilt little brat.'

Patricia ran weeping into the bedroom and slammed the door, locking it from the inside.

'You're a disgrace, Neil Rochester. You treat me like trash!'

Neil tried to force his way in the room. Taking a step back, he barged against the door but was unable to force it open.

'Open this door now. I've had it with you!'

Patricia sat terrified, crouching alongside a dresser in the opposite corner of the room.

'Please Neil, stop it. You're scaring me.'

Neil pounded his fist on the door.

'Fine, then. Have it your way. I'm off out.'

Neil stormed down the stairs and grabbed his mobile phone and coat, slamming the front door. He set off to meet the carefully selected group who would be travelling with him to Marbella.

On the way he fabricated a story designed to explain Gretyl's presence on the trip. Neil wasn't unduly concerned about their reaction; their loyalty to him over the years had been unquestioning. All of them had at one time or another benefitted from their relationship with him.

On arriving, Neil explained to the group that if they could just ride out the week with Gretyl, the village would be rid of her. He also divulged that a specialist had been hired and that incriminating evidence would be planted in her house while she was away.

After half an hour of further planning, Neil returned to the house.

He opened the door quietly, and hearing the beeping sound of the buttons being pressed on the phone upstairs, he sat on the bottom step to listen in on Patricia.

'Jenny, is that you?' Patricia asked, her voice shaking.

'Mum, what is it? Why are you crying? Has dad done something?'

'I'm frightened, Jenny. It's ... oh, I'm sorry. I shouldn't be ringing you.'

'Mum, please. Talk to me, you know you can. We need to talk.'

Jenny had received a number of calls from her mum over the past few years, but she had never heard her mother so distraught. This was different and Jenny was worried.

Patricia continued. 'Your dad ... he's selling up - the house, valuables, everything. He wants to move us to Spain.'

'Mum, that's not like dad at all. Why are you crying? Where are you?'

'I've locked myself in the bedroom. I'm frightened.'

'Mum, listen to me, carefully. Where's dad?'

'He stormed out after trying to knock the door down.'

Neil continued to listen, somewhat removed and indifferent to her cry and his abusive behaviour.

Patricia started to sob again.

'Right, I'm coming over. I'm only an hour away, so pack whatever you need and meet me at the end of the drive. I'll beep three times when I'm outside. Look out for me, mum and don't worry. I'm on my way.'

Neil, tired from the conflict, decided it was time to go so he quietly slipped out of the house.

'If she wants to leave, then off she must go,' he concluded.

CHAPTER 47

Full English Breakfast

Gretyl had woken early Saturday morning, plagued with questions.

'Could I really live without Albert? Will I die alone? How can I get Albert to forgive me? What time do they serve breakfast? I wonder what the fry-ups are like here?'

Food had always been Gretyl's first port of call in times of emotional turbulence.

Gretyl's entrance at the 'eat all you want' breakfast was designed to cause a stir. The other diners looked suitably open-mouthed as she strolled in dolled up to the nines and wearing a Tina Turner style wig.

Having already made several visits to the hot plates, Gretyl was piling the food high again on her final trek. Soon she would be approaching that keenly anticipated state of feeling full and satisfied.

Gretyl walked slowly back to her table, carefully balancing the landfill of hot food on her plate.

'Oh mummy, look. It's a magician,' clapped a young child, approving of the balancing act.

Her health-conscious mother gestured to her husband.

'Honey, we need to move tables. I don't want that rampant carnivore frightening the children. That's not breakfast. It's a sacrifice.'

Like a force of nature, Gretyl began demolishing her final stack of sausage, bacon, egg, black pudding and fried bread.

She continued to chomp away with all the finesse of a hoofed mammal, while the family hurried along to the bottom table.

Snorting with every bite, Gretyl's ritual finished with a loud vibration from her upper esophageal sphincter.

Feeling better, she rose from the table and dragged her suitcase towards the reception front desk.

A young lady sitting there handed Gretyl the bill.

'Minus your £25 deposit, the balance left is £155.95 please. How do you wish to pay?'

Gretyl licked her lips, savouring the moment.

'Pay? Huh. Young lady, I've more than paid after the night I've had in this brothel.'

'Brothel? Oh, erm, we are a hotel, madam. What seems to be the problem?'

'Well, I'm not usually one who likes to complain ... but first you put me in a room with dirty sheets that smell like someone's just died in them. Then I'm woken up repeatedly with loud banging and moaning through the bedroom wall. Randy Rick and Loose Lily must have thought the world was about to end.'

The receptionist checked the room list, eager to find the copulating culprits.

'Oh, I'm very sorry to hear that.'

Gretyl wagged her finger at the girl.

'Please don't interrupt me young lady, I haven't finished yet. Now ... after the torture of sleep deprivation - and you've seen what that's like in Guantanamo Bay - all I needed was a flamin' orange suit and shackles on my feet. I get out of bed to stand under the shower hose, only to be scalded by your water. At this point, I thought my tormentor would appear and try to break me - y'know, drown me with water-boarding and all that stuff. I hurried out of the bath and slipped painfully on my arse ... and no, there wasn't a rubber bath mat inside.'

Gretyl was interrupted by several people laughing and filming the commotion on their mobile phones.

But she continued undaunted.

'I hobble to breakfast to find the food totally unpalatable. I couldn't eat one more sausage. The food was cold, sausages under cooked, eggs raw, milk off, toast moldy, black pudding 'bloody' and service non-existent. That is, unless you count the asylum seeker collecting the plates. Got a work permit, has she?'

Lost for words, the young receptionist pressed the panic button under the counter.

Gretyl picked up her heavy fur coat from the floor and raised her voice.

'Do you want me to repeat myself again? I'm not paying. I'll be suing you for false advertising. Hotel, my arse; I'd have preferred a cell with a bowl of gruel than stay here at this detention centre.'

The young duty manager ran over and tried to calm Gretyl down, ushering her into the office.

'Madam, please. What seems to be the problem?'

'How dare you treat an old woman like this! You'll be hearing from my solicitor. Goodbye.'

Gretyl stormed out of the office and straight to the taxi rank across the road, dragging her belongings behind her.

'Rovers Place, just off the main road, please. You know, the garages at the back.'

'Yep, sure love,' the driver replied.

Gretyl arrived a few minutes later at the lock-up, eager to make an inventory and gather up some items for the new house. She squeezed between the table and chairs and delved into her hoard. It only took her five minutes to conclude that a large van would be needed to shift even one third of this stuff.

CHAPTER 48

Change of Heart

Back at the flat, Albert was up very early, unable to sleep from the stress of the previous day. He'd spent the past hour going over different scenarios. Was he ready to move on from his marriage? Is this what they both wanted? How would she cope without him being around?

It was now 10am Saturday morning and PC Richards arrived at the flat to discuss the fire at the allotment.

'Mr Trollop, after you reported the incident last night, we wanted to update you on the investigation. We've arrested two youths who, while being under the influence of alcohol, committed a number of acts of vandalism. We'd gathered a few eye witness reports identifying them at the scene and after questioning, they admitted to setting fire to your property.'

Albert replied, 'Did my wife have something to do with this? I wouldn't be surprised if she'd bribed them with alcohol.'

Albert was beginning to wonder if Gretyl's recent phone calls were all a smoke screen? Maybe she wanted him to believe she was in Poncey Bridge when really she was in the area, setting fire to his shed.

'Officer, did they say whether someone put them up to it?' Albert asked.

'I don't think so, Mr Trollop. The youths in question told us that they'd been drinking all day and were egging each other on. Unfortunately, this isn't the first time they've been arrested for vandalism and criminal damage. There is sufficient evidence to charge them with the fire, but we would need a statement from you. Is that okay?'

Albert scratched his head.

'That's fine, but are you sure my wife had nothing to do with this?'

'Two youths have admitted starting the fire after a bout of heavy drinking. We've no reason to believe your wife had anything to do with this.'

Albert stood up and shook the officer's hand.

'Thanks for coming to see me this morning. If you don't mind, may I give my statement another time? I have an urgent matter to sort.'

After thanking the police officer again, Albert escorted him to the door.

Grabbing his mobile phone he then dialled Gretyl's number but there was no reply, so he took his bicycle and made his way to the Hunters Inn hotel.

A short ride later, Albert arrived at the reception desk and introduced himself as Gretyl's husband, asking whether she'd checked out of her room.

'Yes, she left about half an hour ago and without paying her bill.'

'Oh, okay. I'll sort that out,' replied Albert.

After hastily settling up, Albert rushed out of the hotel and walked over to the taxi parked up outside.

'Excuse me, but I wonder if you can help me?' asked Albert. 'Did you take my wife to the station this morning? She would be wearing, let me think, it's Saturday, so she'd have her Tina Turner wig on.'

'Yes, about half an hour ago. I'm not really supposed to say any more though - y'know client confidentiality,' replied the driver.

'I completely understand. Look, here's my bus pass. The name's Trollop, Albert Trollop. I'm concerned for my wife and need to know where she is now, if you don't mind.'

'Okay. I do remember the lady. I dropped her off at the garages behind Rovers Place, just off the main road.'

Albert thanked the driver and grabbed his bicycle, making haste towards the garages before turning into Rovers Place. In the distance he could see Gretyl walking out of a lock-up with her hands full.

'Gretyl, what are you doing here? What's all this stuff?'

Caught off guard, Gretyl hurried back inside the garage.

Albert stepped down from the bike and followed her inside.

'What are you doing? Whose place is this?'

Gretyl turned to Albert.

'I didn't think you wanted to see me again, after last night,' she said sullenly.

'Look, love, I'm sorry. I've been under a lot of pressure lately. I was really upset and after the stuff we've been through lately ...'

Gretyl walked over to Albert and tried to hug him.

'It's okay Albert. I forgive you. I guess I deserved some of the backlash. I just thought you'd prefer me out of the way, while you grieved over Stan.'

For a moment Albert wondered if Gretyl had thought staying in Poncey Bridge was the kind thing to do under the circumstances.

Gretyl kissed Albert's cheek.

'I was trying to cheer you up with all the house talk. You know what I'm like. A bull in a china shop, you've said so many times. I just want you to share in my happiness, Albert.'

'So what's all this stuff, Gretyl?'

'Hmm, it's been my little secret, I'm afraid. I was too scared to bring all this stuff back home and didn't want to stress you out, but you know I'm a collector. I just needed more wall space to put this shelving up. And the furniture, well, I just made it look cosy inside, like a front room. Do you like it, dear?'

Albert turned around to stare at the hundreds of items.

'I don't know what to say? There was me thinking you only liked ornaments and wall plates.'

'Oh, Albert, It's so exciting! Some of these paintings might be worth a good few quid in years to come.'

'Well, by the time they're cashed in, we'll probably both be in the ground. Are you saving this stuff for our daughter?'

'Not these treasures. She wouldn't appreciate them, but I have been thinking of opening a shop in the village, selling antiques and stuff. I've even got a name for it - Odds and Sods. What do you think?'

Albert laughed.

'Well, you'd probably sell 'sod-all' of this stuff in a posh village.'

'Less of the cheek, Albert Trollop. These are real treasures and all upmarket gear. Anyway, I've been on the phone to Heather. Told her all about the inheritance and stuff and when we're gone, it's all hers. Money can't buy you happiness, but it helps the kids to stay in touch.'

Gretyl concluded.

'Well, anyway she said she'll visit when I'm back from Marbella ... and there's more wonderful news, Albert. We have a baby grandson, called Connor.'

Heather's relationship with her parents and in particular, her mother, had been strained at the best of times. After Gretyl refused to help out with the cost of her wedding, three years had passed since their last conversation. As a result, Heather didn't send an invitation or bother to inform her of the birth of their first child.

Albert sat down on one of the boxes, trying to take it all in.

'I'm a granddad! That's the best news I've had in a very, very, long time.'

'Love, you're sitting on my box of frogs,' yelled Gretyl.

Albert jumped up.

'Sod the frogs, love. I'm a granddad.'

'Right, that's enough of the family stuff,' Gretyl announced. 'Let's get down to business. I've booked a small van and they'll be here in five minutes to pick up these boxes. Then back to the flat so I can collect my things.'

'Are you moving out for good, Gretyl?'

'For goodness sake, Albert. I'm just taking some bits 'n' pieces to the new house.'

'Sorry, love. I mean, don't you have any plans to spend time at the flat?'

'No, I don't, but I'm not rushing you. I understand how you feel about living here. Would you come back with me so we can talk before I go away on Monday? When I return, I need to see the solicitor and sort out the paperwork. It would really help if you could come with me.'

'I don't know, love. Look, I'll make my way back to the flat now and see you there.'

As Albert set off, Gretyl's mobile phone beeped with a text.

'Job sorted. Flamin' success! Nothing for him to come back to! Mac D's now, Black hoodie, nr. Bathroom. Don't forget £300. Meet me now.'

Gretyl replied, 'Give me 15–20 mins. Discretion advised. We agreed £100! Then we're done.'

After Neil Rochester's visit on Friday morning, Gretyl had taken the trip back to Battersea to look for Michael Corley, a fifteen year old troublemaker from the Estate. Gretyl knew the lad well and took a taxi to visit the different locations where he was likely to hang out, eventually finding him in the Marble Arcade in front of the gaming machines.

The small removal van was already packed with the boxes from the garage. Pulling up by the fast food restaurant, Gretyl asked the driver to wait outside for five minutes.

Gretyl walked into the restaurant and sat down in front of Michael, glaring.

'I asked you to make it look like a robbery!' she snapped.

Gretyl leaned toward Michael.

'Y'know, rough the place up, smash the window, throw stuff around, wreck his plants. Not torch it!'

Michael grinned stupidly.

'Well, a few of us were drunk. After you told me why we were doing it, I thought it would definitely make your husband want to move house.'

'I paid you to do as you were told, not to think! I wish you never did it. You broke my Albert's heart.'

'Well, you put me up to it,' replied Michael.

Gretyl wiped her eyes with a tissue and tried to restrain herself.

'Here's your hundred quid, just as grandma promised.'

'Listen, granny. It was hundred quid, but I'm a big boy now and it should be more like another £200 if you want me to keep me happy.'

'Now don't be greedy,' replied Gretyl. 'You wouldn't want me to tell your daddy about what you were up to in the High Street a few weeks back? Like jewellery, do we?'

'How do you know about that?' said Michael, alarmed.

'Listen young man. When you've lived as long as I've lived, seen the things I've seen and done the things I've done, there's not much that get's past this grandma. Now here's an extra few quid.

Go fetch yourself a happy meal and let's not hear any more of this again.'

Michael sucked his teeth in disapproval.

'Don't be rude to grandma. Show some respect for your elders. Now do we understand each other, young man?'

'Whatever. Yeh. I hear you.'

Gretyl stood up and patted Michael on the head.

'Good lad. You know it makes sense!'

Gretyl jumped back into the van and made her way back to the flat.

She walked in to find Albert packing a small bag of things, apparently ready to travel back to Poncey Bridge with her.

Albert took Gretyl's hand.

'Look, love. I regret some of the things I said to you last night but I hope you understand how I've been feeling lately. I honestly thought you'd set fire to my shed.'

Gretyl picked up a few large boxes with bubble wrap.

'Don't worry about it, love. We all make mistakes.'

Albert smiled apologetically.

'Do me a favour, Can you give me a hand with these boxes please. The driver's gone out for some lunch and we'll be setting off when he's back. If you pack the wall plates, I'll do the frogs. We should be done in an hour or so.'

Albert obliged and walked passed Gretyl, carrying his suitcase to the front door.

'I've decided to come back with you and see what all the fuss is about,' said Albert.

'That's wonderful. Now put your back into it and wrap my plates, will you dear?'

CHAPTER 49

A Bird in the Hand

Arriving mid-afternoon in Poncey Bridge, Albert was impressed by the landscaping and topiary designs in the village with some shrubs and trees geometric in shape and others sculpted in the form of animals.

As far as the property was concerned, Albert was taken aback by the sheer size of it. Though aged in appearance, it was beautifully maintained, from the painted black timber beams and white rendered brickwork, to the colourful palette of hanging baskets adorning the lead decorated windows.

Albert survived Gretyl's whirlwind tour of the house and slumped down in the large wicker chair in the conservatory, gazing at the long stretch of green English garden. No more than a hundred yards away, he was pleased to see a large, steel-framed greenhouse along with what looked like a spacious garage, at least thirty feet long. With plenty of garden to occupy his time, Albert pondered whether this change of life might not be for the best? At least an acre in size, it was certainly large enough to grow his own vegetables.

Albert rested his feet on the pouffe and was soon asleep, exhausted from the busy start to the day.

Gretyl made her way to the garage and, eager to impress Albert, found exactly what she was looking for - garden shears and a pair of step ladders.

Having decided to cut her own box plant into the shape of a cockerel, Gretyl started chopping away at the overgrown sphere that faced the Rochester's property. Despite her non-existent gardening skills, she had neither the patience nor the steady hand to clip her living sculpture into anything remotely decent. This however, didn't stop her trimming away at her *buxus sempervirens* with energy and enthusiasm.

After a mad half hour, her attempt at a cockerel was all but finished.

Albert woke from his short snooze and was surprised to see Gretyl standing on a ladder with a pair of garden shears. He popped outside to enquire what she was doing.

'Hi love. I decided to make a start on my cock. What do you think?' said Gretyl proudly.

Albert looked shocked.

'Erm, it doesn't look like the feathered kind. What were you thinking of?'

Gretyl laughed.

'I thought that was obvious. I wanted to show our neighbours there's a new bird in town.'

'I'd say you're definitely giving the neighbourhood the bird,' Albert replied.

Albert took Gretyl's hand and helped her down the step ladder.

'Look love, I don't want to stifle your newfound hobby but I think you may be sending the wrong message to your neighbours.'

'It's hard to see what you're doing when your head's buried in the bush,' said Gretyl, stepping back to take a better look of her work of art.

'Oh, I see what you mean, Albert. Who'd have thought I would have such natural talent and imagination?'

'Don't worry love. We'll find someone else who can tidy up your bush.'

Neil Rochester stepped out of the house and looked over toward Gretyl's property. As Albert watched him he could see that Neil was staring with a mixture of loathing and disdain at Gretyl's sculpted monstrosity and he smiled momentarily at his wife's creative ineptitude.

Albert waved diplomatically to his new neighbour but Neil missed the gesture.

Having already packed his fold-up bicycle on the van earlier, Albert now wanted to see a bit more of the village so he shouted goodbye to Gretyl from the drive.

'I'll see you later, love. I'm going out for a ride. I'll sort my own tea. Don't wait up.'

The lanes were decorated with flowers and the smell of honeysuckle and roses filled the air. The village high street, adorned with Georgian fronts and bay windows, displayed signs for cream teas, a local theatre group, and church service times.

Outside the post office, a white notice board caught Albert's attention with an advertisement for local dairy ice cream.

He parked his bicycle and pushed the door open to the sound of delightful chimes. Impressed by the display of locally sourced items, he strolled over to the ice cream cabinet.

'Good afternoon. May I have one of your delicious ice creams, please?'

'It'd help if you decided which one, first.'

Mrs Shagpile had put on a hostile tone reserved for those she knew were outsiders.

Albert, shocked by her curt reply, chose to let it pass and looked down at the different tubs of ice cream.

'Could you tell me which flavour this one is, please?' he asked, pointing at a pink tub.

'For goodness sake, the label's on the outside,' Mrs Shagpile retorted.

'I'm sorry, but have I offended you in some way?'

'Well, you're not from around here, are you?' she said, with her back to Albert.

'No. I'm not from here, as you aptly put it.'

'Well, let's be having you, then.'

Mrs Shagpile approached Albert and taking him firmly by the arm, walked him to the front door.

'We're closing now. If you need anything, there's a garage just outside the village.'

Albert shook his head.

'Thank you. I've just moved here with my wife, so I'm sure we'll bump into each other again. Maybe we could all do lunch together. Be seeing you.'

The door slammed shut behind Albert as he walked over to view the notices in the window. In large black ink on white card, the Mown Down Solutions advert caught his attention.

'Now that sounds good,' he thought. 'I might be interested in a gardening community group. Maybe they can give me some advice about sorting Gretyl's topiary.'

Albert walked back into the shop.

'Excuse me, but can you tell me where the Farrell Pub is?'

'Follow the main road over the crossing, turn left and make sure you leave the village. Now for the last time ... we're closed.'

With that Albert set off on his bike for a few early pints at the Farrell Pub.

CHAPTER 50

Mine's a Pint

Following Arti's instructions, Neil walked over to the post office and looked in the window ads for information about their meet that evening.

'Mown Down Solutions - The Farrell pub – Saturday 7 pm - membership fee to be paid upon arrival - Arti, white cap.'

'White cap? He must be wearing a disguise?' Neil reasoned.

It was now 4.45pm and with no one to cook his evening meal, Neil decided to walk back to the house, pick up the Rolls Royce and make his way early to the Farrell Pub, before meeting Arti.

The pub was already full and with no standing space available at the bar, Neil managed to find a small table free by the log fireplace. Holding the glass to his mouth, he closed his eyes and sipped on the creamy, smooth head.

Nearly two hours had passed, and Neil had already dispatched four pints of Guinness.

Neil fidgeted in his chair, uneasy and paranoid with ten grand in his pocket. Already slightly inebriated, he was beginning to feel the centre of attention in the room.

Biting his nails nervously, Neil scanned the pub for anyone wearing a white cap.

Spotting an unkempt and rough looking man wearing a white baseball cap, Neil muttered to himself, 'Very clever ... a hitman disguised as a painter and decorator. This Arti's a professional. Brilliant!'

As the decorator sat down at the bar, Neil addressed him directly, trying hard not to spill his drink as he leaned in.

'I saw your ad in the post office window. I'm the man who called you about the job,' he slurred.

Before the stranger had time to reply, Neil handed him the envelope and said, 'Here's the ten grand you asked for in cash. It's all there.'

He stared at the envelope and then at Neil.

'Rather than take your word for it, I need to check that it's all here if you don't mind,' the man said nervously.

Neil looked surprised.

'Surely you don't expect to count it out at the bar?' he said.

'Don't worry. I'll check it in the men's toilet. I won't be a minute.'

Neil agreed, his eyes glued to the bathroom door, eagerly waiting for his return.

After several minutes Neil was getting nervous.

'What a pillock! Have I just given ten grand to a complete stranger?'

Neil sprung from the chair and ran into the men's bathroom. It was empty. He checked the cubicles. Empty. Noticing a window left wide open, Neil retched into the sink.

Spitting the sick from his mouth, he ran back into the pub and straight out to his car, intent on catching the thief who had run off with his money.

Neil was frantic, looking for anything that resembled a decorator's or a gardener's van. Driving erratically, he pulled over the Rolls Royce and dialled Arti's mobile number, but there was no answer.

Neil left an angry message.

'I've been waiting at the 'you know where' and you've either run off with my ten grand or I've given it to a total stranger, so call me ASAP! I'm going to text you where to meet me tomorrow at 10am. If you don't show, I'll do the job myself and you'll miss out on your ten grand. Oh and if you don't show, you'll be having a visit from a few of 'my friends'.'

Neil made his way home, cursing as he clumsily removed both his car window mirrors on the way.

His life, like his car, seemed to be momentarily spiraling out of control.

And control was the one thing that Neil cherished even more than money.

CHAPTER 51

Blind Date

Arti Chokes pulled up outside the pub in his blacked-out van. Dressed in a white Fred Perry cap, denim jacket, football shirt, jeans and white trainers, he sat down at the bar and ordered a large cognac with ice.

Albert walked over, a little worse for wear, to order his fourth pint of lager.

'Excuse me. Are you Mowing Down Services?' asked Albert.

'Who's asking?' replied Arti.

'I got your message in the post office window. I normally take care of things myself, but I've got a problem back home that needs an expert.'

Arti removed his white cap and placed it on the counter.

'Go on ...'

'Let's just say there's been an accident with some garden shears and I need it tidying up.'

Aware of the nuances, Arti insisted that they go and talk some place more private so he picked up his cap and, with his drink in his hand, walked back to Albert's table.

It didn't take more than a minute before Arti realised he was talking at cross purposes with Albert.

'I'm sorry,' he said. 'You're after a different kind of mowing from the one I offer.'

Arti returned to the bar and knocked back a large bourbon.

He put his white cap back on, hoping he hadn't missed his appointment with Neil Rochester.

Arti sat at the bar and took his mobile phone out of his pocket. His phone was still on silent mode and he noticed that the answer phone symbol had flashed. Arti dialled his voicemail service to listen to the left message.

'Oh, crap,' gulped Arti, realising that he'd missed his appointment with Neil Rochester.

Barely five minutes had passed and Arti had already consumed three more whiskeys. He decided to walk back to Albert's table with a pint of lager for him.

'Mind if I take a seat again? What was it you were saying about your wife? You want her to come by an accident with some garden shears? You want me to take care of her?'

Albert laughed at the picture in his head.

'Cheers, my friend. Yes, you can take care of my wife permanently if it's not too much trouble, though I expect someone else might beat you to it.'

Arti's voice took on a more serious, if slightly slurred tone.

'Seriously, I'd be happy to oblige if you want me to. It's what I do best. Let me introduce myself. I'm Arthur, I'm sixty four years old and I'm a semi-retired hit man.'

Albert laughed out loud. 'That's the funniest introduction I've ever heard! Well, I'm Albert, I'm seventy nine and I'm a fully-retired Formula One Racing Driver.'

Already drunk, both men wallowed in their past adventures for the next hour or so. Albert spoke about Korea and the war years. Arti chattered away with stories of his life as a secret agent.

Being a self-employed loner, the opportunity to tell stories was something that Arti longed for. He couldn't let Doris know about his work. And his only outlet was Internet chat rooms using his alter ego, Mr Sockpuppet. But no one took his espionage storytelling seriously there. He knew that others thought of him as a Walter Mitty character.

'Tell me more,' Arti said falteringly, trying not to slur his words.

His tongue loosened by lager, Albert shared about his wife, the recent loss of his friend, along with the devastating fire at his allotment.

Arti listened intently. He even felt some sympathy for Albert, an emotion he hadn't felt for quite some time.

'Listen, Albert, you're a good man. If you fancy another beer sometime, here's my number. Give me a call when I'm back from my business abroad next week. What's your number? I'll add it to my phone.'

Albert fumbled with the keypad trying to find his number.

Arti reached for the phone.

'It's okay. Here, pass me your mobile and your number will show up on my phone when I dial.'

The two men shook hands outside the pub as they wished each other a garbled goodnight.

Seeing Albert wobbling toward his bike, Arti offered to drive Albert home. He grabbed the bicycle and put it in the back of his van.

'You're a real gent just like my ol' friend Stan, God rest his soul,' Albert said, one word eliding without a pause into the next.

Albert looked up to the roof of the van.

'This one's for you, Stan,' he said, before starting vigorously to sing:

'*Pack up your troubles in your old kit-bag, and smile, smile, smile.*'

CHAPTER 52

Goodbye Canvey

The Soddall family sat in the cramped lounge of their terraced house, each one anticipating the large windfall heading their way.

Dave winked at Sharon, proud of the deal she had helped broker with Neil Rochester.

'Won't be long now and you'll be an international traveller. You can kiss goodbye to the Pot Noodles and microwave dinners then.'

Sharon smiled back as she flicked through her holiday brochures.

'I wonder what Spanish food is like?' she mused.

Kev looked back in disdain.

'It ain't complicated, mum: salad, pizza, pasta, fish, burger and chips.'

Young Kev continued to thumb through different catalogues, folding the pages over in the top corner, anxious to spend thousands of pounds on new trainers, gadgets and Xbox games.

Dave, picking his nose, had popped out earlier to the upmarket Southend-on-Sea Estate Agents. He was now looking at properties in the price range of £300,000.

Sharon reclined on the sofa with her feet on Dave's lap. Reading from a pile of holiday brochures, she circled world cruises and all inclusive holidays in the Caribbean and Mediterranean.

'Dave, look at this. You can cruise the world for ninety days and it's only fifteen grand each. How about that, love? Think of me in all those sexy bikinis.'

Dave flopped out his long, blotchy tongue and rolled it crudely at Sharon.

'All that thinking ain't good for my blood pressure, but I'd die a happy man! Come here and sit on this ol' boy.'

Kev removed his head from his Xbox magazine.

'You two are sooo gross.'

Sharon threw a cushion at Kev.

'If your dad didn't fancy me, you wouldn't be here love.'

Kev picked up the magazines and stomped to his bedroom.

'Shaz, it's funny, ain't it. A few months back, we'd be looking in the newspaper for the cheap caravan holiday vouchers and now we're not batting an eyelid at spending thirty grand on a holiday.'

Sharon paused for a moment.

'Dave, what if it doesn't come off? Are we putting the cart before the horse? We haven't made any money yet.'

Dave sat up on the sofa and gestured for her to sit on his lap again.

'My old man used to say, "Don't count your eggs until the chicks have hatched." Thing is, Sharkie's already had the call from this Rochester bloke saying that it's all a formality and the money should be transferred to Tony next week, so the deal's as good as done. He doesn't get his money unless we do.'

Sharon continued.

'Another thing, Dave, are you sure Tony will pay us?'

'Of course he will. We're family aren't we?' said Dave, confidently.

'But he's never helped us before and we were family then.'

Although Sharon's questions made Dave momentarily uneasy, he felt a new found confidence surging inside his heart as he held Sharon tight.

'Tony might have been the brains of the family, but I've always been the muscle,' he said assertively.

'He wouldn't dare shaft me. He's a crook alright, but he doesn't like violence. He wouldn't dare, love.'

Dave paused and took hold of Sharon's chin and turned her face gently towards his.

'Trust me,' he continued. 'I've laid it on thick with Tony; I told him on the phone that Sharkie has some very dangerous contacts.'

Dave leaned forward and kissed Sharon tenderly on the lips.

'I'm not going to let anyone or anything stand in our way,' he said, as he pulled away from Sharon's mouth.

'It's our time,' he said.

'Yes babe, it's our time', Sharon repeated.

CHAPTER 53

Wax Lyrical

It was Monday morning and only an hour before Gretyl would be leaving for Gatwick Airport with Neil and his party.

Gretyl had been awake since 3am. Overwhelmed with the excitement of her first holiday abroad, her suitcase and bags had been packed with a mix of evening dresses, blouses, skirts and various ill-fitting swimming costumes.

Gretyl was now pacing up and down the house looking for something to do for the next hour.

'Perfume, that's it. I need more perfume!' she chirped.

Gretyl ran upstairs and sifting through the shelves came across a box labeled, 'Stripped-Ease - from head to toe - the perfect solution for hair removal.'

Inside the box was a jar with wax, a wooden spatula and separate cotton strips.

'Legs smooth as a baby's arse. I'm liking that.'

Gretyl was far from a natural blonde. Being very dark, her wiry leg hair insulated her like a layer of fur, while her short and curly overgrowth burst from the confines of her gusset like a neglected topiary.

'If I don't sort this bush out, they'll think I'm a bleedin' Kraut.'

Gretyl unzipped her dress and threw her heavy left leg up onto the bath tub. Opening the pot, she scraped the hard substance with the wooden stick and tried to apply the cold, sticky wax to her crotch area.

'Surely it has to be softer than this? It'd take ages to do me fanny, let alone both legs.'

Gretyl read the back of the pot.

'Ah ... silly cow. I've got to heat the stuff first.'

Walking downstairs, she placed the wax pot in the microwave and set the timer for five minutes. After the ding, she ran back up to the bathroom and, with spatula in hand, spread the hot and sticky wax along her grey squirrel, like marmalade on toast.

'Flamin' Nora! No wonder it takes your hair off!' she yelped.

Gretyl continued with the wooden stick until both legs were covered with generous dollops of scorching wax.

Gretyl sat on the toilet and applied the strips.

'Wait a minute. How long until these things stick? I'll give it another few minutes.'

Gretyl was interrupted by the chime of the doorbell. She covered herself with a towel and ran down the stairs to peep through the stained glassed panel in the door. It was Neil Rochester.

Neil flinched and muttered, 'Dear God! That's the stuff nightmares are made of.'

'What did you say?'

'Erm, I wanted to give you the passport and the £2500 before we get in the minivan. We'll be leaving for the airport in 45 minutes.'

Gretyl snatched the envelope, checking the passport and the cash inside.

'It looks good to me, Mr Rochester.'

She dropped the towel.

'Tell me, how does it look to you?'

Gretyl stood before Neil like a half embalmed mummy, her pink frilly undies stretching half way up her chest.

Neil turned and ran.

Gretyl bellowed from the doorstep, 'You couldn't give me a hand with my legs could you? I'm feeling rather hot.'

Neil did not dare look back.

Gretyl slammed the door and returned to the bathroom.

'Right, off you come, you buggers!'

Pulling the wrong way, she tugged at the strip.

'For cryin' out loud, how hard do you have to pull?'

Gretyl took a deep breath and yanked again, this time screaming as the burning sensation shot through her body, leaving a livid red patch which began to spread across her skin before her eyes. Most of the hair and strip on her crotch still held fast.

'Oh crap. That's worse than bleedin' childbirth. I should have trimmed the hedge first.'

Within seconds blotchy bruising began to appear.

'Maybe if I sit in a hot bath, they'll melt and be easier to remove?'

Gretyl ran a hot bath and rubbed herself with lavender oil.

'That should help'.

Sitting down in the water, Gretyl relaxed while the lavender worked its way into her pores. Stimulated by the aroma, she closed her eyes and began to drift off.

Twenty minutes had passed and Albert walked in through the kitchen door.

Water was dripping over the staircase.

'Gretyl, are you alright?' he shouted.

Gretyl awoke to the sound of running water. Panicking, she turned off the running tap and ripped herself out of the base of the bath, yelping in pain. The wax had dripped around her crotch and stuck to the base of the bath, taking some skin and hair with it.

Albert ran into the bathroom, while Gretyl stood naked with the wax strips fastened to her crotch and legs.

Albert looked shocked.

'What the ... Gretyl, are you okay?'

Gretyl began to cry. 'Oh Albert, I tried to wax and the stuff stuck. Then I must have fallen asleep and now I've torn my bits down there. Oh and I'm leaving in ten minutes for the airport.'

Albert picked a large towel from the cupboard and wrapped it over her shoulders.

'Love, your legs n' bits look awful.'

Gretyl sniffled.

'Thank you, Albert.'

'I don't mean it like that. I'm concerned that you've really burnt your, y'know, wotsit, thingy. I think you need to see a doctor.'

'You've not paid any attention to my wotsit thingy for years, Albert. Anyway, I need to get dressed and get on that plane. I'm not missing a free holiday for anyone. Do me a favour though, love? Go pour your injured wife a stiff glass of sherry for the pain relief.'

'Okay love, a small glass, but I'd stay out of the sun after waxing those pegs. They might think you're German.'

'Oh, I couldn't bear that,' Gretyl sighed.

Gretyl reached down and tried to gently peel the strip still attached to her crotch.

'Oh Albert, it's dried harder than ever.'

Gretyl reached for the trousers that were drying on the radiator.

'I'm going to have to wear these for now and sort out my bits later.'

'Well, you sort yourself and I'll sort the carpet. I think it might have soaked through to the underlay.'

'I'm sorry Albert, but all I can think about is my own underlay right now. I need to be outside in a few minutes.'

Gretyl winced with pain as she carefully inserted each leg into the trousers, the sticky wax adhering to the fabric. She opened the cabinet and withdrew a packet of Paracetamol, popping a few inside her mouth.

Albert returned and passed the small glass of sherry to Gretyl.

'Now listen, love. When you're away, go easy on the drink. You know it's not good for your IBS and judging by your phone call from the train the other day, you can't handle it anymore.'

'Albert, that wasn't alcohol. I think someone must have spiked my coffee. You can't be too careful these days, what with all these date rape drugs.'

At that moment, the doorbell sounded.

Gretyl noticed the relief on her husband's face as he bounded downstairs to answer the door.

Gretyl heard Neil Rochester's voice and grinned as she listened.

'I'm Albert, nice to meet you.'

'I'm Neil Rochester, your next door neighbour. I'll be taking care of your wife while she's away.'

'That's very kind of you … best of luck, you'll need it. The wife can be quite a handful. Give me a call if you have any problems.'

Albert read out his mobile number, while Neil entered it into his phone.

'Thanks for that,' Neil said. 'Because she's new to the village, we wanted to do something a little special for her.'

'Well, it's nice of you. I'm sure the holiday will be a big hit with Gretyl.'

'We always aim to please and will give it our best shot. You can be assured of that.'

Gretyl hobbled to the front door, her legs wide apart and face etched with pain.

Albert offered a modest kiss on Gretyl's cheek.

'Passport? Ticket? Money?' enquired Albert.

Gretyl straightened her blonde 'Marilyn' wig, raised her poorly drawn eyebrows and pouted her thick red lips.

'After all these years, you're suddenly taking an interest in your wife?' she said as she walked out of the house.

Albert waved goodbye as Gretyl pulled her suitcase and carry-on bag toward the mini-van.

Neil lifted Gretyl's luggage and threw it in the back.

'Your seat is here, by the door.'

Gretyl bent over slowly and raised her right leg, stepping inside the Mercedes saloon.

'Oh my ... five strapping men. I'm sure we'll be having some fun together,' Gretyl squealed.

But the five strapping men completely ignored her.

Neil pointed to her fellow passengers.

'Here we have Sleazy, Groggy, Thumper, Dopey and Chunky. They don't talk much so I wouldn't bother them if I were you.'

Gretyl looked around the car at her male companions. She guessed that Sleazy was a single guy who liked nothing more than late night visits from out of town girls. Groggy, she surmised, had a problem with alcohol and was most likely up for drink-driving. Thumper looked like the village thug and was probably Neil's mindless minder. Dopey simply made up the numbers and obviously had an IQ just high enough to breathe, as his nickname indicated. Chunky was a 300lb fatty who was easily persuaded by plates of food and there would be plenty of that in Marbella.

Following her several glasses of sherry and pain killers, Gretyl started to drift into a deep sleep.

Before she started to snore, the last words she thought she heard were Neil's.

'Now lads, Gretyl is a very special guest of ours, so make sure she wants for nothing. She's royalty and we can learn a lot from a lady like her. I for one am glad that she's joined the village. She's classy, very experienced, worldly wise and no doubt could teach us all a thing or two. Let's have it for Gretyl - three cheers - hip hip hooray! Hip hip hooray! Hip hip hooray!'

But Neil had said no such thing.

And Gretyl was not awake.

CHAPTER 54

Diamond Geezer

'Five hundred grand! Five hundred flipping grand!'

Sharon reminded herself of the prize ahead as she gazed at the alluring jewellery in the Duty Free store.

'Soon Sharon, you're gonna get some ...'

But before she had finished her sentence, Sharon heard Sharkie whispering in her ear.

'Sharon ... I've got something I want to show you.'

'You cheeky bugger, we'll be having words if you don't behave yourself.'

Sharkie looked startled.

'No, seriously, I want you to have this.'

He passed her a beautifully decorated silver box wrapped in a red velvet bow.

'Aw, what have you gone and done? That's very sweet of you, but you shouldn't have,' said Sharon.

'Yes, I should,' Sharkie replied. 'I noticed you gazing at the watches earlier and shortly after I pretended to nip to the toilet.'

Sharon opened the box and let out a gasp.

Sharon looked in awe at the watch. It had four diamonds around the bezel, a mother of pearl face and a sterling silver bracelet. She knew it must have cost Sharkie over £500.

'Apart from a kiss, what else could I give you in the airport?' he said softly.

Sharon looked away from Sharkie.

'Trust me, I am flattered 'n' stuff, but like I said, it's purely business. That's all it can be, Sharkie.'

Sharkie rested his manicured fingers on her shoulder.

'Sharon, I don't want to offend you. It's just that you are a very beautiful woman and I want you to know that. There's another life out there for you and I hope you discover it while we are away.'

Sharon's heart beat increased.

'Thank you for treating me like a princess,' she stuttered. 'I just don't want Dave to ...'

Sharkie interrupted.

'Sharon, it's all about you now. Just enjoy the moment. After all, if life isn't about special moments, then what is it about?'

Sharon stared at the watch, stroked it for a moment, and then lifted it up to Sharkie, silently bidding him to put it on her wrist.

Sharon felt a tremor down her arm as he took her hand.

It was impossible to resist him now.

His blue eyes seemed to glow.

'Sharkie, I ...'

Sharkie's kiss caught her by surprise. But when it came, he lingered and she did too, and their lingering felt to her like a lifetime.

Sharon opened her eyes.

Suddenly she thought of Dave and guilt began to displace desire.

Turning away from Sharkie, she walked towards the shops, their bright lights beckoning her like a safe harbour.

CHAPTER 55

Check Out

Neil handed his passport and printed flight ticket confirmation at the Monarch desk.

'There you are my dear.'

The young lady checked the e-ticket and passport.

'I'm sorry Mr Rochester, but your passport is out of date.'

Gretyl chuckled in the background, while the rest of the group gawped, their mouths catching flies.

Neil panicked.

'That can't be? Have you read it properly?'

'I have checked it several times and I'm afraid you won't be able to fly with an expired passport. I'm sorry.'

Neil reached over the counter and snatched back the passport, only to find that it had indeed run out over four months ago.

'You don't understand. I simply have to fly! I am responsible for the travel plans of my group and believe me - they can't be trusted on their own.'

'Well, I was going to suggest that you speak to the Passport Service and see if they can arrange an emergency passport for you, but to my knowledge they do not issue emergency passports for holidays.'

Neil's face turned red with anger.

'This isn't a damn holiday. It's a business trip and an awful lot of money rides on it!'

Gretyl was standing near the desk and interrupted.

'I can assure you dear, Mr Rochester is correct - he stands to lose a lot of money on his little venture.'

Neil spat his words at Gretyl.

'Shut your mouth, Trollop! You've got what you want, so go away and let me take care of business.'

The arguments with the check-in desk now escalated, much to Gretyl's delight.

Gretyl kicked Neil's sports carry-on back into his path.

'They say what goes around, comes around. We'll send you a postcard if you like,' she chuckled.

Neil snatched his leather bag and barged past Gretyl, knocking her to the floor.

Gretyl writhed in pain and with a feeble voice wailed, 'How dare you assault an old woman? Ouch, my hip. I think you've broken something.'

'If only! I'd gladly break every bone in your body and one at a time, given the chance.'

'Well, you can kiss my royal behind, you pathetic wife beater!' Gretyl replied.

Several onlookers stood by, horrified and fascinated.

Two police officers grabbed Neil by his arms while Gretyl was slowly lifted to her feet by one of the Marbella party - the 300lb Chunky, who was now ready for his third breakfast.

As Neil was escorted from the scene, he overheard Gretyl addressing the group.

'Now, let's work this out. It wasn't gonna be any fun with Little Dick, so I say let's go on holiday and have a great time.'

'I'll kill that bitch,' he raged silently.

CHAPTER 56

Tear Away

Barely twenty yards from the top of the escalators, Sharkie spotted Gretyl stepping gingerly off the metal folding steps, her legs straddled apart.

Sharkie laughed.

'Get a load of that Sharon.'

The party now walked together, hoping to spot their hosts for the trip.

Sharon approached Gretyl and held out her hand.

'It's nice to meet you, Mrs Trollop. My name is Sharon Souddalle and I'm here to make your trip a most enjoyable one.'

'How polite and to be greeted by such a pretty lady. I remember you from that posh café in the village when you met his lordship, Mr Rochester.'

Gretyl's face creased as she gently placed her hand on the top of her thigh.

Sharon noticed that Gretyl was in pain.

'Are you okay?' she asked.

'Ah, you know us girls. It's the holiday hair removal thing. Let's just say, between you and me that it's gone a bit 'tits up'.'

While Sharkie greeted the men and took them to the café, Sharon took Gretyl to one side.

'Would you like me to pop into the chemist and get some soothing cream for you?'

Gretyl took hold of Sharon's hand and squeezed it.

'Sweetheart, you have no idea how good that sounds.'

Sharon returned with some tea tree oil and baby lotion.

'If you don't mind me asking, where exactly does it hurt? I've been waxing for years and would be happy to help.'

'I think if we're going to get this personal, we'd better introduce ourselves. What's your first name, dear?'

'It's Sharon.'

'Sharon, my name is Gretyl. And I could do with some help. You see, the silly cow that I am, I tried waxing my legs and bits before leaving for the airport and, well, it's all stuck. I couldn't get the strips off.'

Sharon winced.

'You poor thing. I'll tell you what. Why don't I take you to the ladies? If you like, I'll take a look and see what we can do. The baby lotion might help to remove the strips and the tea tree oil will soothe your skin.'

Sharon helped Gretyl up and handed her the bag from the chemist.

'Here you are. Don't be embarrassed. I'm happy to help, that is, if you wish me to.'

Gretyl thanked Sharon as they hobbled to the disabled toilet. Once inside, she removed her trousers, yelping as she prised her sticky legs from the material.

'You all right?' Sharon asked.

'When you get to my age, love, dignity is the last thing you worry about, especially down there.'

Sharon laughed, trying to make things a little easier for Gretyl.

'Men have it so easy, don't they?' she said. 'What do they know about the stuff us women have to put up with?'

'My husband and I like to wind each other up,' Gretyl replied. 'He bought me some Tena Lady for my birthday last year. I said to him, "No need for that. When I cough, I'm just marking out my territory."'

Sharon took a look at Gretyl's legs. Seeing the clumped and hardened wax around her bikini line, she tried hard not to show her disgust. Taking care of her own private matters was one thing, but an old lady who'd never exfoliated or used a razor, was quite another.

Sharon assessed the damage.

'You should really cut down the length before you apply the wax. If I try to pull this strip by your bikini line, you'll probably pass out.'

'Dear, I'm no stranger to pain. I'm married! So let's just get it over and done with.'

'Gretyl, this hair is over two inches long. I'll need to trim as much as I can first. Let me check my handbag and see if I've anything in my manicure set that will do the job.'

After rummaging through her bag, Sharon was relieved to find a small pair of scissors and held them up like a surgeon with a scalpel.

'I'll try to cut the wax and hair away for you. Now I think the easiest way to do this is if you sit on the edge of the toilet and lift your leg up on my shoulder. I'll kneel down between your legs and start carefully trimming. How does that sound?'

'I really appreciate it, love. I've never had a friend who's prepared to help me like you do.'

After ten minutes, Sharon had managed to remove the strip and wax from both sides of Gretyl's knickers.

'Gretyl, now this is trimmed, I need to clean my scissors. I'll squeeze some of this tea tree oil into your hands and if you rub it on both sides, you'll find it will help, but you might need to do it every few hours or so.'

While Sharon turned on the tap, the call for their flight was announced.

'I'm sorry Gretyl, but I think we might need to take care of your legs when we get to Marbella.'

Gretyl frowned.

'Aw. We've still got a while before the plane leaves. Tell you what, just give 'em a yank and get it over and done with, shall we?'

Sharon noticed the dryer on the wall and wondered if she could warm up Gretyl's legs with the hot air.

'Well, we'd need to get your legs as warm as possible before we try to peel the strips off.'

Sharon placed her hand on Gretyl's leg and pointed to the dryer.

'Do you think you can get your leg up? I need to get you warm before I start rubbing you with baby oil.'

At that moment, a frustrated mother who had been listening to the conversation and waiting patiently for the cubicle started to bang her fist on the door.

'I don't know what you're both doing in there, but maybe you should go and get a room!'

Gretyl chuckled.

'At my age, I'm grateful for any attention I can get.'

Gretyl stood up from the toilet and lifted her leg under the dryer, shouting over its rumble.

'Can you help me, love? That's it, grab hold of it. Get it up.'

'That's sick,' the mother shouted running from the room.

Meanwhile Sharon had managed to hold the weight of Gretyl's legs. Lifting them one at a time so that they were now sufficiently warm, she began to rub them down with generous measures of baby oil.

As she was massaging Gretyl's thighs, the mother returned with two female airport staff who pressed their ears to the door before knocking loudly.

'How does that feel, Gretyl? Are they hot now?'

Gretyl sighed with relief as the oil started to work its magic.

'Love, if only my husband could rub me like that.'

Sharon began to lift the strips as Gretyl panted loudly.

'At this rate, Sharon, it's going to take ages. I tell you what. Just get hold of them, one at a time and yank 'em off.'

With that, the armed guard banged on the door and Gretyl screamed. Sharon had successfully torn away the strip from the shin, complete with the hairs.

'I've got them, Gretyl. I've got the hairs off.'

'Excuse me, this is airport security. Would you please open the door?'

'One moment,' Gretyl shouted, 'I've got me legs in the air and we haven't finished yet ... now, grab hold of the other one, Sharon. That's it girl, you've got hold of 'em ... yank!'

After several more screams, four armed policemen arrived.

Surrounding the toilet, they thumped on the door.

'This is the police. Open the door now.'

Sharon slowly opened the door and stepped out exhausted, revealing Gretyl sitting on the toilet, panting heavily.

'Is it a crime to use the toilet?' Gretyl asked.

'Excuse me madam. It's just that we had complaints of banging and screaming coming from the toilet and it was upsetting members of the public.'

'Well, ain't that great? You're harassing an old lady when you should be looking for terrorists in turbans.'

'Calm down. There's no need for that language, madam. We had no idea your carer was helping you in the toilet.'

'So now you're ageist and I need a carer!'

Sharon cut in, 'Officer, please let me explain ...'

After a few minutes, the police were satisfied with Sharon's explanation and arranged for a wheelchair to be brought for Gretyl.

As Sharon pushed Gretyl outside the door, they ran into Sharkie and his group of five.

Sharkie muttered to Sharon, 'That woman needs a hearse not a wheelchair.'

'Shush, she's alright,' Sharon remonstrated. 'A bit gross, but a lot of fun as well.'

At that moment, Sharkie's phone went off. Seeing that it was Neil Rochester, he switched the loud speaker setting on so that Sharon could hear as well.

'Mr Lovitt. It's Rochester. I'm afraid there's been a bit of a problem. Can you believe that I've been so busy lately, I hadn't checked my passport and it's out of date by only four months? They won't let me fly and by the time I manage to sort a passport, you'll be back home.'

'That's no problem. We'll entertain the party and Miss Soudalle will keep an eye on Mrs Trollop. In fact, she's right here with the lady now.'

Neil shouted with rage at the other end of the telephone and Sharon jumped at the sound.

'He really doesn't like her, does he?' Sharon whispered to Sharkie.

'To be honest, Sharon, she looks a bit of an acquired taste,' Sharkie replied softly.

'We'll keep you posted, Mr Rochester,' Sharkie continued. 'I have your number. You take care.'

With that Sharkie finished the call and ushered the group of men towards the departure gate.

Sharon, pushing Gretyl, brought up the rear.

Gretyl took several painkillers and washed them down her throat with some whiskey from her flask.

'Let's go, Shaz!' she cried. 'Paradise awaits.'

CHAPTER 57

Righty Tighty Lefty Lucy

Gretyl was the last of the party to board and walked slowly down from the nose of the plane until she reached her seat.

'Sharon, this must be mine. Glad it's not by the window. I'll probably need to pee every ten minutes, the way I've been feeling.'

A smartly dressed gentleman who'd been stuck behind Gretyl tried to squeeze past her, only to be pinned tightly between a seat and her prodigious behind.

Gretyl winked.

'Sorry, dear, but it's a long time since I was walked down the aisle.'

The gentleman prised himself from Gretyl's derriere and hurried down the aisle to his seat at the rear of the plane.

Sharon took Gretyl's carry-on bag and with her own small case, tucked it tightly into the overhead compartment.

'Are you excited Gretyl?' asked Sharon.

'Excited? I haven't had this much fun since I saw Mrs Cox fall down the stairs.'

'Oh dear, I hope she was alright.'

'Why? Wicked witches should be punished, don't you think?'

'Oh, I suppose you're right Gretyl.'

'You'll see I'm always right dear. I haven't lived this long only to end up a total retard.'

Gretyl stood up and moved aside as a frail, elderly passenger took the seat next to her.

'My, you are a dainty little one. The seat will be fine for you but I'm not sure I can fit my voluptuous self into this one.'

The old lady turned up her hearing aid.

'Sorry, dear. What was that you were saying? I'm afraid you'll have to speak up quite loudly.'

Gretyl squeezed down next to the old lady, her folds of fat spilling over the seat as she bellowed, 'I was just saying that you are a dainty little one.'

The petite lady cringed in pain.

'Oh dear, please, not quite that loud.'

'Sorry, love. I'm Gretyl and if you need anything on the flight, just let me know. You can have a swig of my whiskey, if you like.'

'Thank you. I'm Mary, nice to meet you. I'm afraid I can't drink alcohol, though. Lucy wouldn't like it.'

Gretyl looked puzzled.

'Well, whoever Lucy is, I wouldn't let her spoil your fun.'

'Oh no, I call my stoma 'Lucy'. My son calls her Vesuvius. The little madam can erupt without warning.'

Mary, glad for the company, continued chatting away.

'I have a friend who's called her stoma, 'Little Richard', because she thinks her one looks like a willy. It's quite funny really.'

Gretyl laughed.

'Well, I suppose there's one benefit. You can stand up and do your business and nobody needs to know. I'll be having a few drinks for little Lucy, don't you worry.'

After the safety demonstration, Gretyl was delighted to hear that the full in-flight service included good food, wine, complimentary drinks, newspapers, TV and even hot towels, though she was puzzled what they were for.

'Ladies and gentleman, this is your captain speaking. Our flight time will be approximately two hours and forty minutes arriving at Malaga airport at 6.10pm local time, with the temperature around 27 degrees.'

Gretyl turned to Mary.

'How exciting! Before we know it, we'll be laying by the pool in our bikinis.'

Gretyl finished off the remaining whiskey in her flask and burped loudly. Placing the headphones over her ears she plugged them into the arm socket of the chair, flicking through all the radio stations until she found one to her liking.

Within moments Gretyl had her eyes closed and was belting out her cacophonous version of Michael Jackson's 'Beat It'.

The next thing Gretyl knew, Sharkie was tapping her on the shoulder. He was sitting behind Gretyl.

'Excuse me Mrs Trollop, but I don't think you realise you're singing very loudly.'

'Au contraire, whatever your name is. I'm warming up the vocals before I get a sing-song going on the plane.'

Sharkie leaned closer to Gretyl and whispered, 'Look, I don't think they'll appreciate it. It's not what you do on a plane!'

Gretyl ignored his comments and the murmurings of other passengers until a flight attendant asked Gretyl to remove her headphones.

'I'm sorry madam, but we've had complaints from passengers about your singing and I'm afraid I'll have to ask you to be quiet please. Now please put your seatbelt on for take off. Thank you.'

Half an hour later, the airbus was cruising at 30,000 feet and Gretyl had already finished four small bottles of Baileys Irish Cream.

She was now intoxicated and drawing attention to herself once again.

'Listen, my lovely,' she exclaimed to a young female flight attendant who had told her to quieten down, 'I was entertaining people before you were an itch in your daddy's crotch. Now let me show you how to throw a party.'

'Well, madam, we don't allow parties on the plane, so I must ask you to keep quiet please.'

Gretyl stood to her feet, turning to the passengers to address them.

'You're going on a holiday, not a piggin' funeral. Now cheer up you miserable lot!'

At this point the flight attendant became firm.

'Madam, it's illegal for any passenger to become intoxicated on our flights. So please calm yourself down. Now would a coffee help?'

Gretyl looked up.

'I can't say I've ever been drunk on coffee dear, so I'll have another two small bottles of Baileys please, if you don't mind of course.'

'Madam, you've had quite enough to drink already and we will not be serving you any more alcohol on the plane.'

But Gretyl was not so easily silenced.

'Well, if you don't want us drunk, love, why do you serve alcohol?'

'If I need to ask you one more time you will be restrained. We will ask for security to meet you upon arrival at the airport and you will be arrested.'

At this point Sharon interjected.

'Excuse me, but I think I can help. We are a small party together, en-route to Marbella. Unfortunately, Mrs Trollop has been in some pain with her legs before boarding the plane and she may have had a few drinks before the flight to ease the pain. I promise to keep an eye on her and will make sure she's no trouble.'

At the familiar sound of Sharon's voice, Gretyl began to grow quiet.

In no time at all, she was asleep and snoring loudly.

Gretyl began to stir ten minutes before landing.

In urgent need of the bathroom, she unclipped her seatbelt and leapt up, knocking the tray of food flying from her table and ignoring the flight attendant's request for her to stay seated.

'I'm not being funny love, but this won't be the only mess you'll have to clean up if I don't reach the toilet right now.'

Gretyl pushed the flight attendant aside and made a dash down the plane. Like an old banger, her exhaust was now blowing lethal clouds of invisible gas.

Gretyl finally returned to her seat and spoke to Mary.

'Oh, sorry dear. I hope I haven't been squashing you in the flight while I've been asleep?'

Mary twisted the nipple valve on her stoma bag.

'Oh, not to worry, I'm sure any squeezing has helped Lucy. She's been playing up all afternoon and I didn't want to wake you. She can be quite a trumpy one when she fills up. I'm afraid I've had to relieve her in the seat, several times. It's a shame we can't open the windows on the plane.'

CHAPTER 58

Old Chemistry

Tony greeted Sharon with a hug in the sultry arrivals hall of Marbella airport.

Sharon smiled uncomfortably and after a brief exchange of pleasantries, she turned away. It must have been at least fifteen years since Sharon had seen Tony. There was awkward chemistry between them at the time and in a moment of vulnerability after a spat with Dave, a consolatory hug soon turned into something else. A number of things changed later that evening, prompting Tony to make his plans abroad. After years of moving around the Mediterranean, he finally settled down in Marbella, living comfortably from his 'criminal' reserves.

Outside the terminal, Tony loaded each piece of luggage into a Mercedes Minivan.

While waiting, the English visitors had been drooling over the strong, tantalising scent of the malt and hops that filled the air from the San Miguel Brewery barely 100 yards away. Now grateful for the air conditioning in the van, they were delighted when Tony passed back a small crate of ice cold beer and snacks.

Sharon texted Dave to tell him of their safe arrival while Gretyl unpacked her newly purchased electronic gadget, along with a multipack of super strength batteries.

Gretyl leaned forward, eager to show Sharon her new toy.

'Take a look at this. It says it's easy to use, takes batteries, lasts for hours and you can use it in the dark. The man at the shop said I should make a film with it. Oh, it's all too much fun.'

Sleazy shouted from the rear of the van.

'Miss Soudalle, save your batteries. I'm solar powered and you can play with me instead.'

'You're hilarious mate,' Sharkie said sarcastically.

Bolstered by half a litre of San Miguel, Gretyl now sat upright and shouted out to Tony who was driving.

'So love, how did you get to own all these posh houses we're staying at? With an accent like yours, did you marry into money, print it or steal it?'

Tony smiled as he looked into his rear view mirror.

'Actually, it's all three. How about you? How did you come by your fortune?' he replied.

'It is believed,' said Gretyl pompously, 'that I'm an heiress with royalty in my veins. True wealth is in the blood, don't you think? If it's absent for any reason, nobility soon brings it back. That's what happened to me.'

Gretyl winked at Sharon.

'For example, take the lovely lady here. I don't know whether she's rich or poor, but she's quality and quality always shines through. Sharon, I believe the best is yet to come for you, my dear.'

Sharon smiled.

'That's one of the loveliest things anyone has ever said to me.'

Sharkie shuffled uncomfortably in his seat.

Sharon looked at her expensive watch, now altered for Spanish time.

'Goodness me, it's a quarter to eight. I'm sure we'll be at the villas anytime soon.'

'I hope so love,' replied Gretyl. 'I fell asleep on the plane and I'm starving.'

Gretyl turned to Tony.

'What grub do you have for us when we get there?'

'Well, Marbella is a gourmet's paradise. Whether you like tapas dishes, paella, pasta, a rich variety of meat or fish, you can literally have what you want.'

Gretyl was unimpressed.

'Crikey. We taught the world how to read, write and speak English and you don't have any real food? I don't do foreign. My irritable bowel disagrees with it.'

Sharon laughed silently.

Sharkie glared at Gretyl.

'Mrs Trollop, you're in Spain. Wouldn't you like to enjoy the Mediterranean cuisine?'

Tony interrupted.

'It's not a problem. We cook a variety of English food, but we can even get you some ready meals from Iceland Supermarket in Puerto Banus, that is, if you want to cook for yourself. There's also an M&S in town.'

'Well, it's good that someone has sense here. Remember, I've got an English gut, not a Spanish one.' Gretyl retorted.

With that, Sharkie leapt in.

'Did you know that Marbella is right next door to Morocco? If you don't like Spanish, how about tasting a bit of North African?'

Gretyl pouted.

'What do you think I am, stupid? Africa isn't in Spain and anyway there's no need for that language.'

The men burst out in laughter.

'And another thing, we didn't defend the English Channel only to be invaded by foreign tripe. Look at London now. We're bombarded with Indian food, kebab houses, Chinese shops and pizza parlours. Nope, foreign food is for foreigners.'

'Mrs Trollop, didn't you know that most of the fruit and vegetables we eat come from Spain and Africa?' Sharkie smirked.

'Not the stuff I eat, dear. It's from my husband's allotment. Now button it, you big poofter.'

Sharkie groaned and in his groan Gretyl thought she heard the words 'five hundred grand'.

Tony pulled up alongside the drive of the largest of the villas, to be greeted with champagne by two scantily dressed male and female waiters.

Walking through to the back patio, a variety of food dishes and alcoholic beverages had been laid out with great care underneath a pergola.

With several hours still to go before sunset, Tony took the opportunity of providing a quick tour of the first property.

'I hope you will enjoy your time with us. We'll have an early breakfast prepared for you and served inside your accommodation from 7am until 8.30am. At midday, you can enjoy a special BBQ lunch by the pool here. After that, we'll take you on a brief tour around Marbella and discuss some ideas with you for your stay. You are here to be spoilt, so enjoy the sun, sea, sand and anything else you wish.'

Sharon smiled and leaned towards Sharkie, and as she did so Gretyl unobtrusively strained to hear what she was about to say.

'You know Sharkie, I've always dreamed of just chilling in a hammock, sipping on some exotic drink, away from the noise of the estate. Then I'd gaze at the stars and listen to the crickets. Their little chirping noises reminding me that I really am on holiday.'

'Did you know,' Sharkie replied, 'that it's only the males that chirp? They do it to attract the females and ward off any other male attention. It's called their courting song and once they've mated, they sing another one. Apparently, the hotter it gets, the more they chirp. Puts a different perspective on things, don't you think? Now would you like me to sing to you under the stars this evening?'

Gretyl decided this was the moment to interrupt Sharkie's mating call.

'Dear, I hadn't put you down as a ladies' man. I thought you were y'know, batting for the other side.'

Sharon laughed.

'What Sharkie? You've got to be kidding me. He's a bit of a predator with the ladies, aren't you dear? I'd watch out if I were you, Gretyl.'

Gretyl raised her eyebrows.

'Honey, my love boat days are well and truly over. This big ol' ship's run aground but I'm looking for some refurbishment!'

Sharkie excused himself and reached for another beer.

Gretyl took Sharon to one side.

'Look dear, please don't think I'm speaking out of turn, but he's no good for you.'

'Oh no, you've misunderstood. We're not an item, we're just working together to sell these villas,' Sharon insisted.

Gretyl raised her eyebrows.

'Hmm, I've seen his kind many a time and I can tell you, he just wants to get you in the sack. He's not right for you my love. You're too good for him.'

'My husband's back home in Essex. He wanted to be here as well, but we thought it best he stay as it was only a short trip - y'know, to keep things simple.'

'Well love, things seem far from simple. What with God's gift to women floating around on his own cloud of Hai Karate, he's like a dog on heat. Another thing, he looks the type that won't take no for an answer. Be careful love.'

'I appreciate that. Thank you. Tell me, are you married?' asked Sharon.

The question seemed to catch Gretyl off guard.

'Er, erm, well I married well over fifty years ago. We're still together, but I'm not sure how or even why, sometimes. I do love the ol' codger, but we have so little in common, I wonder if he misses me at all.'

Sharon put her arm around Gretyl.

'Aw, I'm sure he does. Tell you what, why don't you and I grab a few drinks and go over to our villa? We can have a good girlie chat and then call it a night.'

Sharon walked over to Sharkie and told him they were off to relax, and as she did so Gretyl proudly stood by as she unclipped the bracelet and handed the watch back to Sharkie.

'Sharkie, as lovely as the watch is, it's not for me. Sorry.'

'Flippin' 'eck Sharon, what are you doing? Keep the watch. It's yours! Why are you doing this to me?'

'I think the alarm just went off and I woke up,' Sharon replied.

CHAPTER 59

Dutch Courage

Sharkie had been drinking with the collective since 8am. Furious with Gretyl for tempering Sharon's ardour, he was now desperate to get his own back. So he was sitting with the other five men at the breakfast table. They were all laughing like hyenas while plotting the payback for Gretyl.

The boys agreed they should in their own words 'frighten the life out of the ol' girl'. The whole episode would be recorded on Thumper's iPhone and sent to Neil Rochester for his personal amusement.

The suggestions ranged from strange howling and scratching noises outside Gretyl's window (complete with splattered tomato ketchup), to filling her handbag with as many crickets, cockroaches and other insects as possible. Aware of her irritable bowel, minutely diced pepper and hot spice in her sandwich lunch was also a popular suggestion.

Thumper spoke up in the group.

'May I suggest something a little stronger than a prank, y'know, violence of a more traditional kind?'

Sharkie only resisted shouting his approval by silently chanting his five hundred grand mantra.

Sleazy replied, 'Thumper, you're only good for kicking people's heads in. We need something far more subtle and inconspicuous.'

At this point a loud peal of laughter broke out as Chunky asked to be excused from the mischief should it take place during mealtimes.

As Sharkie leaned back in his chair, he saw Sharon and Gretyl nattering away as they walked through the courtyard ready to enjoy a barbecue lunch.

He could hear Gretyl continuing to whine about her sore legs and Sharon advising her to keep them out of the sun.

He watched angrily as Sharon lent her a sarong to wear as a wrap around her waist. He was disgusted that Gretyl was wearing one of Sharon's newly purchased items from their trip to London.

He turned to the men from Poncey Bridge.

'State of that and the price of fish,' he mocked. 'Have you ever seen anything that wrong?'

Sleazy replied, 'Even my strange fetishes can't compete with that!'

The men burst out laughing together just as the two women approached their table.

Sharkie greeted Sharon and Gretyl.

'Did you two ladies have a nice sleep?'

'I had a lovely continental breakfast this morning, thank you,' replied Sharon.

Sharkie winked at the Poncey five, indicating that it was time for an attack on Gretyl.

'Mrs Trollop, now let me hazard a guess. I'd say you were ... a large greasy fry-up. Am I right?'

Sharkie was emboldened by beer.

But Gretyl was ready to fight back. She had told Sharon earlier that morning that she was expecting plenty of mischief.

'No need to guess where you're concerned love. I'd say you were definitely someone who loves plenty of sausage? Am I right, dear?'

The men applauded.

Sharkie snapped back, 'The only sausage that would touch you is dead meat!'

Sharon interrupted.

'Look boys, there'll be plenty of time for banter later. Now go play with yourselves. Gretyl and I have to talk some girly stuff.'

CHAPTER 60

Hasta La Vista

Arti Chokes had arrived in Marbella early on Tuesday morning, and parked a hired white van opposite a small rented apartment tucked away in the old town.

He unpacked his case, removing a white polo shirt and black trousers, along with the ready-to-stick vinyl logos of a local parcel delivery company he had sourced on the Internet.

Arti, now disguised as a parcel delivery man, had everything in place for Gretyl's execution. He had chosen poison as his preferred method: it was quick, lethal and in his opinion, highly reliable.

He looked out of the bedroom window at La Concha, the formidable mountain sheltering Marbella from the warm northerly winds in summer. Arti figured it was the perfect backdrop for a perfect crime.

Arti opened his pill box, placed a false molar on the table and delicately removed the glass cyanide capsule from the hollow of the tooth. Chewing his dry breakfast of wafers and cheese, he imagined Gretyl's canines cracking open the poisoned vial he intended to insert in her food. It was a risky method of murder, but Arti liked to do things the hard way. He enjoyed the challenge.

Arti made tracks to the villa, ready to stake out Gretyl for as long as was necessary. He had purchased a box of fresh cream tarts early that morning, one of which could contain the vial of cyanide. Arti planned to catch her eating and then discretely slip the poison in her food.

Pulling up outside the villas, Arti peered through his binoculars and spotted Gretyl loading her plate with a large roll and salad. This was the ideal moment for him to make his move, while Gretyl was waiting impatiently to gorge upon the rest of the buffet.

'She'd most likely be the first person to greet me with the package,' Arti deduced.

Arti walked down the passageway and handed Gretyl the package.

'Buenos dias Senora, I'm in a rush if you don't mind. Could you just sign for this parcel while I hold your plate?'

Gretyl handed him her plate while Arti used his thumb to wedge the small glass vial of cyanide inside her salad roll. Gretyl signed the delivery sheet and handed back the clipboard.

'There you are, you fine specimen. You can call on me, anytime,' she winked.

Arti smiled awkwardly.

'Forgive me for interrupting your lunch madam. Buen apetito. May you enjoy it as if it were your last. Hasta la vista.'

Gretyl returned to her lunch as Arti watched on from a secret vantage point behind a wall.

With both hands firmly gripping the bun, she squeezed tightly and bit into the super-sized cheese, ham, piccalilli and mustard salad roll.

Crunch!

Gretyl felt something hard crack in her mouth and threw the plate to the floor screaming. Hyperventilating, she buckled over and fell to the ground, unconscious.

Sharon rushed to her side and tried to roll her into a recovery position.

'Someone quick, call an ambulance. I think she's had a heart attack. Can anyone do the kiss of life?'

Sharkie sneered.

'You can do that, Sharon, but I'm not letting my mouth anywhere near that Trollop. Check her pulse; I'm sure she's fine.'

Arti enjoyed watching the drama unfold. It was all very entertaining but for one slight complication.

'If anyone tries to give her the kiss of life, they'd be likely to cop it as well,' Arti thought.

Arti held his phone upright and after snapping a photo of Gretyl, left for the van, enjoying the sound of raucous laughter from the men by the pool.

Once in the van, Arti reached for his mobile phone to text Neil Rochester.

'The offending weed has been eliminated! Signing off now until payment collection in UK. A. Chokes.'

Arti recalled Albert Trollop's words from the pub.

'Take care of my wife ... permanently.'

Flicking through his contacts list, Arti found Albert's mobile number and texted.

'My cockney friend, your 'trouble and strife' is now pushing up daisies! Enjoy your life, minus the wife! Arti Chokes.'

Arti continued to watch the drama unfold from his van as paramedics promptly arrived and carried Gretyl into the back of an ambulance.

CHAPTER 61

Back from the Dead

Sharon walked over to Sharkie, who was still laughing at Gretyl's demise.

'You heartless pig. Gretyl's dead and all you can do is laugh? I never thought you could stoop so low. I shouldn't be surprised though, 'cause it's all about the money for you, isn't it - me, Gretyl, the whole charade. I've had it. You can take care of your boys. I'm going home.'

Sharkie looked puzzled.

'Sharon, what are you talking about, love? She just fainted after one of the lads put a cockroach in her roll. It was so funny! Didn't you hear the crunch?'

Sharon snapped back.

'She has a phobia of insects, you idiot! She told me last night that she'd probably drop dead if she found one crawling on her, let alone in her mouth. I don't think anything could be worse for her.'

'Let's face it, though,' Sharkie replied, 'I doubt anyone would end up missing Gretyl.'

Sharon ran over to the ambulance to speak to the medic.

'Excuse me sir, but is Gretyl going to be okay? Is she dead?'

Gretyl sat up from the stretcher.

'I'm fine, dear. I must have passed out. I really don't remember what happened?'

Sharon was shocked by Gretyl's bodily resurrection.

'Oh, I'm so glad you are okay. I thought you'd had a heart attack after biting that cockroach.'

Gretyl panicked.

'Cockroach? Was it mincey boy who put it in my lunch? That poof is going to get his comeuppance, I'll tell you.'

Sharon tried to change the subject.

'Gretyl, why don't we go back to the villa and I'll make us a pot of English Tea. How does that sound?'

Gretyl stood up, refusing treatment.

'Let's go Sharon ... now whatever your name is, Pedro, please take your hands off me. I want to get out.'

Sharon walked over to their table and handed Gretyl her handbag.

'Two secs, Gretyl. I need to have a quick word with someone.'

Gretyl took a seat at the table, fully expecting to be able to hear Sharon's conversation.

Sharon grabbed Sharkie's arm.

'What you did this afternoon was way out of order! I expected you to have a bit more brains.'

Sharkie looked embarrassed and pulled Sharon over to one side, away from earshot of the men by the pool.

'Look Sharon, me and the lads were just having a bit of fun. After all, these are the people we have to please.'

'Sharkie, let me make myself real clear now. This is the only decent opportunity my family's ever had to earn some good money and I won't have you ruining it. Do you understand?'

'Sharon, just relax. There's nothing that can stop this deal going through now. Neil wants it, we want it, Tony wants it. It's all done and dusted.'

Sharon replied, 'I've had far too many disappointments in my life to live with my head up my arse! Now remove that head of yours from your hairy bum and let's finish this job properly. Are we agreed?'

'Sharon, I have never seen you so assertive! I just love your feisty spirit.'

'I'm glad we understand each other,' she smirked.

CHAPTER 62

Food or Flight

Arti Chokes was delighted with the speed of his early bird execution and had already packed his suitcase to leave the following morning. With the evening to kill, Arti was pleased to find a complimentary restaurant menu and invitation in the letterbox of the apartment. Only a mile or so outside of town, he decided to enjoy the walk and make his way over for dinner.

Arti spotted the white marbled entrance of the bistro and walked into the restaurant.

'Excuse me. I'd like a table please. I shall be dining alone.'

'I'm sorry sir, but our restaurant is fully booked and is by reservation only.'

Arti seemed a little confused.

'Oh, but this menu was delivered to my apartment earlier today.'

An attractive woman in her late 50s was sat at the bar, swirling her Vodka Martini. She stood up and approached the desk in the reception.

'Excuse me. If the gentleman would like, I'd be more than happy to share my table. I am also dining alone.'

Arti blushed at the offer and was about to politely decline before she continued.

'I'm Monica. I'd be happy for the company this evening. Will you join me?'

Arti thanked Monica and ordered himself a pint of lager and another Martini for the lady.

Throughout his career, Arti had been far from successful with the ladies. His plain and uninteresting appearance had never attracted anyone but his own wife, Doris. Arti was, however, flattered at the attention and sat down, keen to taste the local delicacies.

At that moment Tony entered with the group of five. As he confidently addressed the bistro owner, some of the diners couldn't help hearing him, including Arti.

'Hey, Dino. These are my special guests from England, so put everything on my tab tonight please. Gentleman, you may eat and drink to your heart's content. You are here to have all the fun you want.'

'Tony, we appreciate all this great food and entertainment you're putting on for us,' one of the group said, 'though you missed a real show this morning with Mrs Trollop.'

At the mention of her name, Arti's ears pricked up.

As the men sat down at the table behind him, Arti continued to listen to their conversation at the same time as he feigned interest in Monica.

'Tony, it was hilarious. The boys had come up with a few pranks for a laugh and Thumper here buried a giant cockroach in Gretyl's roll. You ought to have heard the crunch as she bit into it. The ol' girl passed out on the grass. It was so funny, we nearly wet ourselves.'

Tony laughed.

'So there's not much love for Mrs Trollop then?'

'The only disappointment was seeing her come round in the ambulance,' Thumper added. 'But we've got a few other surprises planned for her.'

Tony snickered. 'Classic, lads, classic. Though, we don't want her causing any problems for us with Mr Rochester. After all, these villas will be your holiday homes if you play your cards right.'

'I'll be honest,' Thumper replied, 'she's new money, a tramp who's inherited one of our houses in the village. If I had my way, I'd have her permanently retired, but Neil wanted her on the trip so we could keep an eye on her. Told us that he's got a few little things he wanted to, let's say, plant in her house while she's gone. That's the only reason she's here.'

Tony clapped his hands.

'Ruthless boys, that's ruthless. I love it. Now let's get the drinks in, shall we?'

'Erm, can we order the food first?' replied Chunky.

Tony tried to put his arm around Chunky.

'My friend, I've already ordered all the starters on the menu for us. They should be coming any minute now.'

Throughout the conversation, Arti had begun to glisten with beads of sweat that had started to stud his stoney white forehead.

'Excuse me, Monica. I feel terribly unwell and need to get home. I'm sorry,' he spluttered.

'That's absolutely no problem. I'll give you a lift back to your room if you wish?'

Arti gratefully accepted and made a bathroom visit before his departure. He splashed his face with cold water, staring in the mirror.

'You idiot!' he exclaimed.

Arti reached in his pocket for his mobile phone, ready to text Neil and Albert.

He paused for a moment as he pictured an elated Neil Rochester cracking open his most expensive champagne bottle and celebrating Gretyl's demise.

'I'm just going to have to do the job with my own bare hands. That way, I'll know she's dead. I've already sent Neil a picture of Gretyl face down in the grass, so no point texting. I'll just have to finish what I started.'

CHAPTER 63

Codgers Lane

At 60 Codgers Lane, Poncey Bridge, Albert Trollop was finishing up in the greenhouse, unaware of the new message waiting for him in his text message inbox.

Keen to rest from a productive day's potting in the greenhouse, Albert walked back to the house and reached for his cold tea on the kitchen counter.

'Funny, I thought I might've heard from Gretyl by now,' he mused.

Noticing that the mobile phone was switched off, Albert pressed the power button and was greeted by a few bird-tweet noises and the envelope icon on the screen.

'You have 1 Message'.

Albert pressed the OK button to read the text.

'My cockney friend, your 'trouble and strife' is now pushing up daisies! Enjoy your life, minus the wife! Arti Chokes.'

Albert's head began to spin as his heart pumped wildly. Reaching for his angina spray, he administered it quickly.

'Oh, my dear God!' he screamed. 'Gretyl. I am so sorry.'

Albert gripped the phone tightly.

'Arti, you fool! I was drunk. I didn't literally mean for you to 'take care of her'.'

Albert fell into a chair and began to cry. He'd been married for over fifty years and though the difficult times were many, the thought that Gretyl had died - and that he might have unwittingly caused her death - simply overwhelmed him.

'Should I phone Arti? Maybe it's just a sick joke? Hang on, Albert. If it's not, I'll only implicate myself by calling him back.'

In the end, Albert decided the best course of action was to dial Gretyl's phone.

'Come on love, answer the phone. Answer it Gretyl.'

Albert willed her to pick up, but it was to no avail.

After a brief number of rings, it went to her answer phone. He panicked, unsure what message to leave, before the phone beeped.

'The caller's phone is switched off. Please leave a message.'

Albert replied after the beep.

'Er, Gretyl love, it's Albert. I haven't heard from you since you arrived in Marbella and I'm worried about you. Can you call me as soon as you get this message! Thanks love. Call me. Bye.'

Albert's hands shook as he placed his mobile phone down on the table.

'Wait, I'll go and see the bloke next door. He arranged the trip. He should know if she's okay.'

Albert rushed round to Neil's house and rang his doorbell several times.

'Mr Trollop, how can I help you?' said Neil, surprised by Albert's visit.

'Good evening. It's my wife. I haven't heard from her and I'm worried.'

Neil tried to compose himself.

'Oh Mr Trollop, I'm sure she's fine. I did receive a text yesterday letting me know that they all arrived safely. I tell you what. I'll try to get hold of them later this evening. If I have any news, I'll pop over, maybe first thing in the morning, if that's okay?'

'That would be great. Please let me know as soon as you hear anything. If you can get a message to my wife, please ask her to call me as soon as possible.'

Albert returned to the house, his mind volleying endless questions about Arti and his text.

'Is he really a hit man? Maybe he's just a prankster? If Gretyl's been murdered, wouldn't he or Neil have heard something by now?'

CHAPTER 64

Rolling Pin

It was now 9pm and Arti was parked up in his white van, binoculars in hand, waiting patiently for Gretyl's return to the villa.

He slowly pulled the latex gloves onto his hands and examined his long fingers, like a surgeon about to perform an intricate operation.

On the passenger seat lay a luxurious bunch of flowers which Arti had purchased from a petrol forecourt, while wearing a blonde hairpiece and full beard for disguise. With half a dozen bunches, he tied them together as one gigantic bouquet, thinking it might further conceal his face while he carried them to the door.

Two Mercedes vehicles pulled up outside the villas with the party. Arti had planned that once Gretyl was on her own, he would deliver the flowers and offer to bring them inside. If Sharon was about, he would have to deal with her before strangling Gretyl.

Arti had never throttled anyone before and wondered what degree of strength would be required to choke her. After all, Gretyl's neck looked the size of a male bull - but then he never did things the easy way.

Both the ladies had returned to the villa, while the men joined Sharkie on the property several hundred yards away.

Arti lifted his hand and flexed his long piano fingers.

'Perfect. It's just the women to deal with.'

Before exiting the van, Arti noticed three attractive young women stepping out of a taxi outside Tony's villa. Their smooth legs rode up to their necks, bodies covered with barely enough material to make a small handbag. Arti was delighted: these girls would be an effective distraction to keep the men away from Sharon and Gretyl's villa.

Arti drove the van outside the villa and made his way to the front door with the huge bunch of flowers.

He rang the door bell.

'Hola Senorita. I have flowers to deliver to a beautiful lady. Where would you like me to put them down?'

Sharon laughed at the mobile-speaking shrubbery.

'I expect they're from Sharkie. Put them on the table please.'

Arti shut the front door and carried the flowers over to the dining area, laying them down on the table.

'You should smell the scent of these beautiful flowers,' Arti said.

Sharon lent over towards the roses.

'Your accent is a little strange? It's like a mix of English and erm, not quite Spanish. Am I right?'

As Sharon turned to take the flowers into the kitchen, Arti removed a wooden rolling pin from the inside of his jacket and with one quick swing, struck the back of her head.

Managing to catch her fall, he carefully laid her down on the marble floor and made his way in the direction of a howling noise, which he knew had to be Gretyl trying to sing.

Gretyl screeched:

"Wish me luck as you wave me goodbye

Cheerio, here I go, on my way

Wish me luck as you wave me goodbye

Not a tear, but a cheer, make it gay

Give me a smile I can keep all the while

In my heart while I'm away

Till we meet once again, you and I."

Arti peeped through the crack of the bedroom door and saw Gretyl resting on the bed and reading the local paper. Now was the perfect moment.

He stealthily entered the room and pounced on top of Gretyl, ripping the newspaper in the process. He grabbed her neck and squeezed tightly, gazing at the startled look on her face. Her bulbous eyes seemed to be almost forcing themselves out of their sockets.

Gretyl struggled, desperately trying to resist.

Try as she might, she couldn't find the strength to remove Arti's hands from her throat.

So there was only one course of action left.

Reaching out to the bedside table, she grasped a can of deodorant and sprayed its contents into his eyes.

Arti yelped in agony and jumped off Gretyl, rubbing his eyes furiously.

He tried to see, but the burning was too intense.

He started to grope at thin air, wildly trying to grab what looked like the hazy outline of Gretyl's fat leg as she tried to escape.

Catching hold of her, he dragged Gretyl back in a final attempt to finish her off.

Arti squeezed Gretyl's throat as if it was an empty toothpaste tube.

Her face began to change colour.

Just as he thought he had succeeded in his mission, there was the sound of a loud crack.

Sharon had struck Arti from behind with the rolling pin he'd left on the table.

He was out cold and laying face down on top of Gretyl.

CHAPTER 65

Fly By Night

'Help me love. I've got his crotch stuck in my face.'

Sharon managed to push the unconscious Arti over onto his side and pulled Gretyl up from the floor.

Arti's blonde toupee was now on sideways and his fake beard half torn off from his face. Sharon removed the disguise to take a look at their attacker.

'Flippin' 'eck! Isn't that the delivery driver from this morning? Grab your handbag, passport and money and let's get out of here,' Sharon said.

Sharon and Gretyl seized their handbags and ran to Sharkie's villa. Tony answered the door.

'Sharon, what's happened to your head, love? Are you alright?'

'Where's Sharkie? I need to see him right now.'

'Erm, he's er, having a sleep upstairs. I wouldn't disturb him. I think he's had too much to drink.'

Sharon burst past Tony and with Gretyl in tow stormed up the stairs, heading towards some grunting noises coming from the main bedroom.

Sharon asked Gretyl to wait outside.

She walked in to find Sharkie in bed with two of Carmen's young girlfriends.

Sharon could not contain herself.

'You filthy git! Gretyl and I are being attacked in the villa while you're busy getting your rocks off with a couple of tramps! I'm out of here. Something's not right and I don't want a part of it anymore.'

Sharon was now shaking and at the edge of tears.

Sharkie leapt from the bed and ran over to her, unaware in his drunken stupor that his manhood was dangling and flopping in front of him.

'Sharon, I'm really sorry you've been hurt, but that old cow's had it coming to her.'

Sharkie tried to grab hold of Sharon's arm but she pulled away and scowled at him.

'Do you really want to lose all the money we'd be making on this deal?' he pleaded. 'Look, you can stay with me and she can manage on her own.'

Gretyl barged into the room and unable to hear any more pointed to his exposed member.

'Is that all you've got to offer? I've used toothpicks bigger than that. You can have what's coming to you, right now.'

With all of her might, Gretyl swung her rhinestone-studded handbag into his most prized possession and stared him down.

'A girl should never be without her accessories. Let's see you get by without yours.'

Sharkie was bent double, holding his member with both hands and moaning.

Sharon ran down the stairs crying while Tony tried to console her.

'Sharon, wait love. What do you want me to do for you? Just ask.'

'I want the keys to your car. Gretyl and I are off home. I'll leave it at the airport and text you when you can collect it.'

Tony tried to talk Sharon out of leaving but Sharon wasn't going to budge.

'Tony, listen to me. I think someone is trying to kill Gretyl. I don't feel safe here. If you have a problem with that, I'll get Dave to sort you out.'

Tony backed down and handed Sharon the keys.

'Okay, but it's been a while since you've driven hasn't it? Just take care of my baby. She's brand new, out of the showroom only last week.'

Sharon snatched the keys and ran out onto the drive with Gretyl. She started the car and made headway down the wrong side of the road, toward a petrol garage she'd spotted earlier.

Sharon smiled.

'Don't worry, Gretyl. We'll be home before we know it. If I never see this place again, it will be too soon.'

Sharon needed to ask for directions to the airport, so she pulled into the garage.

'Gretyl, take a look at this will you?' said Sharon, passing her Arti's mobile phone that had fallen out of his pocket and onto the bedroom floor.

'Check for any phone numbers, texts, anything that might give us a clue who's trying to kill you.'

'Dear, I have a good idea who's trying to shut me up. I bet it's that lowlife who lives next door to me. He doesn't want me to blab to the village about the small fortune he'll be earning in this deal. Come to think of it, that must be why he gave me a one way ticket.'

Sharon looked embarrassed.

'Gretyl, I promise you I'd no idea he wanted to hurt you. My role was just to keep everyone happy so the deal could happen.'

'I believe you love, but let me make a few things clear. I've no love for the village. From what I can see, they're a bunch of snobs. In fact, after I'd heard about the deal last week, I was made up when I heard the village was getting shafted. The bitter pill in all of this was that pond scum, Rochester, making money.'

Sharon bit her lip.

'Gretyl, I've got a confession to make. I hope you won't think less of me, but I reckon you'll like what I'm about to tell you. The villas are going to be rubble.'

Gretyl clapped her hands.

'How absolutely flippin' marvellous is that?' she shrieked.

Sharon continued.

'Tony is my brother-in-law and he bought the planning permission from a corrupt official. So the idea was to sell the villas at a knockdown price to Poncey Bridge and for Tony to get his money back. Sharkie and I would make a commission on the deal before they are all destroyed.'

Gretyl laughed.

'My dear, what a truly wonderful scam - taking money from a bunch of mindless morons and earning a wad while selling them a pile of rubble. I love it!'

Sharon looked puzzled.

'So why would you want to stay in the village if it's that bad?'

'I love a good fight, especially when I think the odds are stacked against me. Someone has got to teach those apes a lesson. Apart from the residents, the village is beautiful.'

Sharon laughed.

'While I go and ask for directions, can you check the phone and see if anything points to Neil Rochester?'

'Love, I know you won't believe it, but I'm in my 70s and I've only just learnt how to send a text. Why don't you take a quick look?'

Sharon took the phone back and thumbed through the texts.

'The last one is addressed to someone called Doris. I'll read it out: "See you in a few days. Can't wait to play with my little kitten! Lots of licks! Arthur Meow x."'

Gretyl checked herself in the mirror of the sun visor.

'Sounds like a right pervert, if you ask me.'

Sharon froze as she read another text from the hitman's phone.

'Gretyl, you'll not believe what I've found. He sent a text today to someone in his address book called Neil: "The offending weed has been eliminated! Signing off now until payment collection in UK! A.Chokes."'

Gretyl sighed knowingly.

'When we get home we'll tell the whole story to the police and show them the text. I'll bury that pig. You wait 'till my Albert finds out. He'll have him before the police.'

Sharon nodded her head. 'Do you want me to send a text to your husband and warn him about Neil? Do you know his mobile number?'

'Yeh, that's a good idea love. Let me just find it.'

Sharon moved on to the third text, addressed to someone called Albert.

'My cockney friend, your 'trouble and strife' is now pushing up daisies! Enjoy your life, minus the wife! Arti Chokes.'

Sharon's face went as white as a sheet.

She checked Albert's mobile number against the one in Arti's phone and matched them from the piece of paper that Gretyl had just handed her.

Suddenly Sharon felt nauseous.

'What am I going to do?' she thought. 'I can't text Gretyl's husband if he's involved in it. If I say anything now, she'll lose the plot. I'll tell her when we're nearer to home.'

Sharon needed to buy some time.

'You know what?' she said, 'your Albert will only worry if I send him a text. Why don't we wait till you get home first? You can tell him the whole story then.'

'You're right love. If Albert's going to do anything to him next door, I want to be there to see it.'

CHAPTER 66

Guardian Angel

Doris Chokes was pacing up and down the hall, anxious for Monica to answer her mobile phone.

'Ah, hello Agent Chokes,' replied Monica.

'What's the update on Arti please?'

Under Doris's orders, Monica had been monitoring Arti's movements since he had arrived in Marbella.

For some years, Monica and Doris had formed part of a secret network of female assassins operating mainly in Europe. Known as 'The Cleaners', they were called in to clean up any mess left by their male counterparts.

After witnessing Gretyl's resurrection in the back of the ambulance, Monica had telephoned Doris for further instructions.

'I'm afraid we need a clean-up,' replied Monica.

'Is your cover still intact?'

'Yes. I attached the wireless audio devices underneath the windowsill of the two villas. Tony Soddall made a call to the restaurant, booking a table for the men earlier this evening, so I followed your plan, picked up a restaurant menu, slapped the invitation sticker on and posted it through Arti's letterbox.'

Doris's meticulous attention to detail in her home was only matched by her lethal precision outside of it.

'Yes, he always likes to celebrate with a meal straight after what he thinks is the end of a job!' replied Doris.

Monica continued, 'He arrived at the restaurant while the Poncey Bridge group was there. Naturally Gretyl was the main topic of conversation that evening so after he heard this he went back to the house to pick up his van.'

'So what happened this time?' asked Doris.

'He was hit with a rolling pin which left him unconscious. I witnessed it all from the car, so after the women left the villa, he was quickly extracted and I returned Arti to his apartment.'

Doris sat down in the armchair.

'Did you put the note on his table?' she asked.

'Yes, like you said, if he screws up again, it will be the last time he does,' replied Monica.

Monica watched through her binoculars as Arti looked around the room, rubbing his head.

'He's looking around the room searching for something.'

Arti was fumbling inside his pocket for his mobile. It wasn't there. He checked the hallway and the bathroom but his phone was nowhere to be seen. What he did find however, was a handwritten note on the dining room table.

Monica continued, 'I can confirm that Arti has the note in his hand ... yes, he is reading it now.'

Arti held the note up in front of his face, squinting as he focused on the words.

'What did you write this time, Monica?'

'Oh, I was so impressed that I even memorised it. You want to hear?'

'You bet,' Doris replied.

'Arthur, your guardian angel brought you here, it's time for you to retire. This is the end of your career, no more Arti for hire. Read this warning you must now heed; don't return to the job you failed. This is the end you must concede, or for your sins, you will be jailed. p.s. The cup on the table has boiled water with a couple of tablespoons of salt. Let it cool-off and rinse your eyes with it.'

Doris laughed.

'You've excelled yourself this time!'

After the two had calmed down, Monica continued.

'There are some developments.'

'Tell me more.'

'I can report that the two women have taken a car which, I believe, is en-route to the airport. I can call one of our cleaners and have the mess tidied up before they leave, if you like.'

'No, I'll handle this myself. This is the last time we'll be finishing the job for him. And I'm also sad to say that I'm quite sure this will be our last communiqué.'

Doris sighed as she realised that a chapter of her life had come to an end.

For years she had been cleaning up after her husband, in every sense.

She had never had a problem covering up. Arti thought she was just out on a Saga coach trip or a walking break with friends.

Doris walked into the kitchen and tied the apron around her tiny waist. She reached for the mixing bowl and searched the pantry for some faithful old friends.

'Hmm, time to make a fruitcake to die for.'

CHAPTER 67

Special Offer

After waiting for nearly eight hours at Malaga airport, Sharon and Gretyl had managed to book the last few seats of a flight to Gatwick and touched down in the UK at 8:15am on Wednesday morning.

Tired and in need of a hot shower, the ladies made their way to the taxi rank outside the airport.

'Sharon, I'll really miss my beautiful hairpieces. Can you arrange for my suitcase to be sent back to me? I can't be wearing my Gracie for too long or I'll wear the poor cow out.'

Sharon smiled reassuringly.

'Of course, I'll have Tony send them back straight away. Anyway, I forgot to text him about his new car at the airport so I'll send him a text now. For the life of me, I can't remember where it is in the car park, though.'

'I expect you can't wait to see your husband and boy again? Why don't you give them a call?' Gretyl asked.

'I think it's best to wait for all the drama when I get home.'

They climbed into the taxi and gave Gretyl's address: '60 Codgers Lane, Poncey Bridge'.

As their car drove off, Sharon's attention returned to the text from the hitman to Gretyl's husband.

'What if he tries to kill her when she gets back home?' she thought. 'Hang on though. If he'd wanted to do that, why would he be in cahoots with Neil Rochester?'

As Sharon tried to work out the best course of action, Gretyl took hold of Sharon's hand.

'I owe you my life,' she said. 'What you did for me was more than I could ever repay you for. I won't forget it. I've never had a friend like you before and I'd like us to keep in touch. You could even stay over with us? My Albert would love you.'

Sharon smiled back.

'Of course we'll remain friends. This trip has taught me that all that glitters is not gold. I'd dreamed of getting out of my council house and having a better life for myself, but not at the expense of someone else losing theirs. People come first, not possessions.'

Gretyl smiled sympathetically.

'Now love, I know you had a lot of money riding on this sale,' she said. 'Apart from telling our husbands, maybe we should leave the police out of it until the deal happens. Then you'd still get your money and we can shop Rochester after.'

Before Sharon could reply, she was interrupted by the tweeting noise of a text message in Arti's mobile phone.

The text was from Albert Trollop.

Sharon's heart missed a beat as she opened the message.

'I hope your text was a wind up mate! I was drunk when we met in the pub and was joking when I said 'take care' of my wife! Call me back ASAP! Albert.'

Gretyl looked over at the phone. 'Who's the text message from? Is it Neil Rochester?'

Not wanting to complicate matters further, Sharon turned the phone off.

'Ah, it was nothing, just a two for one special offer at Dominoes. At least we know the bloke likes pizza.'

Gretyl laughed.

'Looking at that dodgy wig and beard he was wearing, I don't think it's the only thing the cross-dressing faggot liked.'

Sharon's relief was palpable. She now knew that Albert had had no intention of really murdering his wife. One thing was clear, however. Neil Rochester was guilty. And it was time for him to get what was coming to him.

CHAPTER 68

Just Desserts

It was 9am and Neil Rochester, accompanied by Reverend Forsythe, knocked on Albert's door. Neil was looking forward to breaking the news of Gretyl's death and showing Albert the photo of Gretyl's corpse.

'Good morning, Mr Trollop. Please forgive the early call, but I have some news about your wife. May I come in please?' Neil asked.

Startled by the sombre appearance of both his visitors, Albert invited the men inside and walked them through to the living room.

'Please, make yourselves comfortable. May I take your coats?'

'Thank you,' Neil replied. 'I am afraid that I have some news that will be very difficult for you to hear. That's why I have brought Reverend Forsythe with me from the village.'

Albert sat down in the rocking chair, his breathing now short and rapid.

'Have you heard from my wife?'

Neil Rochester leaned forward.

'I don't quite know how to say this, but I received some very sad news late last night. I'm afraid your wife has passed away.'

Albert gasped.

It seemed like the whole room was now rocking, not just his chair.

He tried desperately to work out what to say and do.

'Tell them about the text from Arti? Keep my mouth shut? They don't know me, so why would they believe my innocence, if I told them?'

Albert looked up at Neil.

'I feared the worst. I haven't spoken to her since Monday morning and she's never been the silent type. What's happened?'

'It's hard to say, but I was sent a photo of your wife collapsed in the garden. I think it must have been a heart attack. I'm very sorry.'

'Why? Who, who told you? Who sent the photo?' replied Albert.

Neil fidgeted in his chair.

'Erm, it was the owner of the villa. He wanted me to correctly identify her as being one of our party from the village.'

'May I see the photo, please?' Albert asked.

Neil opened the photo from the camera roll in his phone.

'Can you confirm that this is your wife, Gretyl Trollop?'

Albert could tell immediately.

'Yes, that's my Gretyl.'

Neil looked at Reverend Forsythe. 'Sadness and pain come to us all, don't they, Reverend?'

Looking down the spectacles perched on the end of his nose, the vicar spoke.

'That's quite right, Mr Rochester. Death is no respecter of persons, I'm afraid. Whether it's a heart attack, cancer or a car accident, we all go but the way of dust, back to mother earth in a casket, or in the ashes pot.'

Albert excused himself and walked into the kitchen, flicking the kettle on. He couldn't bear to hear another word from a man who only worked one day a week, who was patently not sincere, and who effectively had the cushiest number in the village.

'Can I get you gentleman a cup of tea?' he asked.

'That would be wonderful, Albert. Thank you,' the two men said in unison.

The silence that followed was only disturbed by the tick of the old grandfather clock in the hallway.

Eventually, Albert returned to the lounge with a tray of biscuits and drinks.

'There you are. Well, thank you for taking the time to come and see me. As an old soldier, death was a familiar visitor long ago, but it's never been as unwelcome as it has been this last week. I've just buried my best friend in London and your news couldn't have come at a worse time. I guess I'll need to make arrangements for my wife's body to be brought back here.'

Neil picked up his cup of tea, slowly sipping it from its lip.

'Albert, I hope you don't mind, but we have an excellent funeral director in the village and I've taken the liberty this morning of ringing them for you. In the next twenty four hours, they will be setting in place the necessary arrangements to bring your wife home.'

'That's very kind of you, Mr Rochester,' replied Albert.

At that moment the door bell rang. Albert excused himself and opened the door to a frail and elderly lady who was standing at the entrance with a basket hanging on her arm.

'Good afternoon. Are you Mr Trollop?' asked the woman.

Albert looked at the old lady before him.

'Yes, that's me. And may I ask who you are?'

'Oh I'm sorry. How rude of me. I'm Doris Chokes, one of your neighbours.'

Doris removed her scarf from her neck as she introduced herself.

'I hope you don't mind, but as you are both new to the village, I wanted to welcome you and your wife with one of my home baked cakes.'

Doris passed Albert a white box, wrapped with ribbon.

'I do hope you like fruit cake?'

Albert expressed his surprise at receiving the welcome gift. He was particularly fond of home baking. Not that he saw much of it with Gretyl.

'That's very kind. We both love fruit cake, thank you.'

'Oh, before I go, Mr Trollop. Please promise me that your lovely wife gets the first slice. You will promise me, won't you?'

'Thank you Mrs Chokes. I promise. Goodbye for now.'

Albert closed the door and walked into the lounge, placing the cake box next to the tea pot.

Neil ogled the box.

'Ooh, is that fresh cake, Mr Trollop?'

'Would you like some, Mr Rochester?'

Albert lifted the lid to reveal the fruit cake, its rich smell tantalising Neil as he stared at the glace cherries and its moist, rich filling.

The Reverend suddenly perked up.

'I've already had my breakfast but one can always make room for life's little delicacies.'

Albert popped into the kitchen and returned with three plates and dessert forks. He proceeded to slice the cake with a large knife and cut it into quarters.

'Would you like a big or small piece, gentlemen?'

'I'd like a slither to start with,' Neil replied.

The Reverend licked his lips.

'Well, everyone knows the clergy's penchant for cakes and pastries. It's a large slice for me, Mr Trollop.'

Albert passed the plates and handed each of them a fork. Sitting around a small polished mahogany coffee table, he rested the fruit cake in the centre.

The Reverend helped himself by skillfully manoeuvering a chunk over to his plate.

Neil, on the other hand, was momentarily distracted. He was busy scrutinising the contents of the room, trying to discern their monetary value.

'Mr Rochester, can I pass you a slice?' enquired Albert.

Neil blinked and replied.

'Absolutely! Since my wife went to visit our daughter, I've barely eaten a thing.'

The Reverend made to speak but Albert spoke first.

'By all means finish your cake, but if you don't mind, I'd like to continue the conversation about my wife tomorrow. I need time to take in the news.'

Reverend Forsythe thumbed though the blank pages of his diary and like a poker player kept everything well hidden from the others at the table.

Albert turned to Neil.

'I appreciate you coming over and telling me this news this morning.'

Neil, cramming the entire slither of fruit cake into his mouth and beginning to chew, mumbled his reply.

'Who was it that delivered this delicious cake?' he asked.

'She said she was from the village. Can't remember her name now? Wait, I think she said, Mrs Chokes?'

Neil continued to gorge on the remainder of his cake.

'Chokes? There's no one in the village with that name, but the (munch) name rings a bell? Well, as the good book says ... you've got to (munch) ... love your neighbour as yaaaaaaaaaaaaaargh!'

'Self?' replied the Reverend.

Interrupted by Neil's convulsions, the vicar stared incredulously at Neil and put his plate down on the table.

Neil held his stomach and collapsed head first onto the thick pile of carpet, foaming at the mouth.

'Mrs Chokes! ... Mrs Chokes!' he screamed over and over, each utterance losing volume as Rochester's life ebbed from him.

Albert rushed to his aid and held his hand but it was too late. Albert had seen the look of death many times before, but nothing quite like the terror-filled gaze that was etched on Neil's face as he gasped his last breath.

Albert looked up and noticed the Reverend.

'Whatever you do, don't touch that cake, Reverend. I'm no Sherlock, but it looks like Neil's been poisoned. It must have been that cake?'

The Reverend took a hurried and horrified step away from the table.

'Tell me, do you know anyone called Mrs Chokes from the village?' Albert asked.

'I know every family in this village and I can assure you, there is no one by that name.'

Suddenly the penny dropped.

'She must have been Arthur's wife? Oh Lord above. What am I going to do now?'

Far from offering any comfort or advice, Reverend Forsythe left almost immediately and made it quite clear on his exit that he was unwilling to be a part of any investigation that might arise. This was, after all, not his official day of work.

Albert sat down on the sofa and dialing 999, stared at Neil's pale and lifeless body. In the space of five minutes, two ambulances and three police cars were now parked outside, with lights flashing.

Albert felt unable to take in the enormity of Gretyl's death and that of his neighbour and decided to keep the facts simple for any questioning from the police.

'Officer, I haven't heard from my wife. My neighbour popped over to say that Gretyl had died in Marbella and we were visited by an old lady who simply introduced herself as Mrs Chokes from the village, apparently, delivering a poisoned cake.'

'Do you have any witnesses to back up your story?' asked one of the police officers.

'Yes, the local vicar was here. You can ask him.'

As the police and the ambulance crew began their work, Albert found a quiet corner and sat in a chair, trying to gather his thoughts, trying to find some meaning in all the mayhem.

It was now obvious to him that someone wanted to murder his wife, but if she was really dead in Marbella, then why did Mrs Chokes insist on Gretyl taking the first bite of her cake?

For a brief moment, Albert allowed a simple thought to fester.

'Could my Gretyl really be alive and well?'

CHAPTER 69

Blue Lights

The lights from the Emergency Services could be clearly seen as Sharon and Gretyl's taxi turned onto Codgers Lane.

'Sharon, what are those blue lights flashing? They're not on my drive, are they?' Gretyl asked.

The taxi slowed down as it approached number 60 and Gretyl's hands began to shake as she realised that the blue lights were coming from her driveway.

'Oh, my Albert! Sharon, help me please. Hurry, I need to see Albert right now. They haven't got him, have they?'

Gretyl had already paid the £230 fare upfront for the taxi driver to take her to Poncey Bridge and then return Sharon to her home.

Sharon addressed the driver.

'I'll be back in a minute and I'll pay you extra to wait if you don't mind. I need to make sure my friend is okay before you take me to Canvey Island.'

The taxi driver nodded and Sharon hurried after Gretyl, rushing toward the house.

A police officer stood at the front door and stopped Gretyl.

'Excuse me madam, I'm afraid you won't be able to go in. We have a crime scene here.'

'I live here! My Albert, tell me he's okay? Please tell me, he's okay?'

The officer escorted Gretyl over to the car and introduced her to a female colleague, but she managed to break free and ran back to the house and into the hall, straight into Albert's arms.

'Albert, it's you! Oh my, Albert,' she sobbed.

'Gretyl, I'm so glad you're safe. I can't believe it.'

Sharon was given permission by the senior officer to step inside.

'Gretyl, are you going to be okay? Do you want me to stay with you?' Sharon asked.

Gretyl hugged her tightly and kissed her on the cheek.

'I won't forget you Sharon and I'll never forget what you've done for me.'

Grabbing her handbag, Gretyl took out the cash that Neil had given her for the holiday.

'Look, don't argue with me, but there must be nearly two grand here. Take it, go back home and wait for me to call you. If anyone deserves it, it's you.'

Sharon was stunned. Wiping her eyes she stammered, 'Thank you Gretyl. I'm so glad that Albert is safe. Give me a call when you feel ready. Love you.'

Sharon made her way back to the taxi, tears of relief rolling down her cheeks as she sat down in the back of the taxi.

'I better let some of this out before I get home,' she thought.

Later that day, Neil's body was removed from the house and the police officers informed Albert and Gretyl that they would be returning the following morning.

Gretyl and Albert spent the afternoon comforting each other and sharing their stories. By the time they had finished, the conclusion they had arrived at was crystal clear. Gretyl had caught wind of Neil's scam and knew that he wanted her silenced. She also now realised that he had hired a hitman to kill her. Neil thought the job was finished in Marbella, but the hitman knew it wasn't and sent someone to poison them both at home to complete the mission.

The Trollops tried to relax that evening with a mug of tea in the conservatory. Albert stood up and walked over to the small sofa and sat next to Gretyl.

'Love, I know we don't always see eye to eye. In fact, I'm surprised that either of us can still see at all, the amount of times we've poked each other in the eyeball. In the last few days, both of us could have ended up six feet under. Let's use what's happened to us to make us stronger. Let's both try to make the best of the life we have left.'

Gretyl laid her head on Albert's shoulder.

'You're right love. You and I can make the best of our good fortune. As for this village, they'll be better off without that vermin. Neil's control over this village is now over.'

'Yes,' Albert added, 'I think we can both agree that he got his just desserts.'

CHAPTER 70

Seasons Greetings

It was Christmas Eve and the lights from the Trollops' home could be seen from the main road, which was covered in nearly two feet of snow. An 8ft spruce stood proudly in the centre of the front window, with crystal ornaments draped across its boughs. Hundreds of multi-coloured bulbs lit up the front of the house, while several snowmen patrolled the lawn.

The Soddalls had been out for an evening walk, after spending a long weekend with Albert and Gretyl. Sharon and Dave held hands as they rang the doorbell, while Kevin continued to dig for treasure.

Sharon pulled Kevin's arm away from his face as they stood at the door.

'Kevin, take that finger out of your nose. Santa won't be delivering anything up there, son.'

Gretyl answered the door and immediately pulled several party poppers into the faces of her guests.

'Come in my lovelies. Albert's got his nuts roasting on an open fire.'

Dave laughed.

'I hope they're chestnuts you're talking about. I flippin' love hot roasted chestnuts.'

Kevin taunted his father as they all removed their shoes in the hall.

'Dad, don't be such a muppet. Can't you hear the song? Gretyl means Nat King Cole, not real chestnuts.'

Dave clipped his son around the ear as they entered the lounge and sank into the new, plush settees that Gretyl had ordered especially for Christmas.

Gretyl clapped her hands together, ready for some festive fun.

'Now come here and let's play happy families. Albert, pass Kevin his present first,' she said, excitedly.

Kevin opened the box and withdrew a brand new iPad.

'What a result! Thank you so much. I can't wait to turn this on. Wait a minute. There's a hundred quid iTunes voucher here as well. Nice one.'

Gretyl walked over to the Christmas tree and picked up a small envelope for Sharon.

'This one is for you, love.'

Sharon kissed Gretyl on the cheek and opened her envelope.

'Oh, Gretyl, you shouldn't have. Dave, she's only gone and booked me a three night Spa and Pamper break at Champneys.'

Gretyl bounced on the sofa like an excited child.

'There's more love. Open the booklet.'

Sharon turned the pages and found a cheque made out to her for one thousand pounds.

'Gretyl, you are so unbelievably generous. I really don't know what to say.'

Albert walked over to the tree and picked up a small bag.

'Let's not forget Dave, shall we love?'

Albert passed the bag to Dave, who tore at it like it was his first Christmas.

'Flippin' 'eck! A season ticket for West Ham. Albert, you're gonna have to come with me, mate.'

'Don't worry Dave. I've sorted mine as well. I'll be spending some of my weekends at the flat in London, so it's easy enough for me to travel. Anyway, take a look inside the bag again.'

Dave rummaged inside, like a child in a lucky dip.

'Got it. An envelope.'

He opened the card to find a cheque for one thousand pounds.

Dave stood up, walked over to Albert, and without saying a word hugged him.

Albert looked over at Gretyl's face. She was bursting to give a final, special present to the Soddall family.

Albert winked at Gretyl.

'Go on love, I know you can't wait any longer.'

Gretyl jumped from the settee with the sprightliness of a woman half her age and ran over to the tree.

'Sharon, Dave, young Kevin. Albert and I have been so excited to share this special present with you. It's taken us a long time to sort it and some blood, sweat and tears I can tell you. But believe me when I say, you're all worth it. Now, before I give this to you, we need to go outside, so we are all going to have to dress up warm. Let's go.'

The buzz of excitement filled the air, as Dave and Sharon playfully fought over who could get their wellies on first. Albert and Gretyl were the first out, followed by Sharon, Dave and a lethargic Kevin, who was unimpressed at having to leave his iPad inside and remove his finger from his nose again.

Gretyl walked them down the drive like little soldiers and stopped at the end to give her instruction.

'Now, turn right, walk twenty yards and stop.'

Gretyl had them exactly where she wanted them.

'Now, close your eyes. I'm going to spin you around a few times and when I say ready, open your eyes.'

Gretyl spun them around, one by one and raised her hands in delight.

'Okay, ready. You can open your eyes now.'

Everyone was facing the house next door. Gretyl pressed a button on a small remote control and voila! 62 Codgers Lane lit up with a huge sign on the roof:

'Welcome to the Soddall Family'.

Sharon and Dave looked at each other puzzled, while Kevin was busy checking his Facebook wall on his Smartphone.

Gretyl handed Sharon the front door key.

'This is your new home.'

Sharon stared at Dave, while Dave stared at Albert. Albert grinned and pointed back at Gretyl.

'What's the matter with you both? Go on, go look inside you silly buggers. It's yours.'

Sharon replied, 'Gretyl ... what about your daughter Heather? Wouldn't you like to have little Connor playing next door?'

Gretyl smiled. 'Darlin', I've taken care of it. I love my family but we don't live in each other's pockets. I've sorted them out with a posh bungalow a few miles from here. It's got a swimming pool, a tree house for the little man and a private school only five minutes walk from their home.'

Sharon began to cry again and flung her arms around Gretyl.

'I still can't believe what you've done for us, Gretyl.'

Both families walked down the path together, each footprint announcing their arrival with the crunching of fresh snow.

Sharon turned the key in the front door and walked inside.

Dave turned to Albert. 'I really don't know what to say mate. I just don't know what to say.'

Albert patted him on the shoulder. 'Dave, I'll let Gretyl tell you what happened.'

Gretyl shut the front door behind her and put her hands together, ready to tell her little story.

'Well, my dears. After 'whats his face' got his comeuppance, his lovely wife Patricia came to visit us several months later. After we told her the full story, she gave us first refusal to buy the house so we snapped her hand off. We gave her a fair price and she walked away happy. She's bought a small farm not far from here and lives with her daughter and little girl, we understand.'

Sharon was still crying, overwhelmed with the beauty of the newly decorated and fully refurbished house.

'Gretyl, how on earth did you have the time to do all this decoration? It looks amazing.'

'Well, I have a secret weapon.' replied Gretyl. 'She's called Tracey and she's the new housekeeper. I've asked her to look after both of our properties, so there'll be no housework for you Sharon.'

Sharon stood in the hall, her mouth wide open.

Gretyl continued.

'She actually worked for my half aunt for years and as it turns out, she had some degree in interior design as well, so I told her to go fill the house with stuff you young women like.'

As the ladies continued on to tour the house, Dave pulled Albert to one side.

'Do you mind if I ask you a question, Albert? Just out of interest, why have you decided to keep your council flat in London? It might not be too difficult to travel to West Ham from here.'

Albert motioned with Dave to sit down at the dining room table with him.

'Something special happened to me Dave, when I went back to the flat a few months ago. I'd decided to go and visit my old allotment and see a young friend of mine, Sajan. The last time I saw him was a very sad time for me. You see, my shed was torched and with it, all my precious photos, letters and memories that I kept in a wooden chest there. Let me get to the point. As I walked over to my old plot, a brand new wooden shed stood in its place. Written above it was a sign that said: 'Albert's Shed'. I cried my eyes out when I discovered that Sajan, an eighteen year old lad and his family, had rebuilt my shed, hoping that I might return one day. It was then I realised that London and its people were as much a part of my past as they are an essential part of my future, whatever I have left of it.'

Dave's eyes filled with tears.

Albert continued.

'I've never had a son, but Sajan is the closest thing I've had to one and with his father's blessing, Gretyl and I are paying for his university studies. The way I see it, if the Good Lord has blessed us with the resources to help others, then it must start with the circle of friends he's given us.'

Albert's eyes were sparkling now.

'Dave, we must do the best we can with the cards we're dealt with. I was happy enough without money and I'd gladly give it all away. What really matters in life is loving and caring for each other.'

Albert paused for a moment before concluding.

'If it wasn't for our recent escapades, we would all be missing Gretyl.'